HE RULES WHO CAN

HE RULES
WHO CAN

ARTHUR GILCHRIST
BRODEUR

INTRODUCTION BY
HOWARD ANDREW JONES

COVER BY
ROBERT A. GRAEF

ILLUSTRATED BY
ROGER B. MORRISON

POPULAR PUBLICATIONS · 2021

TABLE OF CONTENTS

INTRODUCTION BY
HOWARD ANDREW JONES

FOR THE MODERN reader many pulp stories are hard to find, but when you serialize one over six issues, tracking the whole thing down becomes six times more challenging, and not just financially. Even should you be so lucky that you find an affordable copy, one or more of the issues might be in such short supply that years could pass before you obtain all the installments. Me, I lucked out. I was able to read the whole saga of *He Rules Who Can* for the first time more than twenty years ago when I purchased a one-of-a-kind set of hand-bound hardbacks from pulp collector and scholar Al Lybeck who loved historical swashbucklers and had preserved his very favorites between sturdy covers. If you're old enough to know what a mix tape is, then you'll know what a gift it could be to get a mix tape from someone with similar taste who had selected songs and artists you weren't very familiar with.

So it was when I first read *He Rules Who Can,* the featured serial in one of these wonderful hardbacks. I'd read some Brodeur I'd enjoyed before, but wow, I'd never read him writing at this level. From start to finish *He Rules Who Can* overflows with forward momentum and scenes of great color, not to mention constant surprises. It's up there with the very finest historicals from the pulps, like one of Harold Lamb's best, or a great Crusader yarn from Robert E. Howard.

Arthur Gilchrist Brodeur was a mainstay in the historical fiction pulps starting in the late teens and through much of the twenties, often writing in concert with his best friend Farnham Bishop. That he was also a professor at UC Berkley and a scholar of Scandinavian studies (his translation of Snorri Sturloson's *The Prose Edda* in 1916 was well received) can hardly be coincidental. His students held him in high regard because when he taught the Norse sagas he presented the people involved as human beings, not remote, mythic figures. Later in life, after he became the founding chairman of UC Berkley's Scandinavian Studies department, and received high honors from the Swedish government for his work, he went on to write the acclaimed *Art of Beowulf* in 1959.

His attention to scholarly detail certainly shows in *He Rules Who Can*. Certainly, some events are simplified and some time scales compressed, and some characters are invented or combined, but for the most part Brodeur holds to the historical record, and when he creates new details he does so with such skill that they blend seamlessly with the facts.

Harald Hardrada, our protagonist, is probably best known to history as the King of Norway (and possibly because of his death upon the Stamford Bridge in 1066), but prior to any of that he spent some fifteen years as a mercenary for the Byzantines and the Rus. And it is Harald's time in the Byzantine Varangian guard that Brodeur celebrates in this thrilling novel. Students of history can delight in the great accuracy taken in even minor details, like the name of Harald's love interest, of Empress Zoe's cosmetics laboratory and even her beauty, said to be truly remarkable as well as lasting long into her middle-years. He brings to life complex figures like John the Eunuch, a scheming figure reminiscent of Richelieu in that he was brilliant, duplicitous, and ruthless and yet devoted first and foremost to the state. Likewise we get Hardrada's fierce rival, Giorgios, captain of the Immortals, a wily, rage-filled villain, yet one so capable and accomplished you can't help but respect him.

Time and again Brodeur skillfully brings the environment to life without bogging his tale down with background lectures, be it the feel of a longship under speed, the splendors of Constantinople—including its hidden passages—or the precise details of the defenses of a city under siege. The scheming and counter scheming of Byzantium are infamous, but have rarely been brought so realistically into focus as they are by Brodeur, whose characters often have ulterior motives and backup plans and long-term goals only achievable by deceitful manipulation. Harald must learn to navigate his way through this environment and yet maintain his stern sense of Norse honor, and much of the story's tension rises from his determination to maintain his word and sense of justice in an environment where lies and half-truths obscure an adversary's purpose.

Those of us who've been lucky enough to read *He Rules Who Can* have been clamoring about it for decades, extolling its excellence and its truly Howardian feel. It is with sincere pleasure that I look forward to the release of this long overdue reprint and not just so that I can compare notes with other readers whom I know will love this half-forgotten gem. Only a little of Brodeur's work has been reprinted in the last decades, and he is long overdue rediscovery by a new generation of readers. I hope that this fine example of his fiction will serve as a gateway to the rest.

— Howard Andrew Jones

HE RULES WHO CAN

*In those medieval days when Constantinople
was the glory of the world, rich, guileful,
corrupt, and dangerous as a nest of
cobras, Harald the Viking and his house-
carles came in search of fortune*

1

MIKLIGARD THE GREAT

IT WAS THE year of our Lord 1038, and the third of the reign, of Michael the Money-Changer.

Openly the crowds of Constantinople hailed Michael as Heaven-born; but it was whispered in the wine-shops that he was born in the gutter. His subjects might have grown fond of him, had he tried to win their affection; but his refusal to show his face among them, his harsh treatment of his empress, whom they loved, and their fear of his brother John, estranged them.

The shadow of John—the monk, the eunuch, the tyrant—lay cold on every heart in the Imperial City. Even the Varangians were afraid of John, though, being men of the North, they feared few things on earth.

They alone sneered at John, even as they alone invariably spoke with reverence of the emperor, being faithful men who drew Michael's pay. If they nourished some doubts of him in their hearts, it was because they, too, gave their first and deepest homage to the empress.

And because John was what he was, a Varangian off duty never walked the streets alone. They went about in pairs, swaggering; a brave sight in their eagle-plumed helmets, their scarlet mantles and silver mail. The soft-faced Greeks would have liked to jeer at their long hair and shaggy blond

beards; but the burly Northern limbs and the two-faced
Varangian axes enforced respect.

The Varangians were the emperor's right arm; John
the Eunuch was his brain—and arm and brain no longer
worked in harmony.

TWO LONG DRAGON-SHIPS swept down the Bosporus,
their oars dipping and rising in slow, powerful strokes.
Their square sails were furled in the teeth of a wind that
piled choppy, smashing waves against their prows. A hot,
westering sun flashed on flung spray and wet oarblades
on mailed breasts and steel caps, and on the white shield
lashed to each masthead—a sign that Vikings came in
peace. The snaky figureheads were drawn back as if to
strike, their painted jaws open to show ivory fangs.

On the foredeck of the larger dragon two men stood
together, shading their eyes against the glowing sun. Both
were tall and strongly made; their armor was fine, their
wind-tossed cloaks of rich blue stuff. The one, Eilif, was of
middle-age, hairy, with flaming red beard and calm eyes.
When he spoke, it was with the rich, deep tones of the
Swede.

The other, Harald Sigurdsson, was young, with the pride
of youth in fine raiment and in his long, silky mustaches.
His fine features would have been handsome but for their
overcool immobility and the quiet hardness of his blue eyes.
The easy poise of his figure suggested sheathed strength
and leashed swiftness. There was about his controlled
gestures a hint of untamed eagerness that sorted ill with
his too perfect restraint.

The elder pointed far down the strait.

"You can see it now if you can bear the sun," he said.

For minutes neither spoke; the eyes of
each probed the other's heart

" 'Tis but a bright loom above the dark of the land—the roofs of the palace. We shall find friends there. When the Norwegian peasants rose against your brother and gave his crown to a Dane, all loyal men who could, fled the land, as you did. Many a stout Norse champion made his way to Mikligard—which the Greeks call Constantinople—and took service in the Varangians."

"I should have done the same," Harald said, "instead of wasting half my youth in Russian Novgorod and Kiev, where iron is more plentiful than gold. Yet the time was not wholly lost, Eilif, since I met you there."

Eilif gestured down the strait. "The emperor's falcons are out," he said. "See! A pamphylian! One of their swift cruisers. She has sighted us."

Harald watched the white speck fly toward them. His eyes narrowed almost imperceptibly.

"Will she fight?" he asked.

The Swede laughed. "There speaks the blood of Norway's

kings! Nay, she will fight only if you force trouble. Remember that a peace shield hangs on your mast, and that you have come hither to make your fortune. You are as good a man of your hands as I have ever seen; but yonder pamphylian could sweep your dragons clean of men in a moment. You have come to a land where a false step means fearful death—and where your cool head will serve you better than your hot heart."

The younger man's face seemed not to change, yet it was somehow harder. Eilif laid a heavy hand on his shoulder.

"You have never sailed this way before," he resumed, very gravely. "I served seven years with the Varangians in my youth, and I tell you that the greatest fool in all this city of Mikligard—or Constantinople—has more cunning than you or I will ever learn. Speak yonder ship gently; she carries doom!"

The cruiser came up at a bowling pace, for all that the current was against her. A brisk breeze filled her two lateen sails; double banks of oars on each side lashed the waves into a smother of spume. The drums that gave the stroke to her galley slaves pounded a swift rhythm. She handled with birdlike grace.

"Never have I seen so swift a ship!" Harald exclaimed. "And I thought my Red Dragon fleet as a gull!"

"She is knife-keeled," the Swede explained, "and built by men who work magic out of books with strange drawings in them. I have seen."

Harald wheeled suddenly, shouting an order. Men sprang to the fighting-compartments between the benches, broke out arms chests, passed arrows, and stood by the rails where their shields hung ready.

"I will not fight unless I must," Harald muttered, "but there is too much gleam of steel on yonder craft to please me."

Without slackening speed the pamphylian drove straight for the gap between the two Norse galleys, lowered sail, and stroked fairly in between them.

"Now!" cried Harald. "If she strikes, we have her!"

"Nay!" Eilif warned. "She has you. Pray that she may not strike. You think to grapple, and lay her aboard on both sides; but—watch yon bronze tubes in her waist. See how one is trained on us, the other on Gray Dragon!"

HARALD, HIS EYES on their challenger's poop, saw a little, strutting man in gold-inlaid corselet and gilt helmet, looking comically like a truculent hermit crab in an overlarge shell. As the Northman, his thin lips curved with laughter, stared, the little Greek hailed again:

"Who are ye? What is your errand?"

Eilif answered, pointing to Harald.

"These be the ships of Harald Sigurdsson, brother to the sainted Olaf, late king over all Norway. I am Eilif, son of Rognvald, Jarl of West Gautland in Sweden. Having served three years in the bodyguard of Jarislcif, King of Holmgard in Russia, we come hither with five hundred picked men, to seek enrollment in the Varangian Guard."

The Greek captain laughed insolently. "There are overmany Varangians now!" he jeered.

"Your emperor is the best judge of that," Harald spoke quietly, in a Greek strongly tinged with Russian.

The Greek's lips curled. "The Heaven-born has other things to do than receive messengers from a barbarian princeling. I will put a pilot aboard you; look to it that ye follow his directions! Otherwise—" He pointed to the long, smooth tubes of bronze commanding the dragons' decks. "Ye have heard of Greek Fire," he concluded.

Harald had, and therefore did not retort. Only the tense muscles of his throat betrayed his anger.

"Send the pilot, then!" he agreed. As a wizened Greek climbed over the Viking craft's oars, Harald turned to Eilif.

"I shall not thrive in this land!" he growled.

The red-bearded Gautlander laughed. "Your time will come," he prophesied. "Once you get your commission in the Varangians, every Greek in Mikligard will grovel to you, save only the imperial household—and the Immortals."

Harald felt a tenseness in Eilif's tone. "Thou likest not those Immortals?" he questioned.

Eilif spat overside. "Dogs, but with sharp teeth," he muttered. "Look you: the emperor has two bodyguards—the Immortals, a corps of young Greek nobles picked for birth, strength, and skill in weapons; and the Varangians, whom he keeps to watch those same noble Greeks, lest they prove as treacherous as they are brave."

"Then he is a fool!" Harald interrupted. "Why not keep the Varangians alone, and thus save the wages of the Immortals if he cannot trust them?"

"No man trusts any other in this empire," rumbled Eilif. "The Immortals cannot be disbanded, being a very ancient corps, honored by the people for their traditions. Yet the Varangians are more trusted than they, for we of the North are known to be true to our wage-giver, whereas a Greek patrician always has his eye on the crown."

The Red Dragon, following the course laid by the pilot,

moved into the quieter waters of the Golden Horn, standing out well past the rocky heights of Old Byzantium. The
house-carles massed in the waist cried out in amazement
at the spectacle opening before them, and Harald himself
drew a sharp breath of admiration. On their port quarter
lifted the great wall of Constantinople: a sweeping line of
stone flanked with towers-some round, some square, some
many-sided, but all agleam with sun-splashed weapons
and armor.

Above its crenellated crest the city—a greater wonder—
soared upward from the water: a heaped mass of brick,
limestone, porphyry and marble; gables, towers, domes,
cupolas in tier on tier, crowned with many tinted tiles, from
the very wall to the comb of the ridge far to the south. The
setting sun turned the myriad roofs and buttresses into a
fairy city, all melting line and glowing color, rose, purple,
amethyst and gold.

Harald stared with all his eyes, his body tense, his nostrils
dilated. Eilif nodded and chuckled.

"Aye; this is Mikligard the Great, coveted and feared by
the kings of the world."

THE RED DRAGON swerved in close to the breakwater,
her smaller consort in her wake. The oar beat dropped,
the longships easing slowly in. The rowers, shipping their
oars, gazed open-mouthed at such a port as they had
never dreamed of, lined with curving piers of marble-
faced masonry, green-veined and highly polished. A dozen
armed guards stood at ease on the stair.

A voice hailed from the wall, in good Norse:

"Who are ye, who come with white shields?"

Eilif caught Harald's surprised glance, and answered it:

"The Varangians are on guard here."

Much pleased, Harald made answer in his own tongue, giving his name and race, the numbers of his crews, and their purpose. The gate swung open while he was yet speaking. Through it pushed two men, one huge, one short and stocky; both in the scarlet and steel of the Varangian Guard.

The big man strode like an eager giant, leaving his fellow with the shorter legs well behind. Burly of limb, broad-featured, yellow of beard and hair, he came with a jingle of mail and clatter of ax on shield that would have shamed a troop of cavalry. His eyes gleamed with joy; his thick arms were spread wide.

"Come to me!" he cried. "Come, little brother to my slain lord and king!"

Harald was smothered in his vast embrace.

"Thiodolf the Skald!" he exclaimed. "Eilif said we should find friends here—but to see thee again—"

"Here is another who has drawn sword for thy brother Olaf!" the big man boomed. "Ulf Uspaksson, the Icelander!"

Harald seized the eagerly offered hand. "To-night we shall drink to old times together. But, first, ye two shall lead me to the emperor."

Thiodolf the "Skald"—warrior-poet and historian of the Norse court—laughed. "So thou wilt become a Varangian? Nay, I am loath to deny thee, but the emperor sees few men these days, and none after vespers. To-morrow I will take thee, though we are more apt to see the Eunuch John— may the saints spew him out!—than the emperor. Now ye shall all come with me to the Frankish Hospice."

"Hospice? Is not that a kind of inn? Where is there an inn to house and feed five hundred?"

Thiodolf and Ulf laughed together.

"By my beard! The Frankish Hospice is a vast guest house, where all who come from the north are housed at the state's charge. It is maintained by a tax on the cargoes of northern traders. Five hundred, say you? There is room for them in the courtyard alone."

"Holy St. Olaf!" cried Harald, crossing himself. "I had not thought to see the like in heaven!"

"It is possible that you will not," Thiodolf retorted. "But this is Mikligard the Great, and much nearer hell than heaven."

2

THE SHADOW

THROUGH A THIRTY-FOOT arch the Northmen strode, its hollow depths lighted by urn-shaped lamps set in niches high above the pavement. As they emerged, a second gate, formed of two leaves of bronze-plated oak, clanged behind them. Its echo filled Harald with a vague sense of disquiet, the foreboding of a man who has lived in the free out-of-doors, and feels himself suddenly shut in.

The sky was now olive-green with approaching night. Lights were leaping out as far as eye could reach. Harald Sigurdsson, amazed, watched them wink on in a line that seemed unending down the long avenue.

The newly arrived Northmen marched like drilled veterans. They were no armed peasants, nor the rude following of a barbarian chief, but the pick of the splendid troops who covered the retreat after King Olaf's last battle. They advanced now in column of fours, leaving scant room for carriages and horse litters to pass, swaggering as if the town were theirs. The crowds hurriedly made way before them, thinking from their very arrogance and their perfect order that they were a regiment of Varangians.

"Here is the Strategium," Thiodolf announced.

They were passing the entrance to an immense square,

stone-paved, empty of all adornment. Open on the west to the street, it was almost entirely closed in on the other three sides by long, square buildings.

"The Strategium is the barracks and parade ground of all the Imperial Guards," Thiodolf explained. "On the north is the armory; on the east, the barracks of the Immortals; on the south, those of the Varangians, with the city prison at its side. All is snug and convenient: a Varangian may pick a quarrel with an Immortal in front of his own door, and be cast into a cell for disorder, all without walking more than a hundred paces."

Something in his manner led Harald to inquire:

"And the Immortal?"

"Immortals are not cast into prison," the skald answered.

Eilif raised his heavy voice: "In my time it went ill with the Immortal who touched one of us!" he boomed. But Thiodolf laid a warning hand on his arm.

"More of this later," he cautioned. "It is not safe to speak of some things in the streets. In these days we Northmen must walk warily."

Past the parade ground they marched, on and on down that straight street from the water front. Now the buildings grew more stately.

Framed in the arches of the south colonnade blazed the white facade they had first seen, in a bath of white light.

"The prefecture of police," Ulf laughed. "The prefect was useless, his men too timid to keep order; wherefore John the Eunuch gave the post of Prefect of Public Safety to Georgios Maniakes, grand commander of the Immortals. Since then peace and law rule in this city—and we Varangians walk more softly."

Thiodolf gestured to the left, leading his guests down
a wide way that opened from the eastern arch. Strange as
he was to cities, Harald at once perceived that this was the
main thoroughfare. The Mese, or "Middle Street," as it was
called, ran through the city from the Golden Gate on the
west to the Palace of the Emperors on the eastern shore.

"This is the Hospice," the skald announced, turning in at
an open archway in the south portico of the Mese. "Wait
here till I return."

The column came to a halt in the street, almost
completely blocking it.

MINUTES PASSED; THEN Thiodolf was back, a second
officer at his side. To him Harald gave his name and titles
in Greek, and was vouched for by Thiodolf and Ulf.

The officer, a tall Englishman, glanced him over coolly,
nodded, and held out his hand.

"I am Aldhelm, captain of the Third Band of the Second
Theme of Varangians, stationed at the Hospice. You are
welcome. Your charges, and those of your men, will be paid
from the public funds for two months. After that, unless
you find employment in the guards, you must pay your own
way. I must tell you that the guards have now well-nigh
their full complement."

"Every man who opens his lips tells me so," Harald
smiled; and, as Northern custom prescribed, gave the officer a gift—one of the two spiral gold armlets that he wore
from wrist to elbow. The Englishman stared a moment,
then smiled back, and took the gift.

"It is so long since I left home," he apologized, "that I
had forgot the ways of our peoples. We shall be friends for
that, son of Sigurd."

Turning, he led the way into a vast hall. Men were dwarfed, well-nigh lost in it. When all his company was within, Harald saw with astonishment that they made a compact group filling less than a twelfth of the interior. And this was but the hall of assembly!

Knots of spearmen in full uniform of silvered mail, plumed helmets, scarlet cloaks, and soft leather boots stood about the wall; for so great a guest house, entertaining so many men, must be well policed. Others, off duty, hung about in little groups.

Here and there among them strolled an officer of Varangians, with a fierce swagger and a searching glance of the eye. Now and then he would stop an applicant for service, shoot a few swift questions at him, and pass on. One or two with whom he spoke stood straighter, with shining faces; many more turned away dejectedly, plucking at their beards.

"They pick those accepted on probation for vacancies in the guard," Aldhelm informed Harald. "These are very few. The lists are full; new men are taken only when detachments are sent on hazardous service, or men are killed in a brawl. I will take you to your quarters."

He led the way into a long passage from which many doorways opened. Here Thiodolf and Ulf looked about them; but Aldhelm led on. Thiodolf chuckled.

"You have indeed made a friend of that Englishman," he muttered to Harald. "He means to lodge you in one of the great suites above stairs."

The Englishman led the way into a vast area open to the night sky, where many lamps flared against the stone, and the waters of a fountain broke in prismatic spray. Across this court yawned a stone archway, within which he halted.

"You shall have these twenty rooms on the right," Aldhelm said. "And the use of this end of the court. The baths are beyond your quarters. Farewell; I must go back."

"By all the saints at once, and the old gods to boot!" swore Thiodolf. "These be the best chambers in the Hospice!"

Harald smiled. "That was the best gold ring that ever came out of Norway," he answered. "We shall do well here."

"Aye," nodded Thiodolf, "the entertainment is good, if ye grow not weary of it ere ye find what ye seek."

HARALD STARED HARD at him. "Thou wert ever a merry man, and reckless," he said. "Yet tonight thou hast croaked of evil like a raven. Speak out, and tell me what is amiss."

Ulf, watching Harald closely, bent forward and almost whispered:

"The truth is that we Varangians are out of favor with the court, and for good reason. We of the north are true to our wage-giver. That wage-giver, here in Mikligard, is the emperor. The old emperor, Romanus, was murdered; and because we are true to the Empress Zoe, his widow, the usurper Michael the Moneychanger, fears us."

He broke off, plainly from a sudden conviction that he had said too much. But Thiodolf, bolder, took up the tale:

"If he is to know anything, Ulf, he should know all. Three years since, the Eunuch John and his brother—who is now emperor—strangled Romanus. At least that is the rumor, and we believe it. Certain it is that they forced Zoe to marry Michael the very night after the murder of her husband. Only through marriage with her could Michael, who is lowborn, gain the crown.

"Michael—at John's bidding, it is said—at once imprisoned the empress in her own apartments, where she has lived in enforced seclusion ever since. But it is John who rules. Michael is sick almost to death. Folk say remorse has eaten his soul. He is seen but seldom, never without John; and then his pale face is painted to hide the shadow of death that clouds it."

Harald's face was placid, but his hands gently smoothed his cloak. By this token Eilif, who understood him, sensed his impatience.

"If I cannot see the emperor, is there none in authority who will receive me?" he asked.

"Aye—the Eunuch John," Thiodolf answered bitterly. "It is he whose shadow darkens all this land. With him I can get you an audience—but you will gain little by it.

"John it was who cut the numbers of the Varangians from thirty to fifteen thousand. He favors the Immortals, and takes away our ancient privileges one by one. It will scarce please him to learn that you have come with five hundred hungry Northmen to seek place in a corps that he already hates. But say to no man what we have told you. John's soft hands clutch half the world, and he sends death to those he mistrusts."

"I shall say nothing. But I tell you this, Thiodolf: see him I will, and from him I shall have what I ask, if I have to tickle his throat with steel!"

The skald started up in alarm. "If such words should become known, it is your own throat that would be tickled, and mine too; and your men would find places on wayside crosses from here to Jerusalem!"

Eilif the Swede looked up, his fingers twitching.

"This John may be an ill man to cross," he said, "but so is Harald. You have seen the ax that Olaf his brother bore?"

Thiodolf nodded. "I remember he called it 'Hell,' and when he went to battle against the pagan Hordlanders he cried out: 'Now shall Hell eat the heathen!' And Hell did."

"It is that same ax Harald has just now laid beside him," Eilif said quietly. "And with five hundred of the best men that ever followed Olaf, it will not be hard for him to make his way anywhere."

Ulf fingered his beard and frowned. "While our roll has been cut in half," he spoke, "there are still thirty thousand Immortals in the empire, not to speak of the eastern troops. And there are generals here, like Georgios Maniakes, who hate Varangians, and are no less skillful than Olaf at his best."

Harald picked up the ax, and felt its edge. "We shall see," he said. "I came here for a purpose, and I mean to gain it. To-morrow, Thiodolf, you shall get me an audience of John."

The skald rose, and Ulf with him. "I will, then. But I pray you speak him fair, or you will never leave the palace. Your house-carles cannot help you: they would not be allowed within the palace gates. What you win here, you must win through cunning; force will not avail. John is the most cunning man in the world. And say nothing of John to any whom you meet. He would hear it."

Harald rose with his guests. "Go not yet," he begged. "Find me some way to get into the palace to-night. It would ease my mind to know something of the ways in— and out—before I speak with this John."

"There is one way," answered Thiodolf; but he seemed

disturbed. "I have my quarters in the Chalke, the citadel of the palace. I will take you there as my guest when I go on duty at midnight."

"Take me now!" Harald laughed. "Then there will be time to see something of this city, and the ways of its folk."

3

GEORGIOS

WHEN HE EMERGED with Thiodolf on the street, Harald found that Ulf was no longer with them. Nor could they see him anywhere among the men who thronged the lighted steps of the Hospice.

"He has grown cautious," Thiodolf shrugged. "We will go without him." He turned to Harald uneasily. "Your men will be quiet at the Hospice? If they start a northern brawl here, you will suffer for it at court."

"Eilif is chief of my house-carles," Harald replied. "They know he is as bad a man to anger as I. They will be like lambs."

Thiodolf muttered; "This is no place for a hothead."

"Eilif says truly," Harald retorted, "that my heart is hot, but my head is cool. Never fear that I will begin what I cannot end. My fears are for you, lest the softness and the treachery of this land have sapped your manhood. When I knew you, you were ever ready to break a head or fire a town. You will find me quick to avenge injury, but slow to make needless trouble."

They walked on in silence along the Mese till they came to a cross street. Here, to the right, a high, carved portal beyond an arcade blazed between two lamp-bearing columns; and from high windows with open ivory shutters poured a flood of light, the reek of wine, and the tumult of excited men.

Harald stopped, tugging at Thiodolf's arm.

"What is here?" he asked. "An ale house? Let us go in."

Thiodolf hesitated. "There may be wild company," he demurred.

At the skald's knock the door opened. A burly Nubian slave, his oiled skin gleaming like black satin, led them into a large hall. A crowd of men were drinking at low tables, and all craned their necks to stare at the newcomers. Harald, sensing hostility in their eyes, felt his anger stir. His face grew masklike; he shook his shoulders to feel the reassuring weight of his ax.

A second black slave hurried up to find them places. When they were seated, Harald began deliberately to return the steady gaze of the company. They deserved his interest.

There were perhaps a hundred men in the place, without reckoning the men and women in the reed-curtained alcoves; and all were plainly men of some consequence. Some were old, richly dressed in long silken robes, their beards carefully trimmed. Some, younger and brisker, bore the air of prosperous merchants.

A few wore tunics and mantles of pure white, and bore gilded wands of office, or leaned these against their seats. In one corner a dozen slender, sinewy men in green sat together, a commingled smell of horse and leather rising from their garments.

But by far the greatest number were young, powerfully framed fellows in splendid armor, all uniformed after one pattern. Their mail was of finest mesh, gilded, over which they wore mantles of yellow silk, edged with purple. Plumed helmets rested on the floor by their chairs; and all wore sword or dagger.

"Who are those?" Harald asked.

Thiodolf purposely misunderstood. "They in white? Palace attendants."

"Nay; they in armor!"

Thiodolf squirmed. "They are Immortals. This tavern draws most of its custom from them and from the charioteers and grooms of the Hippodrome. They stare at us because I am a Varangian, and they love us not."

Harald knew the skald lied, that the hostile glances had been for himself. He perceived at once that the very fact he was a Northman, but not in imperial service, made him fair game for the jealous Immortals. They might try to fasten on him the quarrel they dared not pick with a Varangian officer of the Life Guard.

THE BLACK CAME with their wine, bringing with it roast duck on a silver platter, and almond cakes.

Harald quaffed of the wine, then tore off a leg of duck and gnawed at it. Straightway three Immortals at the table burst into roars of laughter. Others followed suit, till all who could see were rocking with mirth. Seeing that they laughed at him, Harald laid down the food, wiped his hands on the tablecloth, and half rose. His face was expressionless, but his right hand quivered for the feel of his ax.

"Is this the way," he asked, in a calm, loud voice, "that the folks of Constantinople treat guests of the State?"

The laughter died. One Immortal turned to a companion with languid insolence:

"Guests of the State? That is good Greek for beggar!" In clever pantomime he mocked Harald's barbaric fashion of handling his meat. His table-mates were most daintily holding their portions between thumb and forefinger of the left hand, and shaving off tidbits with their knives.

At this open mockery of his manners, Harald's anger flamed; but it showed only in the pinched whiteness of his nostrils.

"Every folk to his own fashions," he observed loudly to Thiodolf. "In our land we eat less like women, fight like men, and are courteous to strangers."

But all at once the tension seemed to slacken. All eyes turned from him. Voices that had pealed in laughter were hushed. Harald pulled the skald's sleeve.

"What now?" he asked.

Thiodolf gestured toward the stage at one end of the room. "There is a great dancer here to-night, the foremost actress in the empire. She is a slave, owned by yonder fat and greasy Syrian, Orontides, whose house this is."

The entire audience—and by this time every seat was filled—sat with eyes glued to a side door giving on the stage. Waiters scurried to and fro from the kitchens, with jugs of Lesbian and Syrian wine, lest any guest thirst during the performance.

"This will be a rare sight!" Thiodolf whispered.

Then the audience was on its feet shouting itself hoarse, clapping and stamping. Rising with them, Harald saw a slender shape glide through the door, poise before the musicians, and leap into a whirl of flying feet and tossing draperies. The music swelled again, the drums muttering a ceaseless accompaniment to the plucked strings and wailing flutes.

The watchers sank into their seats, eyes fixed on the form that flitted and wheeled and posed before them. She danced not after the manner of the Greeks, with slow, graceful postures in time to decorous music, nor in the wriggling contortions of the Orient; but with a wild, rushing grace that seemed to sweep the instruments with her in a whirlwind of sound suited solely to her movements.

Her tiny feet flashed faster than eye could follow; her many-colored draperies, now folding themselves about her close and clinging, now swirling like beating wings, made a riot of glowing hues against which the whiteness of her arms and shoulders now flashed, now stood out like frozen marble.

At last she stopped and the music stopped with her in one crashing chord—so suddenly that the ears and eyes of the beholders, still strained, were utterly confused. She stood there bowing, graceful arms outspread.

THE WALLS ECHOED with tumultuous applause; dignified merchants and mailed warriors alike leaping to their feet and shouting in rapturous enthusiasm. Smiling, she waved her hands to them; and then Orontides, her master, mounted to the stage and took her hand. As at a signal, every man in the place fell silent. The Syrian, leading her on his arm, she descended to the floor and made her way among the tables.

Before each group she stopped; and after she had exchanged a few bantering words with them, the onlookers poured gold and silver into an urn which the Syrian bore in his left hand. Harald saw that the Immortals and the more richly dressed civilians gave large pieces of minted gold, the soldiers especially striving to outdo one another in generosity. His Northern pride stung by their insolence, he resolved, when his turn came, to shame them with his lavishness.

The girl had now reached the table just ahead of Harald's. Its places were occupied by four Immortals, officers, to judge by the rich medallions dangling from their necks, and the fineness of their mail. As she spoke to them, they rose, broke into exclamations of praise and admiration, and poured gold into the Syrian's urn. Orontides smiled and fawned on them.

"Glorious givers!" he cried unctuously. "Hearts of pure gold! Ah, my lord Karaktos! It is such as you who understand art."

The girl moved on, the officers gazing after her with hungry looks. Harald saw her stand before him. When Thiodolf had given two gold pieces, he rose, taking from his neck a chain of massive gold. Dangling it for one moment before the enraptured Orontides, listening in triumph to the exclamations of the other guests, Harald made as if to place the chain in the urn. Then, instead, he flung it about the girl's neck.

A cry of amazement ran through the room, both at the greatness of the gift and the stranger's impudence in giving it to the slave instead of to her master. The Syrian's hand went out greedily, to snatch the chain; but Harald caught the outstretched fingers in his. Orontides whined with pain, and cringed.

The girl smiled, not with the mechanical smile which had acknowledged her other gifts.

"Here," she spoke, in soft, flutelike tones, "is one who understands beauty indeed! Truly this is a prince!"

A murmur of anger and envy rose among the guests. Black looks were darted at the Northman; hands reached for hilts. The Immortal called Karaktos leaped gracefully to his feet and stood at the girl's shoulder.

"Never before have gifts won your favor, Cyra," he said huskily. "If gold will win you, here is that which is worth much gold." He tore a blazing ruby from the folds of his yellow-mantle, and thrust it into the dancer's hand.

Cyra shrank from his eyes. "I want no gift of yours, my lord," she answered, and cast the jewel at his feet. Pouncing like a hawk, Orontides snatched it up and thrust it into his urn. The companions of Karaktos began to smile; but he turned upon them with a fury that sobered them.

"You would take a barbarian's gift, and not mine!" he snarled at the girl. "Thrice have I offered your master much gold for you, and he has refused. Now you fling back at me a stone worth your weight in silver. But your master has taken it, and you are mine, for I have paid for you!"

His hand clutched her shoulder. She pulled away; but he held her fast, drew her to him, and flung one massive arm about her waist.

"Orontides!" she screamed. "I will not be his! Take me away!"

But Orontides had glided from the room, content with his price. Seeing herself abandoned, Cyra struggled madly; but the Immortal was too strong for her. Whipping one hand free, she struck him across the mouth. Mad with the blow and the laughter of his friends, he seized her white throat and shook her fiercely.

So far Harald had watched in quiet, though his eyes were glowing. Now, his cheeks suddenly flushed, he tossed his ax to Thiodolf, and sprang at the Immortal. Warned by the cries of his companions, Karaktos flung the girl from him and turned to meet his assailant. The Greek was a huge man, his bare arms rippling with muscle; and his fury made him doubly terrible. With the swift grace of a trained athlete he met Harald's onrush, catching the Northman's left arm and twisting him half about, reaching with his own left for his opponent's eyes.

Thiodolf, who knew the Greek mode of fighting, and the Greek disregard for fair play, flung himself between the struggling men and the Immortal's friends, with Harald's ax poised. The Greeks reached for hilts, but did not draw; for the lifted ax could strike more swiftly than they could wrench steel from scabbard.

THE FIRST FEEL of his enemy's fingers warned Harald that Karaktos was the stronger man, and knew how to use his body. But Harald had been practiced from youth in the "lordly lore" of Norway, which included wrestling as well as poetry and the use of weapons. In the North he had never met his match, and the Norse schools of fight were the hardest in the world.

He ducked to avoid the gouging fingers, let himself grow suddenly limp and follow the pull of the Greek's right arm, and drove his knee into the Immortal's stomach. Karaktos reeled; but as Harald followed up his advantage, the Greek drove the heel of his left hand into his opponent's face. The blow landed with jarring force, evening the odds.

The two stood apart, staggering. One moment they glared at each other: Karaktos with flaming rage, Harald with the cool relentlessness which was his birthright from ancestors both brave and shrewd. His blue eyes gleamed frostily; his thin lips parted in a smile.

The Greek sprang, swift as light. Swifter still, Harald swerved, thrust one heel behind the other's knee, and drove his right fist to the chin. The blow struck home with a crash of bone. Karaktos hurtled back as if flung from a catapult, and smote the floor with the broad of his back. Harald stood over him, waiting, his breath coming a little hard; but the Greek did not move. He lay asprawl, blood gushing from his nostrils.

Smiling, Harald took his ax from the skald, and gazed about at the onlookers. By their dumb amazement he knew that he had felled one whom the city regarded as a champion.

Then, from all over the room, voices shrilled in fury:

"He has slain Karaktos! The barbarian has killed an Immortal! Strike! Avenge!"

Harald stepped back, the ax resting across his left forearm. Slowly, his eyes glinting defiance, he edged to the wall, and set his shoulders against it. Thiodolf followed with drawn sword.

Only when they had reached this vantage-point did they notice that the girl was gone. Thiodolf grunted scornfully.

"Having raised the storm, she has fled before its fury," he growled. "It is like her kind."

Thiodolf's voice tore through the rising tumult:

"Fools! Would ye murder Varangians? Have ye forgot our privileges?"

One of Karaktos's table companions, a cool-headed veteran, answered maliciously:

"Ye Varangians have few privileges left, now John rules in the palace. And if you are a Varangian, Thiodolf, this stranger is none. He wears not the uniform. Him we may slay; if you defend him, you take your own risks. Have not we Immortals privileges, too? The privilege of avenging our dead?"

The civilians in the crowd howled approval. Mortally afraid of the Varangians when the odds were anything like equal, they asked nothing better than to get a foreigner—especially a Northman—at disadvantage. The Immortals had their private grudge to wreak, their long hatred for the rival corps, and the death of one of their officers. They surged in, brandishing swords and knives. But he who had answered Thiodolf waved them back.

"This is our quarrel!" he cried. "Karaktos was our friend, captain of our own company! Do ye look on while we three avenge him!"

The three advanced, while the rest stood back, their balked bloodlust spending itself in eager gasps and cries.

Harald thrust Thiodolf from him with one great hand.

"Give me room to swing!" he ordered. "I can deal with these!"

"Never!" Thiodolf answered. "They are three to two!"

"Fool!" Harald hissed. "Stand between me and the crowd, lest they rush us!"

Thiodolf obeyed, his sword weaving in his hand, his eyes glaring.

THE THREE GREEKS advanced, side by side, points raised, hilts low. Three paces from their quarry they fell into the swordsman's crouch, left hands wrapped in their mantles to ward his blows. One feinted, hoping to draw Harald's attack in a circling slash of the ax, the others ready to close as the Northman struck. His blows would be heavy, but slow—the ax is not a swift weapon.

Harald read the first man's purpose in his eyes. Instead of warding or slashing, he thrust suddenly with the head of his weapon, as if it were a sword. The ax Hell was broad, its haft prolonged beyond the head in a long horn of trenchant steel. The Greek swiftly turned his feint into a parry; but the ax turned, slid under his guard, and ripped his throat open.

Instantly his two comrades thrust with their long, straight swords, in the dangerous undercut the Greeks had learned from the Roman legions. Harald's ax, still extended, fell to strike one point down; the other flickered home, straight and true to his stomach. But as it flashed he turned slightly, and the steel rings of his birnie dashed it aside. The ax Hell rose and sank; and but one Greek lived to face it.

The crowd, yelling savagely, swarmed closer to Thiodolf's menacing point. Maddened by the fall of their favorites, they were working themselves into the mob-fury that fears nothing and stops at nothing. Thiodolf braced his feet and poised himself.

Harald's remaining foe feinted once, caught the flash of Hell's circling blade, and lost heart. With a cry of fear he cast down his sword and fell at Harald's feet. Spurning him aside, Harald snatched up the sword, hurled it into the nearest faces, and leaped to join Thiodolf. The ax poised again, dripping.

One moment the crowd hung irresolute, dismayed by that red blade; then they moved slowly forward, stumbling over one another's feet, getting each in the other's way, but deadly with hate. The two Northmen set their teeth and stood fast, waiting for the end.

Before their lifted blades and set, grim faces the mob fell silent; but it advanced steadily, slowly to its butcher's work.

A knock sounded at the outer door; sounded again, loud and commanding, but none gave heed. On and on pressed the packed hordes of Greeks, the soldiers in the van with hungry weapons, till the foremost were within striking distance. Steel clashed—

A horn blared in the street outside. As if turned to stone, the furious Immortals dropped their arms and stood. Behind them the mob wavered, angry faces pale with sudden fear.

"The trumpet of Georgios!" Thiodolf gasped hoarsely in Harald's ear.

"Georgios?" The question came through set teeth.

"High Commander of the Immortals, and prefect of public safety. He makes his rounds through the city, with a single attendant, and appears when least expected. All fear him—disobedience to his orders means death on the cross."

Not a man stirred. The door was torn open, and a black-browed giant ripped his way through the throng. Packed as they were, they squeezed aside to make him room, shrinking from the touch of his enormous shoulders. In the doorway behind him stood one man, in the uniform of the Immortals, bearing a brazen trumpet.

The prefect shouldered through them as a bull plows through reeds. His dark face was savage, his beaked nose and jutting chin eloquent of relentless purpose. His sword

was sheathed; but his huge hands, clenching and unclench-
ing, seemed equal to any emergency.

Straight to the Northmen he strode, and stood with his
back to the crowd. His black eyes blazed at the two; and
Thiodolf looked down. Harald met him eye to eye, the
bloody ax still raised.

For all his dominating fierceness, Georgios was first to
shift his gaze. His eyes glanced over the bloody floor, and
rested on the three dead Immortals. He turned again to the
Northmen, noted Thiodolf's bright blade, and the bloody
face of Hell.

"You have done this?" he asked, the sound of his voice
like the roll of thunder before the lightning strikes.

Harald's eyes never left the prefect's face.

"I have done it," he answered calmly, "and done it well."

Georgios glared at him. "For what cause have you, a
stranger and a barbarian, slain three officers of the Emper-
or's Guard?"

"I am a king's son and a king's brother," Harald answered.
"None less than a king may question me. I will give my
reasons to your emperor; though, since men say he is
low-born and I am of the best blood of the North, I will
answer him only as a favor."

THE GRIM GEORGIOS gasped; and the mob, frightened
even to have heard such insolence, stared wide-eyed, each
man at his neighbor. The prefect glanced from Harald's
bloody ax to his determined eyes, and turned away.

"Where is Orontides?" the prefect bellowed.

A cluster of cowed Immortals slunk through the door to
the inner apartments, and returned dragging the trembling

proprietor. Before the feet of Georgios they cast him. He lay grovelling, not daring to speak.

Georgios kicked him roughly. "Pig!" he cried. "Are my officers to be murdered in your sty? Speak, knave, and tell all!"

The Syrian's mouth opened and closed like that of a choking fish; but no words came. Georgios kicked him again.

"Speak, or be crucified!"

Orontides found his voice. "Ah-h!" he sobbed. "Most august lord! Most noble, sovereign prefect! It was no fault of mine. I keep an honest house. But these barbarian dogs—"

Georgios set his iron-shod foot on the Syrian's neck, and pressed his face into the marble mosaic.

"You mean," he asked with ominous quietness, "that these Northmen set on my three men and butchered them?"

Taking the lowered voice as a sign that the prefect's anger was cooling, Orontides gave the answer that he thought would please:

"Even so, my lord. They picked a quarrel, struck when the noble Immortals were unaware—"

Georgios drove his hobnails into the fellow's face. "You lie!" he roared. "I enter to find two hundred men, soldiers and citizens, about to tear apart two armed men. One of these men has slain three of my best officers—a deed notable enough, if he had taken them by surprise. But their bodies lie, one to the right, with no weapon mark on it, and two facing yonder wall, swords still in their dead fists. Their wounds are in front—proof that they set on this stranger, not he on them. Their deaths, then, prove him a brave man, and one as skilled in arms as I have ever seen."

He turned on the cowering crowd.

"Let all civilians get out!" he snapped. "To your homes, and forget what ye have seen! Immortals, bide here!"

Merchants and citizens ran for the door, scrambling into the street as fast as they could. The crestfallen Immortals remained, each trying surreptitiously to slide his sword into its scabbard.

Georgios glared at them. Harald, watching his face in profile, marveled at its utter ferocity. With his enormous frame, his herculean shoulders, and the incredible savagery of his features, he was, indeed, a man to cow the boldest.

"Never have I seen his like!" Harald whispered to Thiodolf.

"He is a devil!" Thiodolf answered in Norse. "Like Thor, whom our heathen grandsires worshiped. Even John the Eunuch fears him."

Before that rigid, silent scowl the Immortals cringed, afraid to move or speak, bunched even as he had first surprised them. Suddenly Georgios thundered:

"Attention!"

Like machines, the huddled men snapped erect, models of soldierly perfection but for their chalk-white faces.

"Ye hares!" the prefect raged at them. "Ye skulking, whimpering cowards! Ye claim to be sons of Greek nobles, men picked from the best of the Empire! And three of your choicest are slain, in fair fight, by one barbarian! And the rest of you, not daring to meet their slayer man to man, egg on a mob to pull him down! Had I known ye were such cravens, I would have clothed ye as women and given ye in charge of the palace eunuchs!"

The men took it, standing stiffly, only their twitching faces showing how his words seared them.

"In column!" he barked. "Right about! March!"

With mechanical precision the men obeyed, faced, filed through the door. When the last of them had departed, Georgios turned to the prostrate Orontides:

"You keep a disorderly house. Tomorrow men will come to give you two hundred lashes. Your tavern will be closed for a month."

Swinging abruptly to Harald, he questioned:

"Now, barbarian, what was the quarrel about?"

Harald scanned him up and down. "You seem a fair man, and strong," he answered. "I will tell you this much, that it was about a woman."

"Her name? Where is she?"

"Her name," Harald returned, "does not matter. I know not where she is. She was not to blame."

GEORGIOS STIRRED ORONTIDES with his foot:

"Her name, jackal!" Orontides, wild with terror of the promised scourging, hoping against hope to win favor and avert punishment, sobbed out:

"It was Cyra, gracious lord. The great dancer, my Persian slave. Do not harm her, my lord—I will pay a king's ransom rather than have her beauty spoiled. She cost me a thousand bezants!"

"Where is she?"

"I know not. Indeed, mighty lord, I know not! She disappeared when the fight began."

"Then she was the woman," Georgios reflected, "who

appeared at my quarters, warned the guard that there was
murder afoot here, and fled before she could be detained.
It matters not; my men will find her."

"Your men have no right to harm her," Harald interposed. "She has done good, not evil."

Georgios scowled blackly at him. "The Varangian here is
of the Life Guard, and so outside my authority," he retorted
angrily. "But you are not yet a Varangian, and with you I
may do as I please. You are already in peril enough for slay-
ing my guardsmen, without endangering yourself yet more
by challenging my authority."

"You mean," Harald asked quietly, "that you will dare lay
hands on me—a free man, and a king's son?"

Georgios turned, his back on him, and called to his
orderly in the entrance way:

"Basil! Arrest this fellow!"

The orderly, a sturdy soldier, advanced on Harald. He
saw the bloody ax, but with no sign of fear he commanded:

"Yield me your weapon!"

With a scornful laugh, Harald slid the ax into the thong
of his leather baldric.

"Come and take it from me!" he challenged.

Thiodolf stood helplessly by, sick with fear for his friend;
he had seen Georgios at work before.

"It were best to give up," he counseled imploringly.

The orderly came on, one hand outstretched. One
moment Harald faced him; the next he whirled unexpectedly on Georgios, caught the prefect's right arm in
a hammerlock, lifted him by main force onto his broad
shoulders, and hurled him full at the orderly. The huge
prefect shot through the air, bowled his man over, and

rolled almost to the door. He was up again instantly, shaking his immense shoulders.

"You shall die for this!" he roared. "I will kill you with my hands!"

This was what Thiodolf had feared.

Georgios rushed. The Norseman, lightly poised, waited. As his enemy closed, Harald pivoted, struck out first with one fist, then with the other, and drove the Greek staggering back. Unused to fist play, though a master wrestler, the prefect came back, shaking his great head, sparring for an opening with clutching hands.

Harald deliberately gave it to him—then danced back, just out of reach of the closing arms. Stooping as if to seize his adversary's knees, Harald straightened suddenly, drove his left fist to the Greek's flank below the ribs, and his right to the throat, with all the power of his upward leap behind it. Dropping his hands, Georgios stood for a moment utterly helpless, his vast chest heaving with pain and loss of breath.

Before he could recover, Harald gave him a knee thrust in the groin; and, as Georgios reeled, followed it with the full force of fist, arm, and shoulder to the jutting jaw. Georgios toppled. Shouldering him bodily, Harald flung him crashing on the marble floor.

"He had done better to keep his troops with him," the victor laughed. "Now to the palace!"

Thiodolf shook his head ruefully. "You can never show yourself in the palace now," he moaned. "Nor in the city. I must find you a safe hiding place till we can smuggle you away. Come—swiftly—"

His voice was drowned by the rush of many feet, the

clank of mail, and the shouting of angry men, all confused together as in the thick of battle. High pitched commands strove to make themselves heard; steel clanged on steel.

"What now?" the skald cried, springing to the door. Harald reached it as soon as he, and burst out laughing. But Thiodolf broke into angry curses.

"This is the end!" he wailed; but the words scarce carried above the din.

IN THE STREET a mass of armed men was fighting furiously, the blows resounding like hammers on a hundred anvils. So many were they that they filled the road from arcade to arcade; and there was scarce room anywhere for a full-armed stroke. This was lucky, else there would have been a savage slaughter. Men cast down their swords for lack of room to use them; and, striving to draw knives, felt their arms pinioned by the sheer press of both friend and foe.

"End it!" Thiodolf bellowed in his friend's ear. "If more fall, there will be a price on your head that will bring the world about your ears!"

Harald stood at gaze, smiling. The sight pleased him. Their backs against the northern arcade opposite, shoulder to shoulder—but with gap after gap showing in their ranks as they were dragged down—struggled those very Immortals whom, but a few minutes since, Georgios had ordered away. Surrounding them, pressing against them, smiting with fist and dagger and smothering them with sheer weight, milled a mass of mailed warriors that Harald recognized as his own house-carles.

A heavy hand smote his shoulder. Wheeling, he saw the

angry eyes and bleeding face of Georgios. The Greek was half doubled up, as if in great pain.

"Call them off!" he roared; and Harald smiled at him derisively.

But the prefect was right: it could do neither Harald nor his men any good to destroy a small force of Immortals in the heart of the Greek capital. At any moment the uproar might be heard by fresh troops, and the Greeks be reenforced.

Snatching up the horn of the still unconscious orderly, Harald blew two quick blasts that ripped through the din and echoed brazenly down the row of stone buildings. Again he blew, and again, ere the frenzied fighters heeded the sound. At last the Norse faced about to learn the meaning of the signal; and Harald bade them give back.

From the thick of the combat an officer detached himself, his torn crimson mantle proclaiming him a Varangian. He was bleeding from the nose, and a knife had laid his cheek open.

"Ulf!" cried Thiodolf. "Fool, what means this?"

The Icelander approached, grinning. As he came up, a flurry in the untangling mass caught the eye of Georgios. As the Norse withdrew, the little line of Greeks—only a dozen or so of them still on their feet—instantly strove to charge on their own account; but in a second Georgios was among them, striking, cursing, bellowing orders:

"Down, ye dogs! Would ye do more mischief? Can ye overcome so many?"

They fell back. The Norse flocked up toward their leader, faces wide agrin, eyes still blazing with the joy of battle.

"What means this?" Harald questioned. He frowned at them; but his lips twitched in spite of him.

Ulf spoke up: "I let you go off alone with Thiodolf," he confessed calmly, "and then followed you with your own fellows. But we lost you in the crowd, and hunted long before we heard a horn, and the shouting of angry men, in this direction.

"When we came up, these men"—he jerked his head toward the bleeding Immortals—"were marching toward the forum. All at once they halted: an officer ordered them back, and they pelted this way. I feared they were after you, and it seems I was right."

HE BROKE OFF, listening.

Georgios was questioning his men, and Olf had caught the end of the reply:

"—Heard my lord shout, and, knowing the barbarian's strength, feared for my lord's safety. As we turned, these ran out from a side street and fell on us. We fought our best, ashamed to be beaten after what my lord had said to us."

Harald saw that the prefect's eye gleamed with pride. The Immortals, spurred by his bitter words in the tavern, had resolved to beat back their overwhelming foe, or die trying.

Far off a horn sounded. Thiodolf caught Harald's arm.

"Flee!" he cried. "This night's work will end in death! Ulf, do thou and Eilif hold the street till I have Harald safe!"

But Harald hung back. "Think you I will leave my lads to perish for me?" he protested. "Who are these who come? More Greeks?"

"Aye. Will it profit your men if you die? On you the freedom of Norway depends. Speed!"

Still Harald hesitated. A glance at the Immortals decided him.

"Ulf! Eilif!" he called. "These Immortals bear no bows. String your staves, and hold them here as long as ye can. If those who reïnforce them be few, keep them in play for an hour; if many, retreat to the Hospice under cover of arrow play. Tarry not too long; ye must not be taken prisoner. Once at the Hospice, Aldheim will surely protect you till I can find a way to join you."

The two nodded understanding.

"Where do you go, lad?" Eilif asked softly.

"To the palace—to speak with the Eunuch before Georgios can poison his ears against me."

Ulf groaned. "You go to death then—but you had best go at once, lest a swifter death come upon you here!"

Yielding to the skald's excited tugs at his arm, Harald turned and sped down the Mese with Thiodolf.

4

JOHN

THEY HAD RUN but a few paces when the great street merged itself in an enormous park, with courts and domes that rose out of luxuriant gardens. They passed the Hippodrome, where the horse races were held; the many-domed majesty of Santa Sophia, the "Great Church" of the emperors; and came at last to the very foot of a long battlemented wall.

Almost north and south it ran the whole breadth of the peninsula, broken only by the massive, tower-flanked gate that opened in their very path. Its bronze leaves stood wide, but a score of full-armed Immortals stood guard within the portal. These challenged at once, and Thiodolf gave the word.

"Pass, Varangian!" growled the officer on duty. "But who comes with thee?"

"My guest," Thiodolf answered. "Who dares stop one vouched for by Thiodolf of the Night Watch?"

The Immortal shook his head, and his men crossed spears before the entrance.

"His Serene Mightiness the Orphanotrophos has commanded that only men in the service shall enter." The

officer spoke curtly, glad for once to have the better of a
Varangian.

Thiodolf stared, dismayed. He must gain Harald
entrance before Ulf and his men could be overpowered by
fresh detachments of Immortals.

"The Orphanotrophos? John?" he echoed. "But he has
never denied me before. Fellow, I relieve you within the
hour, and then I shall admit whom I will. You had best let
us both in now, and I will take all the blame."

The Immortal stared at him suspiciously. "You can wait
the hour!" he retorted. "John is in an ill mood tonight.
Cross him if you will—I dare not."

The skald was about to renew his pleading, struggling
not to seem too urgent, when behind them sounded the
beat of hoofs, galloping madly.

"What now?" he muttered in Harald's ear. "Ulf would
never have given way so soon."

Two mounted men dashed up to the gate, gave the word,
received a salute of grounded spears, and dismounted. A
massive figure thrust Thiodolf rudely aside and vanished
within the gate. The second rider followed with the horses.
It was the prefect's orderly.

"Georgios!" the skald cried in Norse. "He goes to report
to John. Flee, ere men are sent after you!"

But Harald stood his ground. "Never!" he cried. "Never,
till I learn the fate of my men. They would never have let
him pass so soon! Here I am and here I bide."

He had thoughtlessly spoken in Greek, and the officer
of Immortals laughed maliciously.

"Then you will bide till your feet take root. We want no
stray barbarians here."

He was wrong. His words had scarce died when a guardsman from the courtyard shouldered past the watch, and spoke a few words with him. The officer nodded and turned to Harald.

"You are to enter," he grinned.

"Now for it!" Thiodolf gasped. "I warned you."

He passed within the wall. As Harald followed, half a dozen spearmen closed in behind him. When they emerged from the vaulted gateway into the vast imperial inclosure, two of the guards ranged themselves on either hand, the other two remaining close in the rear, spears lowered.

Harald darted quick glances about him, marking the vigilant air of his escort.

"I am under arrest?" he asked.

"You are on your way to the palace prison," a guardsman answered bluntly. "Nay—touch that ax, and three feet of steel pierce your back!"

Perforce Harald dropped his hand, and instantly he was relieved of ax, knife and sword. He walked stolidly on, knowing resistance worse than vain. A hand on his shoulder guided him to the right, where a second gateway opened between thick towers, in a wall three times as high as that they had just passed. This was the Chalke, or House of Bronze, the fortified vestibule of the palace.

At the door they were challenged and passed by a second guard, this time of Varangians. Harald smiled as he met the eyes of their officer—none other than Thiodolf. The skald had misjudged the hour; he had arrived barely in time to take up his watch. This the Immortals at the gate had known; but observing that Thiodolf did not, they had seized the opportunity to annoy a Varangian, and remained on duty just long enough to take Harald into custody, and were just now-being relieved. But for the unexpected coming of Georgios, Harald might have won admittance easily a few moments later. Thiodolf's good-natured face was heavy with distress; but he spoke no word.

AT THE END of a corridor two enormous Nubians, naked to the waist, stood on guard with drawn scimitars before a grille of brazen bars. As the guard drew near, one of the blacks took a heavy key from his girdle, unlocked the door, and signed for the prisoner to enter. Harald was thrust into a cell and the door locked. The guardsmen clanked away.

The cell was small, low-ceiled, and bare, offering no hope of escape. Harald searched it carefully, knocking on the walls, scanning each brick, but could find no weakness. He hailed the Nubian warders, but they neither answered nor gave any sign of having heard.

"Mutes," Harald decided. "Men deprived of tongue and hearing, lest they listen to promises of gold. Truly I have come on a bad errand."

Of a race that wastes no time in lamentation, he resigned himself to what might be in store. That it was death in some painful form he had no doubt. Thiodolf had spoken of crucifixion. Harald had heard of worse fates dealt to captives in Mikligard the Great. Sometimes they were allowed to live, when death was better.

He lay down on his pallet, bending his long legs, for the cell was too small to let him stretch at full length. His last thought was that, if he were doomed to blindness or mutilation, he would find some way to die first—and to take others with him. Then he slept.

He was waked suddenly by the screech of the corridor door on its hinges, and leaped to his feet. A dozen mailed men were at the door, their armor gleaming red in the light of the lamps. At sight of them a faint hope stirred in his heart. They were Varangians.

His cell was opened, and Thiodolf stood at his side. The skald's face was pitifully gloomy, his big hands trembling.

"You must come with me," he said huskily. "I fear it will go ill with you. I have orders to take you to John the Eunuch."

"The very man I came hither to see!" Harald cried. The name was a challenge to his fears. "But what of my house-carles? And Ulf?"

"They are well enough," the skald answered. "Word of them came to John an hour ago; and Ulf sent me a message by one of his men. There was no more fighting. Ulf and your fellows strove to hold Georgios till I could get you clear; but a regiment of Immortals cut them off and held them. When Georgios got away the Immortals marched off, leaving your men to make their way back to the Hospice. That Georgios let them go is proof that the Immortals had brought some order from John."

"That is strange enough," said Harald, his eyes quick with suspicion. "It is stranger that he sends you for me. Why not Immortals?"

"I know not," Thiodolf answered. "Perchance to humiliate us. Would I had not lived to see this day! If it would be of any avail to you, I would die defending you."

Harald looked into his friend's eyes. "It would not help," he breathed; "but—give me your dagger."

Thiodolf laid a hand on the prisoner's shoulder, swung

him about as if to force him through the door, and, cloak-
ing his left hand in his mantle, smuggled a keen-edged
knife into his fingers. The captive slipped it into his belt
under the cloak, and left the cell.

AS HE WALKED in the train of his escort, a daze settled
on him. Disaster had overtaken him swiftly; but a short
while since, he had stood triumphant above the bodies of
his slain foes in the tavern of Orontides; now he walked, a
foredoomed prisoner, to meet his judge. In the unknown
person of that judge all that he had heard of the vast, relentless power of the mighty city seemed incarnate. And the
wielder of that power—the world's most ruthless, most
despotic ruler—was a lowborn eunuch. Aye, such a man
as the meanest thrall in the North would despise; yet in his
flabby fingers a prince of the North must now lay his fate.

Harald walked on and on, as in a fantastic nightmare,
till the exercise and the urgent peril of his position drove
the mists from his brain. His eyes once more focused on
what he saw. His mind became cool and steady again. The
pressure of his right elbow on the knife in his girdle reassured him. At least, whatever lay ahead, he would not die
like a sheep.

A door opened to the right, and a slave bowed before
Thiodolf. Silently the skald led his captive into a small
chamber, with walls veneered in alabaster and lined with
book-laden shelves. Here, on a divan beside a tilted oaken
desk, sat a tall man severely clad in the black gown of a
monk.

"The prisoner, as your Excellency ordered," Thiodolf
announced in a hollow voice.

The tall man nodded, and signaled for the guard to

leave. Marvelling at the monk's readiness to be alone with a dangerous captive, doomed perchance to death, Harald knew himself face to face with the true master of the great empire—the Eunuch John.

Here was the man; and Harald gnawed his lip at the thought that he should meet this mysterious tyrant as a prisoner—not as Viking and prince with the prestige of five hundred swords. Georgios had overmatched him, had seen to it that he came before John a beaten man.

Accustomed to deal with men himself, Harald knew that in his dealings with the Eunuch he must now stand under a heavy disadvantage. John could dictate terms; could, if he desired, refuse Harald's services altogether, or even order him to execution for the death of imperial guards-men. He and his house-carles had spilled too much blood to be forgiven.

The Eunuch's steady gaze did nothing to raise his hopes; yet Harald gave back look for look, since his own life and the lives of his men might depend on his skill in reading this man's character, in outfacing or outwitting him. The longer he searched John's eyes, the more they puzzled and confused him.

The Eunuch was of great height; meager, but with a pot stomach. His face was long, yet fleshy and flaccid, and hairless as an egg. His large brown eye, though dull and expressionless under a high, smooth forehead, yet seemed to conceal smoldering fires. The lips were full, but pale, and firmly set. The nose was big and splayed. His age might be anything between forty and fifty-five.

For minutes neither spoke; the eyes of each probed the

other's heart. At length John opened his lips, and his words came very softly:

"You are a strong man and swift, Harald, son of Sigurd. Ill have you used your strength to butcher the divine emperor's guards and assault the noblest of his officers."

"You know my name?" Harald asked, disregarding the rebuke. His surprise was plain on his face. "I told it not to Georgios."

John's face was a mask. "Your name, your errand, and your forces were reported to me by the captain of the cruiser that put aboard your pilot. Men of mine followed you to the Hospice; my agents saw the quarrel in the tavern of Orontides, the fight in the street, the surrounding of your troops by reenforcements from the barracks of the Immortals.

"By my command they were allowed to return in safety to the Hospice after Georgios had escaped them. Georgios reported to me as soon as he had cast you into prison."

Harald stared. "Verily you are well served! But why did Georgios not have me murdered in my cell?"

"Because none lives, moves, or dies within the walls of this palace without my order!"

The tones were quiet, the man's face calm; yet a triumphant satisfaction was somehow manifest in his manner as he made this boast.

"THEN YOU KNOW," Harald answered, "that all I have done this night was done with good cause. If you threaten me with death or torture, you do so unjustly."

"Death is in store for you," the Eunuch spoke evenly. "Sentence is already passed upon you. What else could follow your deeds of this night? Nay; do not lay hand on your weapon. The hour is not yet."

Harald showed his amazement, and the realization of it made him angry. He could have sworn no man—not even the Varangians who had escorted him from prison—had seen Thiodolf pass the dagger to him. And if they had, being themselves Northmen, they would not betray him.

The Eunuch read his thoughts. "Knowing," he explained, "from the reports brought me that the captain Thiodolf was your friend, I understood he would not send you to me unarmed. You Northmen stand together like no other men on earth. Yet steel cannot help you now; if you kill me, you will not leave these walls alive."

At this threat, Harald's composure returned: he met John's changeless stare with a face equally unmoved, save for a tiny glint in the blue eyes.

"It would be something," he murmured, "to kill my executioner. You are a bold man, to shut yourself in, alone and unguarded, with a Northman whom you have doomed to death."

"He must be bold who would rule," John replied simply.

It came to Harald then that such amazing candor would not be shown to one who had long to live. His brain began to evolve desperate schemes for escape—schemes hopeless from their birth. He knew John must have armed men within call, and the palace teemed with Immortals.

The Eunuch's voice broke in upon his thoughts: "But I am not your executioner; merely your judge. And, if you will permit, a gentle judge." His veiled eyes lifted, and their somber gaze seemed to smite like a blow.

"You mean?" the Norwegian asked.

"I mean that you and I may serve each other. I can revoke the death sentence that I have passed. I can give you life, wealth, honor. You can give me that fine loyalty for which your people are famed, and the bravery and wisdom that I read in your eyes."

Harald stood silent, scarce comprehending. The change from threat to promise, from impending death to glittering hope, was too abrupt. Yet his swift mind adjusted itself; and if John expected a sudden surrender, a glad leap at safety, he was disappointed. His somber brown eyes sank, as if abashed; yet he waited patiently for Harald's reply.

"I have deserved neither punishment nor reward," Harald answered at last. "I have neither done wrong nor rendered service. What is it that you ask of me?"

"You will perform it?"

Harald smiled, feeling that the advantage shifted to him.

"If I choose," he retorted.

The Eunuch was surprised, so surprised that he showed a glimmer of it in his glance. Though the change in his manner was slight, Harald knew he had scored a triumph. He was savagely glad; the man's eternal immobility was beginning to disturb his own calm.

"It is true that you are a king's son," John said slowly. "I am the son of a ship-caulker, and sometimes that is a disadvantage. I will ask nothing of you that you cannot honorably perform. I ask you merely to take supreme command of the Varangian Guards stationed in the city."

"You ask—you offer me—" Harald could not finish.

"Yes, That is what you came for, is it not? A post in the Guards? Have I offered more than you hoped? If it is too little"—there was a hint of mockery in the smooth voice—"I will sign an order admitting all your men to the service."

But now Harald's composure had gone completely. Hitherto he had met the Eunuch's unreadable passivity with a face equally blank. But this. He was staggered. His thoughts raced.

"You come to me," John resumed, "like an answer to prayer." His manner was suddenly frank, even genial. He smiled. The veil of dullness over his brown eyes vanished, leaving them warm and friendly.

"I am a strong man, but I am desperate—driven to bay by traitors. The empire is surrounded by hungry foes without, and sapped from within by the selfish greed of court and Senate. The army is rotten with treason; half its generals of division would sell our Asiatic provinces to our Arab enemies if the bribes offered them were high enough.

"Every great noble plots for the crown; some spend huge sums to rouse the fickle passions of the city mob. The emperor, he who should both punish and defend, is sick to death, more than half mad. Every hour is big with danger—danger to this noblest of cities, to the empire itself."

HE PAUSED. HARALD stared at him, caught in excitement at his disclosures, pulled at by suspicion because they were made to a stranger, yet compelled to sympathy. John resumed:

"The whole burden of the State is on my shoulders. Only I understand its needs; only I have hands on the intricate network of State, church, and military government. I, alone, through my many agents, know what goes on, and why, in every slum and camp and cornfield. Nothing but my firm hand can keep Constantinople safe from invasion, rebellion, ruin. Once I lose my hold, blood will bathe the city, fire and steel ravage the provinces. The lives of millions lie in the hollow of this palm." He extended a soft, pallid hand.

"What will become of them if I perish? Who will protect this people from Moslem scimitars or the tyranny of ambitious nobles, if I fall? Plots surround me everywhere; traitors whisper together in dark corners. Assassins are hired to murder me. The very officers who strut about this palace, who cringe when I pass, intrigue secretly to destroy me, that they may divide the power that drops from my hands. And in all the empire there is not one man whom I can trust—no man who is my friend—none who would not sell me to the highest bidder."

"There is Georgios," Harald reminded him.

John's smoldering eyes flamed. "Aye; there is Georgios Maniakes—aristocrat, splendid soldier, favorite and terror of the people! You have met him: have you looked into his face?"

"I see," Harald murmured. "One told me that even you fear him."

"I do," John admitted. "Yet I must placate him with high position and great honors, for he is the best man in the empire. Aye, the best. The rest are serpents; he is a tiger. And I am like a traveler who walks alone in the desert: still strong, armed against peril—but beaten upon by the sun, assailed by thirst, hunted by savage beasts and yet more savage men."

The utter openness of this confession amazed the close-lipped Northman; and some instinct warned him to beware

of a frankness he had not sought. He gazed shrewdly at the
Greek; but the brown eyes were dull again, as if filmed to
protect the thoughts behind.

"And so," John ended, "I need a man who is faithful and
strong, brave and wise. Among your countrymen in the
guard I could find many who are brave and loyal; none who
unite these virtues with the power to rule and the brain to
lead. You are such a man—the first I have known. I have
read you to-night; and I never read men wrongly."

Harald pondered. The man attracted him; but there was
also something about him which inexplicably repelled.
Great he undoubtedly was; his words rang true. Yes—
Harald recalled with misgiving the tyranny, the crimes,
of which Ulf and Thiodolf had accused John. They were
shrewd men. Was it possible that they had misjudged the
Eunuch?

"You have made me a great offer," Harald said at length.
"I am tempted to take it. The alternative is death?"

"Death," John affirmed, once more impenetrably aloof.

"I will speak as openly as you," Harald announced. "You
make me this offer partly because you have me in your
power, and rely on my gratitude to keep me faithful; partly
because we Northmen have high repute for loyalty. In that
you are right. Among my people, he who takes wages keeps
faith with his lord—till death, or till his service is ended
by mutual agreement.

"But the Varangians are the emperor's guard; not you,
but the emperor will be my wage giver. To him I will be
faithful. What assurance have I that loyalty to you is loyalty
to him?"

"I am the emperor's brother," John reminded him. "All my thoughts, all my efforts, are bent to serve him."

Harald stood thoughtful, watching the unchanging features. How much truth was behind the evil reports of him, reports which contrasted so sharply with the Eunuch's own confession? John seemed to have bared his inmost soul. Yet who could read those veiled eyes?

"I AM OF good blood," Harald resumed, "and I would not undertake an unworthy service. Gold tempts me as it tempts any man, and glory tempts me more; but I have an honest name to keep clean. You say you are of low birth; then so is your brother the emperor. Men say his sole claim to the crown is his marriage to the empress. It is whispered that you and he murdered the old emperor to place yourselves in power."

As he spoke, he watched John narrowly. The Greek met his gaze with unmoved candor.

"Lies," he said gently. "All lies. If these things were true, you would die for speaking them."

Harald was pleased. He liked the Eunuch better for denying without defending or explaining himself. He was almost ready to believe John sincere.

"Your word is as good as another's," he admitted, "and your knowledge of the truth is better. One more thing: you say your own officers are turbulent, rebellious, and so unfit for your trust. I come of a race as turbulent as any on earth. My brother died at the hands of his own mutinous subjects. We of the North keep faith with our master, unless he wrongs us—and not you, but the emperor, would be my master. If you and the emperor keep faith with me,

I will serve you to the last drop of my blood. If you do me an injury, you had best slay me before I slay you."

John met the young, fierce eyes with a friendly smile.

"It is a good bargain," he answered, "and will be truly kept. To-morrow your five hundred men shall be enrolled in the Emperor's Life Guards, and you shall take rank as Patrician of the Empire and Commander of all Varangians within the walls. In time—if you satisfy me—I will make you Grand Heteriarch, supreme general of all Varangians in the empire, including the armies now on service in Persia. The Immortals remain under command of Georgios, and I will make peace between you."

Harald raised a hand. "That is all very well," he broke in, "but I have heard that you have taken away the privileges of the Varangians. I have no wish to command troops that stand discredited."

John sighed, a trifle impatiently. "Those Varangians! I have indeed shown them some harshness, but they deserved it. They are rude, rough barbarians, intolerant of control. They hate me, and have refused to carry out orders, because they believe the slander you but now repeated—the old lie that I plotted the former emperor's death.

"They know not that the Empress Zoe alone both planned and carried out the murder. To check her wicked folly, I was forced to marry her to my brother, and to see to it that he, not Zoe, wielded the imperial power. Regarding her as their true ruler, the Varangians believe that I wrongfully withhold her rights from her. Ever since I shut her up within her apartments they have broken all bounds of discipline. For these reasons I have had to hold them in check.

"They are good soldiers—the best in the world; but they need a strong and loyal commander. You are the man to rule them. It will be your task to punish insubordination, to restore discipline, and to make your men once more the finest, most trustworthy, and most cherished troops in the imperial service. If you do this, I will make you great and rich beyond your dreams."

Harald's face was as blank as John's, but his thoughts were troubled. Was it true that the empress was a murderess, a wicked, light-minded woman, who must be restrained from ruining the empire? Or was this Eunuch a crafty, ambitious intriguer, betraying his sovereign to gain supreme power for himself, through his sick, shadowy brother? None could read the answer in that flabby, changeless face. But to Harald, proud with the sensitive, outrageous self-respect of his race, the answer was all-important. He could serve a noble-minded statesman; he could not serve a rascal and a hypocrite.

Time alone could show the truth. Meanwhile, there was death on one side, greatness on the other. He could preserve his independence, at least in his own heart, by maintaining that he served, not John, but John's imperial brother.

"I accept!" he said.

John rose, his mask melting into an expression of delight. From a casket on his desk he took a medallion of gold, richly chased, on a silver chain.

"The symbol of your authority," he explained, "the medallion of a Prefect of Varangians. You are now supreme, under me, in the city."

Harald laughed. "And Georgios?" he asked.

John laughed too—a high, thin chuckle that came from his throat, with no change in the muscles of his face.

"You have said that I fear Georgios. Well, so I do; but—he, as well, fears me. Leave Georgios to me!"

5

HE RULES WHO CAN

RETURNING TO HIS desk, John thrust with his foot against a metal knob protruding from the floor. Somewhere outside a gong clanged. The door opened, framing the big figure of Thiodolf.

The skald's bluff features lightened as he saw Harald standing at ease, unharmed. Then his eyes caught the medallion at his friend's neck, and his mouth opened in a soundless gasp.

"Restore to the prefect his weapons," John commanded.

Thiodolf strode off. In the passage he turned to stare once more.

John uttered his thin chuckle. "More than he will gasp, when you enter on your work," he said.

Thiodolf was back straightway, as if he had not had far to go. In silence he girded Harald's sword about him, hung the ax Hell about his neck, and handed him his knife.

"Now return the weapon he lent you, Prefect!" the Eunuch ordered.

Thiodolf started back in alarm; then, as Harald gave back his knife, the skald turned on him a look of such reproach that Harald could not restrain his laughter.

"I told him not, by the holy beard of St. Olaf!" he vowed.

"Did not you yourself say to me that you and I were babes in cunning beside John the Orphanotrophos?"

Thiodolf's jaw dropped. "He is a wizard, possessed by seven fiends!" he muttered in Norse. Unaware of this hearty characterization, John raised one hand in the benedictory gesture of the Greek Church.

"You may go!" he said; and he turned from them as one who has lost interest.

The two Northmen walked down the long passage, each revolving his own thoughts. Harald's face was set and stern, his brow furrowed; while the skald, never raising his eyes from the pavement, seemed to bear a burden of care and anger. At length they readied the guardroom of the Chalke, where the Varangians on duty first stared, then sprang to attention with a crash of grounded spears.

Thiodolf faced Harald, and saluted. "Farewell, my friend!" he said in slow, bitter tones. "Hail, Prefect!"

Harald caught his arm and swung him half about. "Peace, foolish one! Are we any the less friends because one of us gives orders and the other takes them? Come, walk with me, and I will teach you wisdom."

Thiodolf shook his head. "If the prefect will excuse me, I am on duty here."

"Then my first order is that you depute command to your next in rank, and attend me. Make haste!"

Thiodolf gave the necessary order and followed Harald to the gate. When they had passed through it, the prefect slowed his pace, and laid one arm about his friend's shoulders.

"Tell me, old comrade," he urged, "why my good fortune

grieves you. Would it have pleased you better to have me slain? That was the choice the Eunuch gave me."

"If he had had you slain," the skald replied in a troubled voice, "I should have died avenging you. If he had appointed you to a captaincy, I would have been pleased enough. But to find you in his confidence— It is no joy to me to see you, a good Norwegian and the brother of my sainted king, selling yourself to such as John—a murderer, a traitor, a lowborn dog!"

"Do you not take orders from him?" Harald smiled.

"Aye, because I must, having entered the imperial service. He was but a despised palace servant then; when he came to power, I had no choice but to do as he bade, or die. But you—you enter, not the imperial service only, but John's— otherwise he would never have made you Prefect."

"NAY!" HARALD PROTESTED. "I serve not him, but the emperor."

"Who is no better than he, and sick and mad to boot! They are both murderers."

"John denies that," Harald answered thoughtfully. "And I have no doubt he knows, better than you, whether his hand or Zoe's slew the old emperor. But that we shall learn in time. If I ever find it was he, then I shall find means to withdraw honorably from my office. And I mean to discover the truth about him."

Thiodolf was silent for awhile. At last he said, somewhat sullenly:

"You have the title of Prefect; but think you the Varangians will obey one placed over them by John, whom they hate? You will be lucky if you live a month among them."

"They will kiss my feet if I bid them!" Harald declared, laughing.

"There speaks Olaf's brother!" Thiodolf smiled at last on his friend. "Yet, if you do succeed in mastering them—and they are wild wolves of the North—you will still have John to deal with. Believe me, he means but to use you. Disobey him once, or cease to be useful to him, and you will be found some dark night with a knife in your back, or a draft of poison in your belly."

"I have told him," Harald answered, "that if he injures me, he will do well to slay me quickly. I think that he and I understand each other. Fear not for me, old friend."

Thiodolf looked at the new Prefect long and earnestly. "I pray you may come out of this with life and honor," he said doubtfully. "But heed one thing: beware of Georgios! When he hears you have been made a Prefect instead of a corpse, he will tear the empire apart to ruin you."

"I have taken his measure and found it short," Harald declared.

"Then yours is shorter than I thought, if you believe that. Nay; you have done no more than make a fool of him, and won his enmity. He is as dangerous as John. But this is not the way to the barracks!"

"I go not to the barracks to-night, but to the Hospice. I take over my duties to-morrow. Now I would sleep."

With a quick motion Thiodolf caught his arm and drew him back against the building. They were at a cross-street, far down which the lights of the Strategium shone. From the darkened corner of the arcade a figure lurched across their path, almost plunging into them; and as he turned

*"Ha! It is thou, brawler! Dost thou challenge
my right to give orders here?"*

the corner, a lamp above him shone full on the staggering
form. It was an officer of Immortals.

The corner lamp revealed them to him in the same
moment. He reeled back, staring into Harald's face, and
at the medallion on his breast. Then, with a choked cry, he
dodged past them and ran toward the palace.

The Northmen looked at each other. "That," said
Thiodolf slowly, "is the man who fled before your ax in the
tavern. He will go straight to Georgios."

"Let him," said Harald shortly. "Farewell now; I must
not keep you longer from your post. Come to me at the
Strategium to-morrow."

WHEN THE NORTHMEN had gone, John the Eunuch sat
alone for a space, his full lips touched with the ghost of
a smile. His right hand played with the ends of the cord
about his monk's robe; the fingers of his left stroked his
chin thoughtfully. At last he rose, and stepped softly to
the rear wall of his chamber, listening with his ear close to

its alabaster surface. His hands fumbled at the juncture of the wall with a huge inset book cabinet; and suddenly the entire case swung inward, leaving a passageway. Into this he stepped, revolving the cabinet till it closed the entrance.

He had to stoop to avoid striking his head against the low ceiling of the hidden passage; but familiarity enabled him to slip through it with catlike swiftness. A door at the farther end admitted him into a second chamber, much like his own, but smaller.

The room was square and austere. No window opened from it; only an airshaft above gave access to the light and air of day. With flint and steel John lighted a candle. Its rays showed a desk littered with manuscripts in Greek; cases of books; and in one corner a row of flasks, a chemical alembic, and jars sealed with wax. Along one wall stood a low couch, on which slept a young man.

John bent over him, holding the light high. Under his scrutiny the other awoke, blinked, and smiled up at him. John smiled back, his eyes warm with affection.

"I did not mean to wake you, Constantine," he said. "But it is better; I am glad of a chance to talk to you. The time will soon be ripe."

Constantine sat up in bed, and took John's hand. He was of about thirty years, very handsome, with an almost womanish beauty and large, cunning eyes.

"The time cannot come too soon," he answered in a soft, musical voice. "The studies you have assigned me are fascinating, but I long for action."

"You shall have it. My plans grow clearer. I have found a man to play off against Georgios, though it may be hard to keep Georgios from murdering him before I am ready to pit them against each other. Now that my way becomes plain, I can use you in a higher capacity than that of my clerk."

"Why have you not told me what you mean to do with me?" Constantine questioned. "More than a year has passed since you summoned me from Paphlagonia. I came hither with high hopes. With one brother wearing the imperial crown, and another his chief minister, had I not the right to dream that I, too, might become great? Yet you have kept me hidden here, copying records and dispatches, and studying the things you bade me learn. And for all your promises, I have seen no more of the city or palace than this secret chamber."

John frowned. "It would have ruined all to let men know of you too soon. You are too like Michael in feature not to be recognized as his brother. In a few days I shall have Georgios out of the way; then it will not matter if all men know you.

"Moreover, I did not wish Michael to know you were here, lest he guess I meant you for his successor. Now he is too sick to care. Zoe loved Michael once, but her treatment at his hands and mine has quenched her ardor. She is almost ready to recognize another emperor when he dies."

Constantine glanced up quickly. "Is it so near, then?"

John shrugged. "I cannot tell. He is very weak; he had another seizure yesterday. He may linger a year, or he may die to-morrow."

THE PALLID, DELICATE face of Constantine grew sullen. "It is wearisome here," he complained. "Give me my freedom now!"

John stroked the young man's cheek solicitously. "Soon,

very soon. I have need of your cunning, which I sometimes think is as great as mine. But you must wait till I can send Georgios away, and till Harald the Northman has sapped the earth under his feet."

"A Northman? But you have told me that the Northmen hate you, and regard Zoe as their true ruler."

"Even so," John agreed. "But this Northman is in the hollow of my hand. I have saved his life from Georgios; I have given him rank and opportunity. A king's son himself, new to our service, he has little use for an empress whom he has never seen. He is the best of tools: strong enough not to break in my hand, shrewd enough to know that I can make him great or ruin him. He has all to hope for from me, nothing from our enemies."

Constantine pondered. "This is very well," he answered, "but you have won to power by knowing men. You saw this Northman, and knew he would serve your purpose. How am I to become worthy to succeed our brother if you keep me here, away from the world? How am I to learn to read men, unless I move among them?"

John's smile caressed him. "Patience, little brother! He must be patient who would rule.

"For five and thirty long and bitter years I bore the scorn of men: a slave, a eunuch, a thing to order about. Now all men fear and obey me.

"So shall you be great, if you but school yourself in my teachings. You are young, strong, handsome—you will not need to wait for power to come with age. And you will have me by your side, to counsel you if your own wisdom fails."

Searchingly Constantine looked at his elder brother;

and something in that look made John drop his eyes, lest the youth know he had read his thoughts.

"Farewell now; I must sleep," he said.

As he entered his own chamber, and closed the secret entrance again, he scowled savagely.

"The young snake will bite me, if I watch him not," he muttered. "After all I have planned for him! He sees too clearly that I mean to rule through him when Michael is gone; and he purposes to rule without me. Truly this Northman has come to me as a gift from Heaven!"

He glanced about, as if to make sure that the room was indeed empty. It was the furtive glance of a man who has weaknesses to conceal. Then, from a cabinet with wooden doors, he drew a tall flask of fine Venetian glass, and a golden goblet. Filling the cup, he drank off the wine in one great gulp.

Many times he filled and drained the cup, his white cheeks flushing more and more. Not till the flask was empty did he put it away again, with the goblet. Then he flung himself on his bed.

A THUNDERING IN his ears, his temples throbbing with his surfeit of wine, the Eunuch struggled from his couch. A moment he listened; then, rising, he tiptoed to an onyx stand, poured water into a silver basin, and laved his eyes and cheeks. Not till his face was dry did he call his servant.

The slave, at his gesture, flung wide the door. Daylight flooded into the room from its two glazed windows, and reflected dazzlingly from the mail of him who entered.

If John was startled, none might know it.

"Welcome, noble Georgios!" he cried, and waved the

intruder to a cushioned seat. "What seek ye of me, Lord Prefect?"

His manner was almost fawning; but there was no humility in his dulled eyes.

Georgios Maniakes glared at him, one hand upraised as if to strike. The Prefect of Immortals, "the Lion of the Purple City," as men called him, was in a most leonine fury.

"What is this I hear?" he roared. "I bring you a man to be killed, and you heap him with honors! He has slain the emperor's guards, and you make him chief over guardsmen! He has insulted me, and you make him my equal! Was this what you promised me? By St. George of Cappadocia, this is not to be borne!"

The Eunuch smiled ingratiatingly, shrugging his lean shoulders.

"Ah, Lord Prefect, if you but understood! Were the culprit but a barbarian mercenary, he should have died on the cross, as you desired. But a king's son, the darling of every Varangian—"

"The son of a savage princeling, no more to be considered than a dog!" the Prefect thundered. "The darling of his own spears—but what he is to men who never knew him, as most of the Varangians do not? And he has laid his hands on me—"

John's shoulders straightened. He assumed a dignity that, for all his ugliness of body, sat on him well.

"You speak of things you do not comprehend," he answered. "Even those Varangians who never saw him know who he is: the scion of a royal race, whom all of them respect.

"You know not how these Northerners hold together. If

I had slain him, the whole corps would have been in rebellion. I could not tell you this last night, when you were too raw with injured pride to listen; but now I tell you I have only done that which was best for the realm, and for you."

"For me!" The face of Georgios was livid. His eyes played like lightnings. "Let me judge what is good for me, and do you keep your hands off!

"I am a Greek patrician, of blood that has given this people emperors. And you give an upstart stranger—my enemy—honors equal to mine!"

Once more the Eunuch smiled. "Not so, my lord. I have given him danger, which may end in his death. I have given him work to do which must be done, if the empire is to stand. When he has done it there are dark, deep cells; there is steel; there is poison." He paused, and Georgios eagerly broke in:

"You mean that when you have done with him, I may have him?"

John bowed. "No less. In the meantime you must not harm him, must not plot against him, must not block his path. If you do, purposes no less dear to you than to me will perish. Leave him to me, for now; rest assured your vengeance shall be satisfied. And now, that you may know how much I value you, how richly I would reward your great deserts, I have resolved to bestow on you—at the express bidding of the emperor—the governorship of the Theme of Bulgaria."

Georgios started. "Theodamas has failed, then?"

"Aye; he has not succeeded in crushing the Bulgar revolt. If you win where he has lost, I can promise you the ministry of defense. Whether you succeed or fail, all spoil taken is yours. I know you will not fail, for there is no general like you."

Georgios ran one great hand through his shock of black hair. The Eunuch's promise had taken the fire from his anger, and he felt like a pricked bladder.

"Theodamas has had all too few men in his command to win battles," he muttered.

"I saw to that," John chuckled. "I meant him to fail, that you might win more glory as his successor. You shall have two more divisions of Immortals, men whom you have trained, and who worship you. With them you must win matchless glory. It may be that the barbarian will be ripe to pluck when you return from the campaign."

"When do I march?"

"It were best," John answered softly, "for you to leave as soon as you can equip your men and stock your wagon trains. In that way your quarrel with the barbarian will be forgotten, and he will be the riper to fall into your hands."

Georgios fixed the Eunuch with a blazing stare; but John's brown eyes were dulled and unwavering. With a bow that held scant measure of reverence, Georgios strode away.

THE SOUTH COURT of the Strategium, where the Varangians were housed, seethed with armored men; strong-sinewed men, big and blond; men who bore themselves arrogantly; men scarred of face and intolerant of eye.

Some warriors paced to and fro, scowling; some leaned wide shoulders against the brick wall and grinned; but by far the most had their heads together, talking in couples, in groups, in companies—and most of them spoke in undertones. Some few, surrounded by excited friends, cursed and shouted loudly. The air was charged with resentment and expectancy.

Two stood apart from the rest, angry of face, their voices bitter.

"It is an insult, Svioslav!" So spoke the smaller of the pair, a thick-set officer wearing the copper medallion of a captain. His companion, a huge Russian, tugged fiercely at his drooping mustaches.

"Such an insult as no man of this corps has yet had to bear!" he snarled. "An insult to all of us, and thrice an insult to me!"

"You will resent it?"

The Russian turned hot eyes on his friend. "Have I ever failed to avenge my wrongs, Rotlieb?"

Rotlieb, a fox-haired Frank, glanced about, to make certain that none heard them.

"We Varangians choose our own Prefect," he muttered. "It is our oldest privilege. Yet the cursed Eunuch has kept us without a leader for these three years, forcing us to take our orders from him; and now a message bidding all officers of the corps assemble, to receive the orders of their new Prefect! A Prefect we have had no part in choosing; one who has neither camped nor fought with us; a stranger, and an unbreeched boy!"

The Russian growled in his throat, like a great mastiff. "Who is this Harald Sigurdsson?" he cried. "What has given him the right to command us? May I be impaled on the devil's tail if it be not this same Eunuch's work! Let him come! We be here, as he bade us. We will show him that Varangians obey no Prefect not of their own election!"

His voice rose with his swelling anger. Others, hearing, strolled up to the pair.

"Would John leave anything undone to humiliate us, think you?" one called; and a murmur of rage ran through the court.

Svioslav the Russian spun round to face the speaker. "Aye; but this! To place a new-come stranger over us—a stripling! To pass over men who have grown gray with years and red with wounds in the service!"

The captain Rotlieb nodded wisely. "We may be sure the Eunuch but waited to find a man who would carry out his will, without question, as none of us would do. Doubtless he has found this Norwegian one after his own black heart."

A dark-browed man, tall and lean, shouldered his way forward, and thrust one knotty fist under the Frank's nose.

"Smell this, dog of the Rhine!" he bellowed. "It can smash a skull or swing a biting blade! Though I like this breach of our rights no more than you, I will have the heart of him who dares miscall the brother of King Olaf the Holy!"

The Frank dropped one hand to his sword; but with the lean man's eyes on him, he did not draw. His antagonist stood tense for awhile, then turned away with a short laugh.

"It takes a man to outface Erik of Valdres!" he boasted. "We be old sword-wolves, we Norwegians!"

Others crowded about him, some shouting angrily, some laughing and clapping him on the back. Ugly names were hurled back and forth; hands tightened on hilts. Blood might have been shed had not the Russian taken the situation into his own hands. Snatching up a shield, he beat upon its metal boss till the court was filled with the clangor. Understanding, the angry men dropped their quarrels and turned to hear him.

"Fools!" he cried. "Will ye shed blood for a stranger, and so give the Greeks cause for laughter? This is my affair and Aldhelm's—no other's. Aldhelm is not here yet; therefore it is my affair alone, till he comes. Ye prate of your rights; but it is my rights which suffer, and I know how to take care of them. Leave this Harald in my hands, which are strong enough to deal with ten such unfledged goslings!"

Shouts of applause greeted him. "Northman's way! Northman's way!" they cried, rattling their scabbards. "So should a Prefect be chosen. Man against man, and the best man to rule!"

ERIK OF VALDRES shrugged his lean shoulders. "So be it!" he grinned. "Yet thou wilt not find Harald Sigurdsson such easy plucking, Svioslav. And if he should fall at thy hands, know this—there be other good Norwegians here to avenge him. He is our royal blood."

The Russian giant laughed uproariously. "When I have done with him, I will take each Norwegian here, one after the other, and crack them in my fingers!"

Amid the uproar that followed his boast came three men, scarce noticed by the excited Varangians. Only the dark Norseman, Erik of Valdres, ran forward to greet them.

"Ill doings, brothers!" he spoke swiftly. "Is it true that John has made Harald Sigurdsson our Prefect?"

The tallest of the three nodded shortly. "It is true. I had it from Harald's own lips, and heard John give him the title."

"Then we who served with Olaf must stand behind him, Thiodolf," Erik said with fiery eagerness. "All the Norwegians here wish him well, though they like not the manner in which he is set above us; and the rest are bitter that the Eunuch should defy our privileges. Svioslav is in one of his killing rages. He will strike as soon as Harald shows himself."

Thiodolf the Skald glanced at the two with him. "Svioslav has cause," he answered, "he and Aldhelm had a better right to be chosen than any other. What say you, Ulf?"

"Aye," the squat Icelander agreed. "Svioslav is oldest theme-commander in the service, and a mighty champion. And though Aldhelm the Englishman is but a captain, he is second to none either as soldier or as leader of men. All men know our choice of a Prefect would have lain between these two."

"Aldhelm would have won," spoke the third man, a tall, square-made captain, very handsome, with cold, green eyes. "The Russian's seniority would help him little in an election, for his savage fury has made him few friends among us who like not to be bullied. You say truly, Erik: blood will be spilled over this. Be it our task to see that it is spilled in fair fight, not in foul murder."

Thiodolf struck hands with him. "Well said, Halldor! Yet I think Harald will need none of our help, if it come to sword-strokes. In case he does, let us quickly draw the Norwegians and Icelanders together."

They mingled with the crowd, picking out their own countrymen, whispering a word here and there. The Norsemen began to draw apart; and soon the others, noticing, began also to collect, taking position by the Russian.

Into the gathering storm strode a calm-eyed man, very

tall, who, seeing what was toward, stopped in the arched entrance-way. A shout went up from Svioslav's backers:

"Aldhelm! This way! To thy friends!"

Aldhelm advanced a few paces, surveying them coolly.

"What is your will?" he asked.

Svioslav pressed forward to meet him, thrusting his own well-wishers aside with rough shoves of his arms.

"Look you, Aldhelm! Here are thou and I, the best men in the Guard, scorned for a stranger! Our comrades would have chosen one of us Prefect. Wilt thou endure such an injury?"

Aldhelm stared at him. There was no friendliness in his eyes.

"Harald Sigurdsson is my friend," he answered. "It is true that I had some hopes of the election—if John would ever let it be held—but I am too much the soldier to rebel when a better man is put in my place. I have just come from the Hospice, with word for you all that our Prefect is on his way hither."

Svioslav laughed nastily. "Some men fear death more than dishonor!" he sneered. "Eat as much dirt as thou wilt, Englishman; I will maintain my rights with my sword!"

ALDHELM STEPPED FORWARD instantly, his hand leaping to the hilt. The Russian, glad of the chance to crush one rival before dealing with another, drew blade and rushed at him. The Varangians all swarmed around, forming in a great circle, that all might see. The bright blades rose and clashed.

Even as steel rang on steel, they who faced the door raised a cry. A lithe figure stood poised in the archway, at gaze. Like an arrow loosed from the string he shot through

the circle, whirled a gleaming ax, and smote up the blades
of the fighters.

Aldhelm, recognizing the intruder, stepped aside with
a smile; but Svioslav turned on him with an angry bellow:

"For that thou shalt die!"

The ax-bearer dodged a fierce slash, sprang in, and
caught Svioslav by the beard. At sight of the terrible bully
thus set at defiance, the throng gasped. Desperately the
Russian strove to shorten steel, wrenching to and fro to
tear away from the iron fingers; but each time he would
have thrust, his tormentor, grasping him close to the chin,
flung his head up so violently that he could not see to
strike. Svioslav's eyes filled with tears of pain.

His captor smiled on the yelling crowd. "I am Harald
Sigurdsson, your Prefect!" he announced. "I hear that some
of you will not accept me. It is good old Northern custom
for him who disputes a chief's right to settle the matter
by steel."

They fell silent, staring at him—all save Svioslav, who
tugged and jabbed vainly, spitting curses. Whenever he
raised his sword, Harald swung him off balance, so that
the stroke went wild. The bully, dangling helpless by the
roots of his own beard, frothed with harmless rage. The rest
glanced one at another, as men who have seen the heavens
fall. At last they broke into a shout of applause:

"Well spoken, Sigurdsson! Northman's way! Steel to
steel, and we obey the victor!"

He had won them—or the most of them—by his bold
appeal to the trial by combat, love of which was deep in
every Northern heart; yet, but for his bearding of Svioslav—which amazed them and set them to laughing at the

same time—he could not have gained their ear so easily. Only a few, hangers-on of the Russian, cried out against him. Glaring at one of these, Rotlieb the Frank, Harald cried:

"Wilt thou come against me? I will split thee with one hand while I swing this goat with the other!"

Rotlieb backed against the wall. He spoke growlingly, afraid to fight.

"It is Svioslav's affair, now Aldhelm will not fight."

Harald waited; then, as none other spoke, he asked innocently:

"Where is this Svioslav? I hear him not."

The Russian shrieked in baffled rage; the Varangians laughed almost as one man; and Harald looked at his captive with assumed astonishment.

"Ha! It is thou, brawler! Dost thou challenge my right to give orders here?"

Svioslav, who had not let go his sword, suddenly ceased his struggles, going limp in Harald's grasp. Then, with lightning speed, he dashed his hilt upward at his persecutor's face. So swift was the stroke that Harald barely avoided it, the heavy pommel bruising his cheek. Leaping back, he raised the ax Hell.

The two blades met, the advantage with the nimble sword. Svioslav slashed in furiously to win ere Harald could recover. In and out the point flashed, barely parried each time; yet its parrying maddened the Russian. He struck again and again, his reckless attack forcing the Northman to remain on the defensive. Harald could gain neither room nor time for a sweep of his massive weapon. Svioslav's backers howled their glee; while the rest of the Varangians waited, anxious and glowering.

At last Harald dropped on one knee, his chest laboring for breath. Exulting, the Russian raised his sword for a backstroke that would end the fight. As the gray steel rose, Harald flung himself forward, left hand touching the pavement, and drove all the length and the lean power of his body into a thrust with the pointed flange of the ax.

The sharp steel tore a fearful gash in the Russian's thigh. Pain, and the sheer force of the blow, sent him staggering backward, so that his stroke ended in a crash of steel against the stone floor, as the sword smashed in a shiver of flying metal.

Harald bent over his foe, who lay, cursing, in a pool of blood. When the guardsmen's cheers died down, he asked:

"Do you obey, or die?"

Svioslav glared up at him, his eyes red with hate. "I obey!" he snarled.

Harald lifted him up. "Tend his wound, one of you!" he ordered.

Men came forward; but ere they reached him Svioslav flung himself on Harald, his broad knife flashing from its sheath. Suspecting no treachery Harald had turned away. A cry from Thiodolf warned him. He wheeled, took the knife in his shoulder, and dashed his shortened ax into the Russian's throat. Svioslav dropped, his neck half severed. Bleeding from the dead man's stroke, Harald faced the throng, his wet ax lifted.

"Who else challenges?" he cried.

NONE SPOKE. ALL stared, amazed, at him who had slain

the foremost champion of the guard. At length Erik of Valdres drew sword, and clashed mightily on his shield.

"Skoal, Harald, Prefect and Champion!" he roared. "Skoal!"

From five hundred throats the cry reechoed:

"Skoal, Harald! Skoal! Skoal!"

Harald smiled, though his wound burned.

"Such is the world's way," he said. "He rules who can. John rules in Mikligard, and I rule you.

"Ye have thought I was John's slave, to make you do his will. Know that I am no man's slave, and do what is good in my own eyes. So long as John plays fair with me and mine, I—and you—obey him. Ye are my men. Let John but wrong the least of you, and I will avenge you as I would myself. Now hear my orders:

"Ye have rebelled against discipline. For that, every band in the corps shall drill four hours each day, in full equipment. Ye must learn to obey, whether ye like it or no. Having now a Prefect of your own race, ye have no cause to complain. Ye shall find me a just master, though somewhat hard—which is for your own good. Are ye content?"

Rotlieb the Frank thrust himself forward.

"By sword and shield!" he panted. "Thou art a man! We ask nothing better than to have a man over us. Had we known thee before, there would have been no trouble. We are content!"

"Good!" Harald answered. "John the Orphanotrophos has sent me word that Georgios Maniakes, being about to leave the city, is giving up his prefecture. Aldhelm the Englishman will henceforth act as Commander of the Third Theme and Prefect of Police."

Aldhelm looked at him incredulously. "You mean," he asked, "that I, who am but a captain, am to have authority over a thousand? And police power within the walls?"

"More than that!" Harald smiled upon him. "As Prefect you shall have six full themes of a thousand each. We cannot have the city less well policed than before Georgios left it. Nor could I do less for a man who might have stood in my shoes."

Aldhelm grasped his hand and wrung it hard.

"Ulf Uspaksson, and Thiodolf," Harald continued, "keep their present posts at the palace, save that each receives the rank of commander. Halldor the Icelander takes charge of the military camp between the inner and the outer walls; Eilif Rognvaldsson is in command of the barracks. Erik of Valdres goes on duty at the Zeugma Port.

"Now heed one thing: two divisions of Immortals are to march with Georgios. That leaves but a handful within the city, and three bands to share duty with us at the palace. Ye see that John has once more full confidence in us. See to it that he has no cause to repent his trust! There is to be no brawling, either with citizens or with Immortals. It will go hard with him who breaks my command!"

His eyes, grown hard and cold, swept their faces.

Ulf Uspaksson stood a-tiptoe to whisper into Thiodolf's ear:

"Our new-hatched Prefect crows lustily. He dares much, to lay such command on men like these. What if Svioslav's friends had rushed him?"

Aldhelm the Englishman answered quietly: "I came later than you three; I spoke last with him before he arrived here. He trusted to win over all, and he succeeded. If he had failed, Eilif Rognvaldsson and the five hundred who followed Harald from Russia wait with drawn swords just beyond the entrance. A single shout from Harald, and they would have rushed in like hungry wolves."

Halldor turned his ice-green eyes on Thiodolf. "Here is a man indeed, oh, skald! Brave, generous, and cunning. Make a song of his deeds swiftly, lest they outstrip your power to tell of them!"

Thiodolf glanced toward Harald, whom the Varangian officers surrounded, eager to clasp his hand.

"It will be a good song," he mused, "and the refrain will be: 'He rules who can!'"

6

THE SLAVE

WITHIN A FORTNIGHT Harald's wound had healed, for the Russian's knife had been almost stopped by the tough links of his mail shirt. Harald had never let it interfere with his work, which demanded all his time.

Each morning, with the help of Greek clerks furnished by John, he transacted the business of his office: received reports from his subordinates, heard complaints, planned the work of the day; and—when time permitted—listened to one of his clerks read aloud from the military treatises of the great Greek generals, Bardas and Nicephorus Phokas.

In the afternoon, inspecting the bands at drill, and making the rounds of the sub-stations of police.

In the evening he went to the palace, to render account of his duties to John. This was ordinarily a mere formality; though at times the Orphanotrophos gave him shrewd advice, or plied him with questions. To all appearances John was his stanch friend.

Of all the new Prefect's tasks, that which most fascinated him was the study of Greek military tactics. He had had no more understanding of the advanced methods of the East than of its complicated drill. War in the North was a matter of simple formations, in which dogged courage and brawn counted far more than discipline.

In Constantinople the soldier was more than a mere fighter: he was a trained unit in a perfect machine. The common soldier in the Varangian ranks knew more of warfare as a science than his Prefect; and Harald felt the full depth of his ignorance as soon as he first saw his own men at drill. Straightway he set about learning this new art; and he learned fast.

WHILE YET THE westering sun flashed on the spears of Georgios and his departing hosts, Aldhelm took over the prefecture of police. The gleaming building off the Forum of Constantine still reeked with the perfumes of the Immortals who had been stationed there, but the bleak room which had been Georgios's office was Spartan in its severe virility and order. Records and files were neatly stowed in cabinets about the walls; the tilted desk was clean, the furniture rough and simple.

"St. Guthlac make me as good a man and as stanch an officer!" Aldhelm breathed, as he ran through the taped manuscripts.

A fortnight it may have been after he had taken charge, Aldhelm came early to the prefecture, to find Harald waiting him in the court. The Norseman wrung Aldhelm's hand, and glanced about curiously.

"All in good order here," he approved. "There has been no trouble in the city since you took command. A good beginning!"

"Townsfolk walk warily when Varangians are in control," Aldhelm smiled.

"Aye, when the Varangians themselves are kept in hand. Have you a map of the city?"

Aldhelm drew forth a huge parchment roll, and laid it flat on his desk. Harald bent over it, studying it closely.

"Here are all twelve quarters of the city plainly marked," he mused. "I shall expect you to station two bands in each, and hold the rest in reserve."

"It has been done," Aldhelm answered.

Harald laughed. "You are matchless, Englishman! Each band is how strong? Seventy men?"

"Sixty to seventy. The proper strength of a band is one hundred; but, since the Varangians are apt to be used as troops on the frontiers, at least thirty men in each band are armorers, wagoners, cooks, and engineers. In these last years of peace, John the Eunuch saved wages by dismissing all these."

"I SHALL RESTORE them," Harald said, "but not with mere workmen. Within ten days every band in your command shall be recruited to full strength by trained soldiers."

"Then who," asked Aldhelm, "shall cook, drive, dig, and repair in time of war?"

"There are soldiers who can do these things, and yet fight well, too. In my country all men are both craftsmen and fighters. Henceforth every man taken into the corps shall be first of all a warrior. If there are not enough transport men and engineers among them, I will train them. With two full bands in each district, and four thousand in reserve, you should be able to master any trouble that may arise. If there is need, I can send you help from the Strategium."

Aldhelm thought it over. "There is more to this than good policing," he said at last. "In this way you hold all Constantinople in the hollow of your hand. Aye, even the palace, which is full of your guardsmen. Save for a handful of Immortals, your troops alone garrison the walls."

"Aye," said Harald, "till Georgios returns from Bulgaria, or till John orders one of the Greek generals to march in his troops from the provinces. There are two hundred thousand men garrisoned in the provinces, from Africa to Thrace."

"None the less, it means that you are master of the empire. If John chooses to bring in troops, you can seize him ere they arrive."

"All of which John understands," Harald reminded the Englishman. "He knows I will obey his orders while he keeps faith with me. Unless he is a fool—and he is not—he has nothing to fear."

Aldhelm studied him. "You will be a great man," he said, "if you are not murdered. Yet I fear greatly for you. John is not the man to give such power to another without protection for himself that we know not of."

A Varangian entered, saluting:

"One Demetrios, a Syrian, with a petition for the Prefect."

Aldhelm glanced at Harald, who nodded assent. The soldier, with small respect, herded in an undersized, furtive-eyed man in vivid blue silk. He had no more than crossed the threshold and caught sight of the two officers than he flung himself flat on the floor, beating his forehead in self-abasement. The guard who admitted him stood by scornfully, his toes itching.

"Get up!" Aldhelm commanded with contempt. "Are you a man, who grovels like a worm?"

The Syrian raised himself to his knees, pouring out a flood of adulation:

"Oh, mighty ones! Oh, Glories of the Age! Suns of Valor, Blessed—"

"Enough!" roared Aldhelm. "What is your desire?"

"Justice, most noble—"

"You shall have it. Speak, and be brief."

His glances roving from Harald to Aldhelm, the Syrian spoke, pouring out his words in a desperate torrent.

"I am a brother to Orontides, who owns the Tavern of the Seven Delights," he began. "This morning my servants brought me word that they had seen, in the Nestorian quarter, a slave who had fled from my brother's household. I sped thither at once, with my men, to seize her.

"When we would have taken her, the dogs who dwell there fell on us with staves. We fought like lions, and would have conquered, had not your police laid hands on us all. Us who were wronged they beat, no less than the Persian knaves who withheld our own from us. I alone escaped, to hasten hither to the fount of justice. The slave is ours, oh, Prefect! Give her to us!"

He paused for lack of breath.

"There is no report on this," Aldhelm said. "Go you, Orm, and ask if the men are on their way hither."

The Varangian departed, to return almost at once.

"They come," he announced.

HARD ON HIS words rose a clamor and a wailing, and a dozen soldiers thrust in a motley crowd of men and women. Two burly fellows in torn tunics, battered and bleeding, were plainly the servants of Demetrios; the rest, bearded, black-gowned men and women with flushed faces and coifs all awry, were Nestorians—Persian Christians. One girl alone wore no coif, and her robes were half torn from her back. At sight of her Harald sprang from his seat.

It was Cyra, the dancing girl, who had unwittingly plunged him from the revelry of a tavern into a cell, and thence into sudden greatness. Aldhelm, noticing his interest, pointed to her.

"Is this the slave?" he asked.

"Please, your Mightiness, it is!" Demetrios panted.

Aldhelm addressed the girl gently:

"Are you truly the slave of Orontides, as this man says?"

Cyra, drawing her torn garments about her, knelt at his feet.

"I was his slave, my lord; but one generous beyond my poor power to praise gave me a rich gift; and because of this the Greek captain Karaktos, being angered, bought me from my master for a jewel." She paused, and cast a timid glance at Harald.

Aldhelm turned on Demetrios. "Do you acknowledge the sale?"

"Never, most mighty lord! The wench lies."

Aldhelm frowned, tugging at his beard.

"One of you lies," he said. "If I can learn which one, there will be punishment."

The Nestorians burst into cries of protest, till Aldhelm waved furiously for silence. Demetrios, glancing from one to another of the Prefects, saw Harald smile, and, misreading his amusement for a sign of favor, flung himself at Harald's feet.

"Oh, Prince of the Age!" he implored. "Well of Mercy undefiled! To you I appeal! Give me this slave who is my brother's. Behold, even now my brother lies sick unto death, having been cruelly beaten by the tyrant Georgios—and his tavern closed for a month—all because of thee! Grant justice! Command that she be restored to him, lest he die in poverty!"

Harald laughed scornfully. "Thou fool!" he replied. "Not I, but the Prefect of Police, has authority in this case."

"But thou art his master, and he thy servant!" the Syrian pleaded. "Command him, and he will obey. See, lord"—he pulled from his fouled ropes a heavy purse—"here is much gold! I can pay the worth of the slave. Give her to us, and all this shall be thine."

Aldhelm got to his feet, white with fury; but Harald held him back.

"Let me deal with him," he urged. "The dog has tried to bribe me." He towered above the frightened Demetrios, glaring savagely down on him.

"Justice is not to be bought in Constantinople while I am Prefect!" he said sternly. "By trying to chaffer with the law thou hast confessed thyself in the wrong. I myself saw the Greek buy this girl from thy brother; and afterward I killed the Greek. Therefore she is either free—her owner having died without heirs—or my slave, the spoils of my victory. If she is mine, I will not sell her; if she is free, she cannot be bought. Speak thou, Prefect Aldhelm! Is she mine, or free?"

Aldhelm, marking the twisted face of Demetrios, in which fury strove with craven fear, laughed aloud. He strove to read Harald's flashing eyes, and read them aright.

"Hear judgment in thy case, oh, Syrian!" he pronounced. "The girl is free by the law. None may buy of sell her. She is dismissed. But first thou, who hast insulted justice and sought to bribe thy betters, shalt suffer sentence. I condemn thee to pay the contents of thy purse to this girl, whom thou hast wronged by seeking to enslave her."

Demetrios struggled to his feet, white as ashes. Both his trembling hands clutched the purse, folding it to his breast. The breath whistled through his nostrils.

A Varangian snatched the purse from him, and handed it to Cyra.

"Thrust him hence and dismiss these!" Aldhelm commanded. The soldiers instantly cleared the court; the Persians, as they departed, calling down blessings from heaven on the most just of Prefects.

Cyra alone lingered. She clasped Harald's feet.

"For liberty, and for the means of life, I thank thee!" she breathed. "Would that I might repay thee!" Rising, she glided out.

Harald turned to his friend. "Well judged, oh, Upright One!" he laughed. The Prefect of Police snorted.

"Foul beast!" he cursed. "I know something of his kind. They will find some way to strike at you for this; for they will blame you, as my master. Poison, or a knife thrust in the back."

"I will watch them," Harald answered carelessly. "Am I not guarded by thousands?"

Aldhelm shook his head gravely. "Walk warily after dark," he cautioned.

Harald nodded. "It might be well to give orders that Orontides may not reopen his tavern for yet another month," he said. "It will teach these swine that we have the upper hand of them."

IN THE EVENING Harald found John awaiting him at the palace with less than his wonted urbanity. The Eunuch drew him into his study, sent away his servant, and fixed Harald with his unreadable eyes.

"Why have you ordered the companies on police duty recruited?" he asked pointedly.

"They were all too few to keep so many thousands of folk of different, jealous races in order." Harald spoke carelessly, being sure of his ground.

"Georgios kept order by the sheer terror of his name."

"I have no name as yet among the folk," Harald objected. "Give me time, and I will make my word stronger than another man's blow. Just now, when thousands of troops have been sent to Bulgaria, only the arms of my Varangians keep the lawless in check"

"Let it pass." John waved the subject from him. "It was unwise to anger Demetrios the Syrian."

Harald stared at him; but the Eunuch's eyes were veiled.

"You are well informed," Harald replied.

John waved one soft hand. "I confirmed the decision of your Prefect of Police," he said, "but I urge you to revoke your additional sentence against Orontides. He has been punished enough. Let him open his tavern. It brings in much revenue."

"How?"

John smiled mysteriously. "A place of such ill fame for drinking and dicing pays well to be let alone. Orontides takes in much gold, and is generous with it to those who are generous to him."

Harald shrugged. "I but extended the sentence Georgios imposed on him. So far as I can judge, Orontides is a fat snake, with venom in his jaws. Aldhelm reports that his records are full of charges against him. Varangians have been killed in his house."

"And Immortals," added John with unsmiling humor. "It is true; yet his gold is good."

Harald was slow to understand; yet he had some faint perception that Orontides had bought the Eunuch's favor.

"If I change my decision," he objected, "men will say that my word is like a veering wind. Only by enforcing my judgments can I hold respect."

John frowned. "Then you refuse to pardon him?"

"I must refuse. He is a foul dog, deserving punishment."

John threw himself back in his chair, his dark eyes glowing. There was no expression in his features, but his anger was plain. Then, suddenly, he said:

"Let it pass. I will not interfere with your authority. You are a zealous officer, and in all I have heard of your doings, I find much to praise and little to blame."

Harald's own wrath was slowly rising.

"You seem to have heard in detail of my doings," he retorted.

John looked mysterious. "I have many eyes," he said.

"Say spies rather!" Harald spoke warmly, forgetting that resentment was a poor weapon against this man. "Can you not trust me? I would have told you all, had you given me time to speak."

"I trust no one," John spoke lightly. "Had I done so, I had been dead ere this. It is true that my spies watch you, as they watch all men, all things. It is my business to know all that moves or breathes in this empire. Hold it not against me. I watch you no more than others."

As Harald departed, he thought earnestly upon the Eunuch's frank confession.

"It behooves me to be wary," he reflected. "Those Greek clerks? But no! None of them knew of these things to-day."

He quickened his pace, suddenly furious. "He has spies among my own Varangians!" he muttered.

Arrived at the Strategium, he found Eilif awaiting him.

"Word from Aldhelm," the Gautlander reported. "The girl Cyra has been stolen from the Persian quarter."

"When?" Harald cried, his anger blazing. "Who has dared defy my order?"

"Two hours ago her countrymen reported at the Prefecture that many men had come, with weapons, and carried her off. Six men were killed in the fight over her."

"What has Aldhelm done?"

"Sent orders to every sub-Prefecture in the city to have all Constantinople combed for her. Give a Varangian free rein to search, and he will turn every house within the city walls inside out. She will be found, doubt it not."

"Turn out a thousand men from the barracks, and aid in the search!" Harald commanded. "If a hair of her head is harmed, I will open the belly of every Syrian in the town! My honor is concerned in this thing!"

7

INTRIGUE

HAD HE DONE as his temper urged him, Harald would have rushed into the city at the head of his Varangians, and stormed house after house to find the dancing girl. Such was the Northman's way; and it would have served on Norse soil. But the thousands on thousands of houses in the Greek capital, many of them of several stories, daunted him; he might search for months, and be none the wiser. Prudently he swallowed his anger, and did the only possible thing: hastening to the Prefecture of Police, he waited there, with Aldhelm, for reports from the thousands of men searching the city.

The hours passed, each with its messenger; but no news of discovery, no hint that promised success.

The Syrian's house was the first to be searched; that of his brother Orontides the second. Each had been ransacked to the very vaults, to no avail. Orontides still lay groaning in his chamber, attended by a few servants; beyond these, no one could be found in the showy marble palace that was his home.

The abode of Demetrios was empty, save for a wrinkled caretaker, who declared, in an ecstasy of fear, that his master had left the city for his native land. Inquiry at the gates revealed that he had indeed departed, with all his household; but the girl Cyra had not been with him.

The Persians among whom she had been living were questioned over and over. Their tale remained the same: soon after the fall of darkness armed men had broken into the quarter, rushed the house where Cyra lodged, and carried her off.

"Bring me any man who bears wounds," Harald commanded; and most zealously his police carried out the order. A procession of cursing, struggling men, mostly Syrians, was dragged to the prefecture—some with broken limbs, some with knife cuts, some with bruises; but all denied knowledge of Cyra or Demetrios.

The night passed, and a little after the dawn Aldhelm, sleepy but cool with the stolid coolness of his race, reached for the map. His broad fingers traced along the Propontine shore, and came to rest on a halfmoon-like indentation in the coastline.

"A Sicilian galley awaits for her clearance here," he observed.

"What of her?" Harald asked.

"You have ordered that she be permitted to sail this afternoon."

"Aye. She is a peaceful merchantman."

"But she is Moslem; and the Syrians of this city are Moslem renegades, or Moslems who pretend Christianity for trade advantages. No confessing Mohammedan is allowed within the walls."

Harald leaped up, with a shouted order to the guard:

"Run to the barracks! Fetch Eilif hither with two hundred men. Speed!"

"You are quick in decision, Northman!" Aldhelm
exclaimed. "Aye, and prudent; for if the girl has indeed
been smuggled aboard that galley, the crew will fight to
keep her. Yet Demetrios and all his servants—"

"Have fled my wrath, while his paid agents bore her to
the unbelievers!" Harald broke in fiercely. "That I understand. But how he expects to get her again—"

"He has doubtless sold her to them," Aldhelm replied.
"The Moslems pay well for Christian women. Understanding well that he could not hope to keep her, the Syrian took
his chance to sell her for a high price."

Eilif burst into the court with clanging mail.

"Whither do we go?" he called out cheerfully. "I have
tenscore of your house-carles without. Are there blows to
strike?"

"Follow on, and see!"

DOWN THE LONG Mese the Northmen sped, marching at
the double, their mail and their iron-bound shields clanging like a hundred anvils.

The crowds, accustomed to give way before armed men,
broke from their path and piled up in arcades, between the
arches of which they peered in excited curiosity.

Vehicles sped to right and left till they almost collided
with the masonry, leaving a clear road for the troops.
Happily the hour was so early that most of the townsfolk
were not out; else the throng would have been too dense
to yield ready passage.

Pointing to the right, Harald led the way down a well-
paved military road, straight to the westernmost port.
On either side of them olive trees raised their gnarled
branches and lancelike leaves, through which the morn-

ing sun filtered as they left the palace behind. Before them faint cries were wafted on the sea breeze, with the creak of cordage and the mingled smell of brine and tar.

His eagerness winging his feet, Harald drew well ahead. Suddenly he cried out in fury, pointing. Eilif, hastening to him, saw a long, lean, lateen-rigged ship draw out from the shore, her sails furled slantwise of the mast, her oars dipping easily to give her seaway.

"She sails!" he cried. "Without order!"

"She will not sail far, then," Eilif answered coolly. "You forget that the shore-watch acts under your orders now."

Harald seemed not to hear him. Crying his men on, he rushed down the slope. Pressing hard after, they followed him to the gated guard-tower, only to see the Sicilian strike into a faster beat, her oars lashing the blue sea to creamy foam.

Eilif stared in amazement. Not a fire-tube turned on her to check her unlicensed departure; not a voice challenged.

Harald burst into the tower like a whirlwind. To him ran the officer of the watch—Varangians all.

"Loose on yonder galley!" Harald commanded. "Stop her, or answer to me!"

"She has her clearance!" the captain of the guard answered, his broad features agape with consternation.

Harald raised his ax. "Obey, or die!"

Springing to the wall, the officer summoned his men to the fire-tubes. The long bronze muzzles swung up, focused, spat forth the red tongues of flame with a hiss of compressed air. Fire burst out angrily on the surface of the water, a furlong behind the fleeing ship.

"She is beyond our range!" the captain groaned.

"Launch a cruiser!" roared Harald.

One was already launched, in waiting for any emergency. With short, deep shouts, the Northmen thronged the quay and sprang over her gunwales. She was a fleet pamphylian, built like an arrow, oared to overhaul anything with sails. Drums beat to give time to the rowers; swords and spears flashed from her deck, her thin prow cut like a lance through the water.

On her foredeck Harald stood like a statue of vengeance, his keen eyes straining after the Sicilian. She had a fair start, and, like her pursuer, was built for speed; but her oars were fewer. Slowly, so slowly that Harald gnawed his lips with impatience, the slender pamphylian cut down her quarry's lead.

The breeze grew stiffer, beating the water into choppy waves that smashed against the prows. Faster and faster grew the drumbeat; and in the pursuers' ears, borne by the head wind, thrummed the *nakers* of the Moslems. Like a bird the galley skimmed over the whitening crests; like a swift sea-eagle the pamphylian swooped down on her.

"Good boats, these!" Eilif grunted to his lord; and Harald, licking his lips, gave no answer. His hands whitened on Hell's haft; her thin blade gleamed evilly in the mounting sun.

MAILED MEN CLUSTERED in the Sicilian's stern, their helmets glittering above white turbans. "Merchantman!" Harald scoffed. "She bears all too many spears for a trader."

"Those are bowmen yonder," Eilif observed. "And we have few archers with us. Shall we train the forward fire-tube on her?"

Harald shook his head. "If we do, she will burn before

we can take the woman off. Have the men ranged their shields along the gunwales?"

"Aye. But their arrows will sweep us from stem to stern. You had best take cover, Harald."

Harald laughed in his face, a savage laugh. Yet he turned on his heel and walked aft. Eilif stared at his back.

"There is blood on the wind," he muttered. "When Harald leaves the post of danger, it is to brew death."

He was right. The pamphylian veered off suddenly, heeling over as she swept into an angle to her former course. With a yell of exultation the Moslems saw her turn, and put fresh strength into their oars. They leaped ahead, while the pursuer seemed to drop far behind; but in a little while the pamphylian swung back to her former course.

Now she was drawing, not close behind, but parallel with her prey, and safely out of arrow flight. Slowly the stern of the galley drew closer, then, with a mighty spurt, she drew abreast.

But Harald was not content. On and on, the drums thudding furiously, the hundred oarsmen gasping as they pulled, she forged ahead, and on her poop the fire-tube lifted.

Harald hailed in Greek, shouting between cupped hands: "Heave to, or we burn you!"

Faced with the menace of the terrible Greek fire, which, as they now lay, would sweep his boat from stem to stern with all the force of the wind behind it, the Moorish captain obeyed perforce. His exhausted oarsmen slumped over their handles, barely stroking enough to keep her head into the wind; and the grim pamphylian drifted down on her.

"You have a Persian woman on board," Harald shouted. "Send her, with your captain, aboard us."

There was nothing for it but to obey. Slowly the Moors lowered a boat; unwillingly the Moslem captain descended into her, accompanied by a muffled figure. A few strokes, and they were under the loom of the pamphylian's side. A rope ladder was thrown down, and the Moor made to mount; but Harald waved him back.

"The girl first!" he ordered, smiling at his foe's angry glare.

With trembling feet Cyra mounted, and almost fell into Harald's arms.

He thrust her upon Eilif.

"Take her away," he commanded. "Make her comfortable."

THE MOSLEM OFFICER, who had now reached the deck, turned angrily on his captor.

"By what right do you stop me?" he demanded fiercely. "I have my clearance."

"Your name?" Harald countered.

"How does it concern you?"

The Mohammedan was a tall, lean man, clad from head to foot in close-meshed mail, the curtains of his turban-wound helmet swaying below his well-trimmed, grizzled beard. His eyes were hot, his features thin and fanatical.

"It concerns me that your life is in my hands," Harald answered. "This is my authority." He showed the gold medallion that marked him Prefect of Varangians.

The Moslem bowed grudgingly. "My name is Yusuf ben Mirza," he said.

"You say you have your clearance. Show me your papers."

Ben Mirza handed over a parchment scroll, which Harald examined. He could make nothing of the Greek writing, but the seal was that of John the Eunuch. Passing the parchment to Eilif, he asked:

"What does this say? You can read these bird tracks."

The Gautlander spelled out the scroll laboriously, reading aloud, one great finger following the words.

"It is authority to sail, signed by the Orphanotrophos," he answered.

Harald frowned. "Then a power higher than mine forbids me to interfere with you," he confessed. "Nevertheless the girl, being free, goes back to the city with us."

"Take her at your peril!" Yusuf warned. "I have bought her in fair trade, for the Emir's harem."

"Who was the seller?"

"A Syrian. What matters it?"

"The Syrian is a fugitive from the law," Harald explained. "He had no right to sell her. You have been cheated. A free resident of the city cannot be sold; moreover, the law of this land forbids the sale of a Christian to an unbeliever."

Ben Mirza fixed him with glittering eyes. "Nonetheless you had best give her back," he said ominously. "I am the agent of the Emir of Sicily, with whom your emperor is at peace."

"Aye," Harald retorted. "An agent who comes with many spears, claiming to be a merchant. You may go now—without the girl."

The Moslem swung on his heel, but at the rail turned for an instant.

"If war breaks out again between us," he cried, "may we two meet in battle!"

"You are a strong man," Harald observed appreciatively. "May God grant it!"

"**WHAT WILL YOU** do with her?" asked Aldhelm.

Harald did not know. "You are right, Englishman: she is safe here in the Prefecture, but this is not the place for a woman. She is not safe in the city—so much we have seen already. Nor do I know this country well enough to find a refuge for her."

Aldhelm fingered his yellow beard. "In a land like this," he reflected, "no refuge is sacred enough, none safe from intrigue and bribery, save—the cloister."

"You would make a nun of her?"

"I know she is not the sort of whom nuns are made," Aldhelm admitted. "She is too fair. Have you noted her hands? Never have I seen a woman with such tiny palms, such tapering fingers."

"I see she must not stay here," Harald smiled. "Nor elsewhere among men, if her beauty turns even your cold head. Which nunnery shall we send her to? There are many."

Aldhelm thought. "Take her to the Patriarch," he advised, "and ask him to find a cloister for her."

"I will take her to-night!" Harald declared, and he rose.

The better to escape attention, Harald went unattended, his mail wrapped in a wide cloak. Cyra was heavily veiled. It was no rare thing for girls of the lower classes to walk out with soldiers; and Harald hoped to attract no curious eyes. But he had forgotten the inimitable grace that clothed the Persian girl's every movement. One who had seen her close could hardly mistake her undulating walk, the perfection of the dancing girl's training.

The streets were crowded, as always in the evening.

Every one who passed turned to stare at the tall soldier and the graceful woman with him. Now and then men laughed significantly, or flung gibes at them. Harald became anxious, and Cyra shrank closer to him.

Suddenly Cyra shrieked. Wheeling, tugging at his ax, Harald felt her snatched from him. Even as he got his weapon clear, a knife smashed against the mail above his ribs.

Cyra was struggling in the grasp of two men. The crowds about them had vanished as if by magic at the first outcry, leaving the two surrounded by cloaked figures. Whirling his ax, Harald leaped for the two who held the girl. Instantly four men flung themselves in his way, short swords out-thrust. Others closed in behind and on his flanks.

He did not wait for them to carry the fight to him. Two chopping jabs sent the men on his left reeling back, and he sprang in to Cyra's aid. The great ax rose and fell. One fellow, releasing his grasp of her too late, died as he reached for his weapon; the other fled.

Even as a blow from behind sheared the steel rings protecting his left shoulder, Harald turned, and became on the instant a fighting madman. His ax whirled, slashed, bit—so fast, so terribly, that the assassins had no chance to work in concert. Again and again their strokes went home; but the fine mesh of his mail turned all but that first blow at his shoulder, and that had not gone deep.

The first ax stroke told him they were unarmored: such assassins relied on surprise to effect their purpose. His savage onslaught overbore such little courage as was in them. Suddenly he realized that he stood fighting the air, with no enemy before him. Cyra lay in a huddle at his feet, one of the dead assailants sprawled headless across her ankles.

Flinging the body aside, Harald lifted her gently up, and bore her toward the darkened portico of the Patriarch's palace. She came to in his arms; and, still thinking herself in the grasp of the ruffians, she struggled gallantly. With a few gruff words he quieted her.

BEATING ON THE oaken entrance door with his dagger haft, Harald waited long to be admitted. At last the great door creaked, and opened scarcely an inch.

"Who comes?" quavered the frightened voice. A round, scared eye peered through the crevice. Harald thrust at the door with his foot, but it did not give, being set on a massive chain.

"The Prefect of Varangians!" he announced himself reluctantly. He had been in no mind to admit his identity to any save the Patriarch in person; too many eyes seemed to be upon him in this intrigue-ridden city.

There was no answer, but the door did not close. He listened for the sound of feet or voices, but none came. He was about to hammer on the door again when it opened wide. Scarcely had he borne the girl through it before it was closed again, and bolted. A cringing old man in rich livery stood before him.

"This way, my lord," the servant mumbled. Following him through the long corridor, Harald saw that the Patriarch kept no state, despite the silver edging on his servant's robes. The house was old and shabby, the soft-piled rugs on the floor were worn almost to rags, and heavy with dust. Into a large atrium they passed, in the style of the last Roman emperors; and from this into a retired chamber where, on a high raised seat, an old man sat alone.

As they entered the old man rose, and dismissed the servant. He was very tall, with the head of an aged lion. His eyes had once been fine; now they were dim with years and hot with repressed bitterness. His long, white beard, carefully tended, flowed down over sunken cheeks and rested on a tarnished robe.

"I have heard of you," he said at once to Harald, waving aside all formal greeting. "Men call you honest, though you serve John, the enemy of God."

Harald set Cyra down. She stood trembling, with downcast eyes, her little hands twisting.

He turned to face the Patriarch. "I serve not John, but the emperor," he answered.

"He, too, is God's enemy!" The Patriarch's voice vibrated with passion. "And on him God's wrath rests even now, weighing him down with the sickness of death!"

He paused, to search Harald's face. "What is your will with me?" he resumed, his tone sullen, as of one who has had to bear much, and without patience to bear it well.

Harald extended his hand in a gesture toward Cyra. "She is a free woman, whose beauty is her danger," he said. "Four times, the last time tonight, I have saved her from those who would enslave her. I have brought her here that your holiness may find a place for her in some nunnery."

The Patriarch looked long at Cyra, his old eyes unwinking. There was no trace of kindness in them. He spoke at last:

"She is the dancing girl of Orontides. I know somewhat of her. Is she willing to take the vows?"

Harald was astonished. How did this retired old man, who, though he was official head of the Greek Church, lived in a sort of exile, watched and suspected by the court—how did he know Cyra, the dancing girl?

The Patriarch answered the unspoken question. "I have my agents," he said in a dull voice; and then, tremulously, he broke out, his voice hot with passion:

"How should I live—I, who am hated by the jackals in the palace—if I did not keep an everlasting eye on my foes? They spy on me, seeking every chance to make accusation against me. Only by setting spies on them do I keep myself safe. Some day God will place in these feeble hands the instrument of His vengeance!"

HE ROSE, TREMBLING, almost tottering, but strong in his passion. To Harald's eyes he was only an old man in fear of deadly peril; nor had Harald come on the Patriarch's account, but on Cyra's.

"We must not trouble you then, holy father," he said. "I will find some other refuge for her. Let us go with your blessing."

The Patriarch silenced him with a gesture. "I fear you not, Prefect," he said, more quietly. "If you were not the kind of man I could trust, you would not have risked your life to help this girl. I asked if she desired to take the vows?"

Cyra flung herself on her knees before the grim old man.

"Oh, my father!" she cried. "If there is peace, if there be safety, in the cloister, let me hide behind its walls!"

Assailed by sudden doubts, Harald turned to the Patriarch.

"Is there surely safety in the cloister?" he asked.

The old priest smiled, the grin of a wolf at bay.

"Many are the shames the Eunuch has heaped upon the church," he replied. "But he has not yet dared the infamy of violating the cloister. It is safe."

He clapped his hands for his servant. When the old steward shuffled in, he signed to the girl to go with him.

"Place her in sanctuary in my private shrine," he ordered, "till we can find a place for her among the sisterhood of St. Helena."

With a last look backward at Harald, Cyra departed; and Harald would have gone also, but the Patriarch forbade.

"Be not so quickly gone," he said, his hot eyes burning. "I am told you are the son and brother of kings. It is even said that your elder brother is a saint of the Roman Church."

"It is so, father."

The Patriarch's glance flashed fire.

"Then why," he demanded, "why do you serve men who have mocked the sacraments, laid murderous hands on God's anointed, and defied His majesty?"

Before the old man's wrath Harald felt himself shaken. He crossed himself.

"Do you not know," the relentless voice echoed in his ears like the knell of doom; "do you not know that he who calls himself emperor, aided by his brother the Eunuch, murdered their prince, and through an infamous marriage took unlawful possession of the throne?"

Recovering his self-control with an effort, Harald faced the accusing eyes.

"I have heard this," he answered, "but John himself told me it was a lie."

"Told you, no doubt," the patriarch said scornfully, "that the empress herself slew her husband, and that John forced her to marry his brother that her mad folly might be curbed. Aye! That is the tale he told the people; and there are those who believe him. Fools! Hear now the truth:

"The emperor was an old man, too old to keep a woman's love. John was a mere palace eunuch, whose low birth justified his menial rank. Knowing the empress for a weak, vain woman, he found a place at court for his brother Michael, who now is emperor, and whose beauty quickly brought him into favor. The empress saw him, and loved him. They were lovers long before the emperor died.

"John grew in rank and honors as the empress's love for his brother increased. At last he secured a place in her own household, and fanned the flame of her wicked love. From that day the emperor grew sick—by slow poison, which John administered. But when his death came not swiftly enough, John and Michael strangled him in his bath.

"Before he was cold, they forced the empress to marry Michael. Aye, with hands yet hot from the hideous crime, the usurper succeeded both to the throne and to the wife of his victim."

HE PAUSED, STUDYING Harald's face. The repulsion he saw there satisfied him.

"Can you," he went on, his words slowly falling; "can you, the blood brother to a saint of God, serve such men as these?"

Harald fought hard for calm. "You—you know this to be true?"

"Zoe has confessed to me. And now, by giving you power, John has placed in your hands the means to effect God's vengeance."

Harald was struck with a horrible suspicion. Did the mad patriarch dream—?

"You"—the Prefect breathed thickly—"you would have me slay him?"

"Is it not your duty to slay God's enemy?" the old man asked implacably.

Harald glanced helplessly about him.

"I have sworn an oath," he said, striving for firmness. "An oath to serve the emperor faithfully, unless he or his brother plays me false. How can I break my pledged word? Or how can I be false, even to a villain, if he trusts me?"

"How if the emperor is no emperor, but a usurper?" the patriarch questioned with tireless malice. "Is not your duty to the throne rather than to a slave who sits upon it? Zoe is empress; nor can a wicked marriage make a king of him who married her."

"I could give up my commission," Harald said, more to himself than to the aroused old man. But the patriarch would have none of that.

"To do so," he retorted, "were to give up the advantage God has given you. As Prefect, you command thousands of men—enough to force the murderers from the palace, to place them on the scaffold. Your duty to the empress demands it.

"She is weak, if you will; nay, she has been wicked: but she has atoned her sin through bitter suffering. You, who are a servant of the imperial crown, must cast her persecutors from power, and set her free."

The Prefect stood silent, overborne. The fierce old voice resumed:

"Because I know the truth, I, too, am a prisoner. Only on

holy days, when I must celebrate service in the cathedral, am I allowed to leave this house—and then under strong guard, lest any speak with me. John would kill me if he dared, but he fears the people. They cared little for the slain emperor, but they will not see their anointed bishop perish.

"But I am cunning." His hot eyes narrowed. "Through a secret way my spies leave me and come to me—a way through which I might escape, did not God demand my presence here. Every holy day I show myself to the people, at John's order—lest the people think me murdered, and rebel against him to avenge me. But with none am I allowed to speak."

"THEN HOW WAS I allowed to enter?" Harald asked.

"Men were sent to stop you," the patriarch replied. "Men who, day by day and night by night, have stood watch to keep me from departing or others from visiting me."

"You mean," Harald exclaimed, scarce believing, "that they who fell on me to-night—"

"Were sent by John. Aye. And for all your strength they would have slain you, being many, had they not been ordered but to beat you helpless and take the girl away. The Eunuch meant no more, this time, than to keep you from me. Even now his hirelings report that you beat them off, and are with me."

Harald's anger leaped to life, smothering his indecision. "If you are right, then John has already lifted his hand against me, and so absolved me from further service to him!"

"And you may now slay him without breaking your oath!" the patriarch concluded eagerly. His very eagerness gave Harald pause.

"If you are right," he repeated. "But you may be deceived. "Nay, be not angry with me, father. Before I risk my honor I must be sure. I have too much to lose to strike blindly."

The patriarch fell to brooding sullenly. At length he seemed to reach a decision.

"You must be sure," he agreed, with a touch of bitter irony. "But what will it take to make you sure? Will it suffice if you hear, from the very lips of the empress, the truth of what I have told you? And if you get proof that John himself inspired the attack on you—what then?"

Harald's own eyes glowed. "Prove these things," he replied. "But prove them, and I will hack the dog to bits!"

"There speaks a brave, an honorable man." The priest sighed, and the wrinkles between his white brows showed more plainly. "It will be hard to get you an audience with the empress, for John keeps her more closely watched even than he does me. He would have you killed if you were caught in the women's quarter of the palace. But I will find a way. Kneel now, and receive my blessing."

Harald knelt, but his soul had little peace in that blessing. He was too shaken by what he had heard, too deeply caught in the whirlpool of rage and doubt.

The great door closed behind him, and he stood once more in the light-pricked streets of the city. But the evening air could not cool his brow; and though his thoughts whirled, his eyes watched vigilantly for any that might follow him.

No one followed. When he reached the spot where he had been attacked, there was no trace of the fight. The dead were gone, the very blood removed.

In the shabby palace he had just left, the patriarch once more summoned his steward.

"Get word to-morrow to the eunuch Zodatas," he commanded. "Bid him find the girl Cyra a place in Zoe's service."

The steward bowed, but stayed to question. "Will not John—"

"Zodatas will see to that. Nor does John care greatly what women are about the empress, so long as none of them leaves her presence without his spies close at heel. None will refuse the girl entrance; it will be escape she cannot hope for. Now go; and see to it!"

8

THE EMPRESS ZOE

"GEORGIOS HAS ENDED the Bulgarian revolt."

"You have had messengers?" asked Constantine.

John the Eunuch nodded. "The swiftest, most resourceful men I could lay hands on. They marched with him; and whenever they had news important to me, two of them would desert and ride for Adrianople. Thus I have kept touch with him, without his knowledge.

"This very day came the last, with word that Georgios has crushed the enemy, captured their king, and crucified two thousand of their bravest soldiers. Moreover, he gave orders for two divisions of Immortals to march back to the city at once."

Constantine fixed his large eyes on his brother.

"But you made him governor of the province!" he exclaimed. "He has no right to leave it till you send his successor."

The two were seated in Constantine's hidden apartment. The secret door was closed; but John, seated close to the panel, had his ear constantly to a tube of thin metal running down from the ceiling and through to his own chamber.

"Georgios does not trust me," he explained. "Knowing

that the emperor cannot live long, and mad with ambition to snatch the crown for himself, he means to be here when Michael dies. He will come within five days, with forty thousand of the best troops in the world."

"What will you do? Play the barbarian against him?"

"Harald?" John fell to musing. "I know not. I had meant to, but I am no longer sure of him. He visited the Patriarch last night."

Constantine smiled thinly. "I told you you should have poisoned that priest."

There were condescension and a little scorn in John's answer:

"Until you learn what may not be done in Constantinople you are not fit to rule. If the Patriarch dies, all men will say that I murdered him. You can oppress this people, rob them, torture them, and yet be safe from their wrath; but lay a finger on their bishop, and they will tear you limb from limb."

The young man's eyes glittered; and John was swift to see his resentment, though his calm face did not change.

"Having seen the Patriarch," John went on, "the Northman has certainly heard things he should never have known. He will doubt me, perhaps let himself be used as a tool against me. I must win back his trust before I dare put him against Georgios. And there is more."

"Yes?" Constantine prodded, as John paused longer than his eagerness could brook. He strummed lightly with his fingers on the table.

"I have told you of Harald's interest in the girl Cyra," John continued. "The Syrians were bitter over her loss. Therefore I sent Demetrios out of the city, and had my

"Barbarian!" she screamed. "Northern beast! Go hence!"

agents steal her. They sold her to Yusuf ben Mirza, the Sicilian merchant, for a princely sum; and the purchase price I sent to Demetrios."

"Shrewdly done!" Constantine applauded. "Unless the Northman suspects."

"I fear he does. He stopped ben Mirza's galley, took the girl off, and bore her to the Patriarch's palace."

Constantine pursed his full lips. "You must get her from the Patriarch, and quickly!" he exclaimed.

"Why?"

"It is plain the Northman loves her, else he would not have taken so much trouble on her account. As long as she is there he will visit the Patriarch often, to see her. Thus he will be as wax in the Patriarch's hands, and can be molded into a dangerous tool against you. Who knows but they conspire together already?"

John smiled, a smile that touched his lips alone.

"You prove yourself worthy of my teaching, little brother. But Cyra is no longer with the Patriarch."

"Ha! Then you have already removed her?"

"I have done nothing: I did not need to. She is in the palace now. Zoe has created her second lady in waiting."

"But how came she there?" Constantine demanded.

John shook his head; his deep eyes glowed. "Would that I knew! There is constant communication between the empress and the Patriarch; how, I have never discovered. Every entrance to the palace is guarded; my eunuchs watch the empress night and day; yet there Cyra is. Last night she was with the Patriarch; this morning, with Zoe: and my eunuchs and Immortals swear that no one has entered the palace inclosure!"

"ONE OF YOUR men is in the Patriarch's pay," said Constantine at once.

John's lips curled delicately. "So much is clear; yes, but which?" He shrugged. "After all, there is no danger in the girl, so long as she is watched."

Constantine regarded his brother approvingly. "She was set to spy," he said; "and you have turned the spy into a harmless prisoner. Will the Patriarch tell Harald where he has placed her?"

"I think not. He would scarce confess to the Northman that he has exposed her to the danger of my wrath."

"Then," Constantine's eyes gleamed craftily, "if the Patriarch and the Northman conspire together, we have but to tell Harald that the Patriarch has placed her with Zoe, and he will be angered against the priest."

"Even so. The Patriarch has overreached himself, and played into my hand. But that is not all. Yusuf ben Mirza was no ordinary trader. He was a secret envoy from the emir of Sicily. Cyra was destined for the emir's harem. You know enough of those Moslems to understand what that means. The emir will accuse me of bad faith, and war will break out again. Our possessions in Italy will be in danger."

"Send the girl secretly to him then," counseled Constantine. "She is in your hands."

John fixed the young man with his inscrutable eyes. "What if I want war?" he asked.

Constantine gazed back at him, letting the implications of the question sink into his mind. "I see," he said at last, his handsome face bright with admiration of his brother's craft. "I see! If there is war, and if Georgios becomes dangerous to you—"

"Georgios, or the Northman either. You have guessed rightly, little brother. Now comes the time when I must use you. True, Georgios will soon return; but I shall get him out of our way again. Meantime we can keep you out of his sight. Harald, filled with the suspicions poured into his ear by the Patriarch, will come hither to demand speech with the empress herself, thinking to learn the truth from her own lips. He will come soon, for it is not in his nature to delay. You will now go to her, and give her my command to answer only as is written here."

He handed Constantine a tiny scroll. "She is to destroy this as soon as she has learned its contents, and her answers to the barbarian must be just what this contains. Tell her, if she disobeys, I will have her glorious hair shaved and thrust her into a nunnery. Such a fate will frighten her worse than death, for she is a vain woman and hopes still to regain power and the admiration of men."

Constantine took the scroll, but did not rise. His dainty features turned sullen.

"You tell me you have need of me," he sulked, "and then bid me run on an errand any servant could perform."

"Not so. You are unknown to her, and to all others in the city. By sending a messenger she has never seen I arouse her curiosity and so command her unconscious respect.

"Moreover, you are much like Michael as he was when she first loved him. The sooner she sees you, the sooner she will be ripe for our plucking. She must learn to love you as she once loved Michael, for you can gain the crown only through marriage with her. Blessed be the Providence that made you handsome!

"Now go, and fail not. Your future and mine—nay, our very lives—depend on Harald's accepting as true the tale I bid Zoe tell him. You are to witness the audience, unsuspected by Harald, and report to me. When Georgios arrives I will have other work for you—work worthy of your powers."

CONSTANTINE'S FACE CLEARED. He rose and left the chamber—not by the secret panel into his brother's room, but by a small door opposite, well concealed behind a hanging. It led into a passage between the inner and outer courses of the wall.

John also departed. Even as he touched the panel his ear caught a slight ringing sound, as if thin metal had been lightly struck. He bent to the tube behind him, listened, and whispered back through it. Then he slid through the panel into his own chamber, closed the secret door and seated himself. Through the outer door a servant entered, announcing:

"The Prefect of Varangians!"

"Admit him!" John ordered.

If he had expected a whirlwind of wrath, an injured barbarian bursting with deceived pride, he was disappointed. Harald entered with quiet dignity, his face and manner composed. John bade him welcome with his usual calm urbanity. With studied strategy he did not wait for the other to attack.

"Be seated, prefect. You have come to report the seizure of the Moslem galley? It was seen from the palace walls. I am told that a free woman of this city was a captive aboard her. You did well to bring her back. Have you put her in a place of safety?"

Harald had inherited an outward poise that almost perfectly concealed the most violent turmoil in his heart; but the Eunuch's words so took him by surprise that his eyes showed their amazement before he could control them.

"The woman was Cyra, whom I refused to the Syrian, Demetrios," he answered. "The dog had her stolen, and sold her to the Moslems. I have found her a refuge—with the Patriarch, who has agreed to place her in a nunnery."

John nodded amiably. "That is well. She will be safe there."

Harald was dumfounded. He had expected some sign of anger at this admission. But John sat there smiling.

Harald attacked from another quarter. In swift, short sentences he told of the ambush into which he had fallen, and his successful defense.

John's face grew anxious. "Those Syrians are dangerous,"

he said. "I warned you against their vengeance. Have you found trace of them?"

With a grim smile the Prefect answered: "My police unearthed three of them this morning, all bearing the marks of my ax. I had them hanged."

"It was well done," John commended. "It was a happy thought of mine, to give our Varangians into such strong hands as yours." He looked at Harald, as if expecting more.

Having striven hard to force the issue, and found neither anger nor resistance, Harald was flung back on his last resource—which meant that he must show his mind, fully and frankly, to the cunning Eunuch. He hesitated, but there was no other course unless he consented to give up his search for truth. He laid bold hands on the situation.

"I have heard evil tales," he plunged in bluntly, "which bear out the reports you once denied to me concerning the former emperor's death. I have come to ask you to give me audience with the Empress Zoe. If you value or expect my loyalty, you will not deny me."

Now John's complacency indeed dropped from him; but his flaccid features showed only disappointment.

"I had hoped," he said in hurt tones, "that you believed me; that I had at last found an officer who trusted me as I trust him. Nay, I will not refuse: you may see the empress now. Lest you still doubt me, I will permit you to speak with her without my presence. I will guide you to her apartments and then retire."

Harald was speechless. Was this the cunning trickery of which the Patriarch had warned him? John spoke with all seeming frankness; he even permitted a free interview with that empress whom he was said to guard so carefully. With a few words of embarrassed gratitude Harald followed the Orphanotrophos down the corridor to the Chalke.

ONCE MORE THEY crossed the court which Harald had first seen the night of his arrest. Its fountains, flowers and heavy scents made the air, imprisoned between painted walls, almost stifling. The sun poured down upon them unrelieved, for the hour was noon. Then from that sunken oven they passed into the southernmost of the three great houses that formed the imperial palace: the Theophylakton. The sunshine struck like a blow as they passed into it, blazing back from a thousand facets of bright mosaic on floor and walls.

Harald had thought himself accustomed to the luxury of this more than half Oriental city; but involuntarily he halted in amazement at what was now revealed. He was in the first of a series of apartments, each of which opened into others through doorways so wide that a vista of the most gorgeous splendor opened before him while yet he stared immediately about him.

The rooms were spacious, the high ceilings beamed with aromatic cedar into which designs of vines and twining flowers were set—the stems of gold, tendrils of jade and amber, flowers of silver, fruits of clustered gems.

The walls were of white marble, pure and flawless, divided into broad panels. Some of these were inlaid with mosaic, in which each stone was a jewel—the designs not formal, but representing flowering meadows, hunting scenes, festal processions. Others were chiseled deep and delicately, their cunning tracery filled in with gold, as the Moors set sword blades. Jeweled lamps hung from the beams. The furniture was of finest woods, polished, and inlaid with ivory and mother-of-pearl. The ransom of an empire was in every room.

"The Empress's apartments," John breathed reverently. "The Emperor has a second suite off the west court, more sumptuous than this."

Room followed room, each more beautiful than the last; and in each the marvelous decoration was so varied that the eye grew weary with sheer loveliness. At length the two men came to a chamber larger than all the others, ending in a huge bowed window, unglazed, giving on the gardens. Far out, and below, Harald saw the blue water; between its creamy foreshore and themselves lay a vast stretch of emerald grass, glowing flowers, and fantastic shrubs.

Dazed as he was by all this splendor, Harald yet had eyes for the white-robed eunuchs that stood at each door, the cluster of mailed Immortals in the northeast corner of the terrace. Here and there, in all directions, the sun glinted from other mailed breasts and backs. The Empress was indeed watched, then—or were these guards of honor?

A woman rose from a cushioned seat between the windows and passed through one to a flight of marble stairs that gave access to the gardens. Harald saw that she was tall, young, and moved with an exquisite grace. As he started to follow, John drew him back.

"The Empress must first give permission," he whispered.

Harald watched the woman move across the garden, her rich robes gleaming with tissue of gold, her unbound hair falling in a rich, brown, waving cataract to her knees. Straight across the lawns she passed, then turned, and was lost to sight among the shrubs.

Presently she returned, and Harald saw her face. He

thought her the loveliest woman he had ever seen. Her eyes, large and deeply black, were somber; her features were so purely chiseled as to seem austere, had they not been relieved by the soft, warm curve of her lips. Her bare arms were round and supple. She paused at the top of the stairs and spoke in a rich, soft voice:

"The Empress Zoe, heaven-descended, Porphyrogenita, consents to receive you."

John bowed low, backed away, and answered, his voice humble:

"The Prefect of Varangians alone craves audience. I will withdraw my most unworthy person."

Lost in wonder at the girl's beauty, Harald followed her as she turned back down the stairs. He had eyes only for her; but his brain, as if strangely distinct from his senses, was busy framing the speeches he must make to the great if imprisoned Empress.

He scarce noticed how or where his way led. He knew only that he suddenly stood in a bower of riotous bloom, where fountains hissed and spattered, and women and eunuchs clustered about a cushion-heaped divan. And on the divan lay the Empress.

OF NECESSITY HE turned his eyes from his lovely guide to pay homage to Zoe; nor was he less affected by the sight of her. He had expected to find her worn with grief and fear, haggard-eyed; but Zoe, the heaven-descended, showed no trace of the cruel treatment the Patriarch had said she suffered.

She was slenderly made, most delicately shaped. Her hands, idly engaged with a most transparent tissue of embroidery, were long and exquisite. Her face was marvelously fair, of the most perfect texture. Its color was faint, soft; it seemed that anything so fine must melt at a touch. It was like the incredible soft bloom of a fruit too ripe that the slightest contact will bruise or spoil.

Her eyes were full, dark, startlingly alive; they rested on her visitor with a calm assurance that only her royalty saved from insolence; and yet Harald was stirred by a questioning, almost avid, curiosity in them.

She waited for the Prefect to prostrate himself; and when he merely bowed, conscious of his own kingly blood, her dark eyes burned as they watched him, and the soft lips set. The women about her stirred a little fearfully, but Harald saw from the corner of his eye that the somber beauty of his guide was touched of a sudden with a trace of mischief.

At last, in a languid, cool voice, Zoe spoke:

"Your desire, Prefect?"

Recalled to himself, Harald bowed again, realizing keenly that he had come on a difficult errand. "Did you, or did you not, murder your first husband?" It was no question to put to a queen. If she was indeed John's victim, it would be cruel, and in any case insolent. He did the bravest thing of his life when, with a long-drawn breath, he asked in a voice he scarce recognized as his own:

"Is it true, as I have been told, O heaven-born, that the late Emperor was murdered—with your gracious knowledge?"

The moment he had spoken he felt ridiculous, as well as brutal.

The Empress sat up, with a supple swiftness that was almost tigerish. Her large eyes glanced away, just for an instant. Following their direction, Harald saw a white-robed figure, with its head veiled, leaning idly against a tree. It would be within earshot only if they raised their voices. To Harald's amazement, Zoe's voice was full and loud as she answered, her glance darting scorn:

"Murdered? Say, rather, thrust out of my way, like the worm he was! He died at my command, that a better man might sit on his throne. The ingrate whom I put in his place has repaid me with cruelty and shame; but my hand at least gave to my people a ruler who knew how to govern. How does it concern you, Prefect?"

Harald met the full shock of her eyes, and saw in them neither remorse nor shame for the foul deed which she confessed. Rather she seemed to glory in it. Her look was haughty, self-assured; aye, and something more that puzzled him.

As her eyes rested on the Northman something smoldered in their depths which made him uneasy, but which he could not read. Her gaze lingered; then she smiled dazzlingly, and sank back on her cushions.

"What else?" she asked lightly.

Harald was sickened. He had lived a hard life, full of blows and struggle; he had seen men slain by hundreds on bloody fields, and had spilled his share of blood. He had known all the horror of war, of burning towns; but never before had he heard, or dreamed to hear, a beautiful woman, an Empress, confess, with arrogant pride in the deed, to the murder of her husband.

He turned away, his face hard.

"Nothing more," he said, and strode from her presence.

He had not quite reached the stair, when he heard some

one breathe, pantingly, behind him. It was the beautiful girl who had guided him to Zoe. He turned and looked into her dark eyes. They were not somber now, but pleading.

"We shall see each other again, Prefect," she whispered.

Then she stepped past him, and so up the stair, making pretense to show him the way. He caught a half-veiled glance and the ghost of a smile. As he was watching her graceful figure cross the green lawn his mind was unexpectedly diverted by two things that did little to calm his spirit.

First, a white-clad figure—a man, by the gait—muffled to the eyes, was entering the roofed passage between the two wings of the palace. The unknown could be none other than he who had leaned against the tree during Harald's brief audience with Zoe. Nothing of his face could be seen; but once, as he adjusted the folds of his cloak about his face, Harald saw the gleam of a large emerald on his finger. The Immortals on guard made way before him.

Then, coming from an apartment near by, Harald saw a girl, who passed him, bearing a golden flagon. Instantly he recognized her dainty steps, though she was halfway down the stairs before she looked up, and so gave him a glimpse of her face in semi-profile. It was Cyra.

His mind whirling, he took one step as if to follow her, but a hand grasped his arm, and he looked into the eyes of an Immortal.

"The audience is ended, Prefect. This way!" the man directed. Harald followed the guard, with wildly racing thoughts. At the inner court, John came forward to meet him. The Eunuch's eyes were kindly, questioning. Harald met his gaze and felt its friendliness.

"I am satisfied," he said sadly. "The Empress has confessed."

John thrust out a soft hand, and Harald took it.

9

THE SECRET WAY

EAGER TO STAMP his will on Harald's shaken mind, John pressed him to dine with him in the palace; but Harald declined. "I have had as much as I can bear," he excused himself. "Another time, mayhap."

Nor could the Eunuch alter his resolve, and so shrewdly contented himself with lodging one last shaft in the Prefect's troubled mind.

"You have heard for yourself," he said, "how false are the evil rumors my enemies have spread concerning me. They have probably told you also that I hold the Patriarch a prisoner. You may now see that that also is a lie. Go, if you will, to his palace; none will stop you. That old man is most holy, but age and brooding have cracked his brain." And, smiling kindly, he turned away.

So deeply had Zoe's confession affected Harald that the very air of the city became hateful to him. He plunged into new labors to distract his thoughts, spending all his energy on the perfecting of the small but magnificent army of his Varangians. From the Frankish Hospice he drew every stout champion that applied for a post, swelling the ranks faster than uniforms could be provided. Weapons and mail each man brought with him; but the new recruits presented a most motley appearance. As fast as enrolled they were assigned to different themes, to be trained and absorbed into the routine of the service as fast as possible.

After a fortnight John summoned him to the palace. Twilight was deepening into dark, and the keen night wind from the Black Sea was swirling the dust of the streets into acrid clouds when Harald reached the Chalke. He found the Eunuch in his chambers, seated by a table loaded with food and drink and set for three.

John rose with outstretched hand. "You have come in the moment of time, Prefect. I have great news. But first we shall dine."

He turned and rapped on the secret panel. Instantly it swung open, and Constantine glided into the room.

"This is my brother," John smiled. "I have called him into our council, since he is now to help me bear the burdens of my office. Sit now, and eat. May the meal bring peace!"

The three took their places. Harald surveyed Constantine with frank curiosity. He did not like the fellow's eyes, but he was a merry table companion. John was more amiable than Harald had ever known him.

Throughout the meal Constantine joked and laughed; but he lost no chance to scrutinize Harald as he drank toast after toast to him. John also drank heavily, though he was usually a secret rather than an open drinker. Harald answered briefly to the talk of the others; his mind was still too troubled to enjoy the feast.

At last the servants tiptoed in and cleared the board, leaving only the wine. When they had gone, John filled the embossed golden beakers all around.

"I have called you hither because the time has come for action, Prefect. We are at war."

Harald pushed back his chair, a somber light kindling in his eyes. After the detestable Greek intrigue of the last four months his soul cried out for release, and war was greatly to his mind.

"With whom?" he asked.

"With the Moors. The Emir of Sicily has done homage to the Egyptian Khalif, to secure troops for an invasion of the empire. Their fleets have landed at Bari, and ravaged our colonies on the heel of Italy. You know the cause—the girl Cyra, whom you rescued from the Sicilian galley."

The Eunuch paused, with a direct smile at Harald. "She is now in the palace," he continued. "The Patriarch sent her hither, to attend on the Empress. What do you think now of the rumors that I hold him in confinement? You see, he has free access to the royal family."

"WE SPOKE OF war," said Harald, sick of all Greeks.

"Aye, truly. We must act at once, or we shall lose the little that is left to us in the Mediterranean. Moreover, Georgios is coming back. He should have been here days ago; but fever overtook him on the way, forcing him to stop at Adrianopole. Now he is well enough to march. When he comes there will be civil war, unless—"

"Civil war?" Harald broke in abruptly.

"Aye. The Emperor is dying; slowly, indeed, but dying. When Georgios comes the truth cannot be hidden from him. Georgios is of noble blood, and has long coveted the crown. The Emperor's death will give him his chance to strike. What with the Moslems in the west, and rebellion at home, the empire will be in fearful peril. I look to you to save her."

"How?"

John fixed his dark eyes on his guest. "By taking joint command with Georgios in Italy."

"With Georgios?" Harald asked. "If he intends to seize the crown, how can you send him to Italy? He will not go."

"Mayhap," said John. "But you wonder why I do not send the provincial troops to invade Sicily, and keep you here to interpose your Varangians between the throne and the troops of Georgios."

"It would be good sense," Harald agreed.

"Not so, Prefect. If Georgios thought you stood between him and the crown he would join battle with you at once. Whoever won, the best of the Varangians and the best of the Immortals would be destroyed in a bloody war. When two such terrible forces as these assail each other, the result is mutual annihilation.

"No; to save the finest troops in the empire, I must make them fight side by side. Therefore you and Georgios must both go to Italy. I will summon the provincials, who are numerous, but none too trustworthy, to hold the new conquests of Georgios in Bulgaria."

"And leave the city unguarded?" It was Constantine who spoke, a thought too eagerly. As John brought his glowing eyes to bear on his brother, the young man sat back, feigning indifference.

John tapped Harald lightly on the arm. "Nay; not unguarded. What I shall do is fraught with peril to you, Prefect; but it is the only way to save the empire. In the short months of your service you have raised the strength of the Varangians to twenty-four thousand; you have dispensed with the non-combatant strength of the corps, choosing each man for his courage and strength, and making the troops themselves their own smiths, grooms, farriers, cooks, and drivers.

"That seemed to me perilous, but it may save us now. Your corps, in fighting men, numbers two divisions. Georgios marches hither with two divisions of Immortals. I will send him with his entire force to Sicily, as commander of the land forces; you, with one division of Varangians, will sail in charge of the fleet. I will lend you skilled crews and men to man the fire tubes. Your second division of Varangians I will hold here to guard the capital."

"Where, then, is the danger to me?" Harald asked.

"Georgios hates you. He asked me to grant him your death on his return to the city. I pretended to agree; but now I shall refuse, on the ground that he has left his province without authority. I will calm his anger by promising him the crown when the Moors are beaten; the Emperor will surely die before then.

"But when Michael dies, I shall place the crown on the head of Constantine here. When you and Georgios return he will find the throne occupied. The provincial troops will be summoned from Bulgaria: they, with your Varangians, will suffice to hold Georgios in check. Stay—we will make our triumph sure. You command the fleet: when the war in Italy is ended you will train your fire tubes on his troops as they embark, place him under arrest, and bring him back in chains."

"Then the danger to me is that, before we are ready to sail back, his two divisions will fall on my one?"

"Nay; he will scarce do that. His one encounter with your

Northmen has taught him the cost of facing them in open battle. Here, in the city, with the crown the price of victory, he would risk it; but not in Sicily, where victory would but mean a second war with Varangians on his return hither. Your danger lies in his craftiness. He will seek to put you out of the way by stealth. You must be ever on your guard."

HARALD DRAINED HIS wine in a mighty gulp. "I like it not!" he declared bluntly. "You promised my life to Georgios, and now deny it. Am I a slave to be treated thus? What can I expect of him but hate? And having broken your word to him once you trick him again, by promising the crown and issuing secret orders for his arrest.

"How can you expect loyalty from your generals when you break faith with them at every turn?"

John laughed unpleasantly. "How would you deal with Georgios?" he asked, with something near derision. "One must promise what he asks, to keep him quiet; but to keep such promises were to destroy the empire. He never gave me loyalty; always threats, which could be quieted only by promises.

"As for your life—only my promise to give it him on his return prevented him from taking it before he left. But for me, you would have been cold and rotten already. Now I ask you for some return. When I made you Prefect, I told you I needed a man whom I could trust, to save the realm. Since then you have proved yourself an able officer; but you have done nothing that any able officer might not have done. Now I ask you, for the first time, to show your courage and devotion in the Emperor's service. Will you do it?"

Harald reached out his cup for more wine, drained it, and wrung out his mustaches.

"I keep my promises," he answered. "You may count on me to obey your instructions to the letter."

John pledged him in a full beaker. "So speaks a true man!" he said. "Prepare to sail within the week."

HE WILL NOT go to the Patriarch now!" John exulted.

Constantine sat silent till the clank of Harald's mail died away.

"Why not?" he asked moodily.

"Because I have convinced him that the Patriarch is a crack-brained fool; and because the Patriarch deceived him in the matter of Cyra, after promising to put her in a nunnery."

"Mayhap," the young man answered. "But one can never tell what these barbarians will do. I take it ill that so much of your plans should hinge upon this raw savage."

"It may be," John guessed, a bit ironically, "that you would have preferred to sail with Georgios yourself."

"Why not? If I could not match swords with him, I could at least outwit him."

"Man to man, yes," John admitted. "But this is a matter for force. The Varangians are the only soldiers alive who could stand up against the Immortals if Georgios forces a fight, and Varangians would never obey you. Rest easy, lad; all I do is for you. When you are Emperor, you will thank me."

"If the barbarian does not make himself Emperor first," Constantine sulked.

John arched his eyebrows. "So that is the trouble? Fear not; he is loyal."

THE EUNUCH WAS wrong for once: Harald went straight from his presence to the Patriarch. The aged priest admit-

ted him without delay this time; his old eyes were aflame
with eagerness.

"You have convinced yourself of the truth?" he asked,
ready to interpret the visit favorably. "You are with me?"

Harald passed over the question. "Where is Cyra?" he
demanded.

"Did I not agree to place her in a cloister?"

"I am tired of the lies men feed me here!" Harald
exclaimed with an impatient gesture. "She is in the palace,
in attendance on the Empress. You sent her there—not
out of danger, but into it. Nor have you lied there alone.
You told me the Empress was innocent of her husband's
murder. In my very ears she confessed it—boasted of
it. That is none of my affair, but Cyra is. Why have you
deceived me?"

For an instant the Patriarch's eyes fell; but they rose
almost at once, flashing fanatic fire.

"What matters one woman, a base-born foreigner?" he
cried. "I placed her where she could serve our cause. She is
devoted to you—would give her very life to save you from
dishonor. When you know all that is in store for you, you
will thank me on your knees for what I have done!"

"I have not asked you to do anything for me," Harald
retorted. "If anything is in store for me I will win it by
honest service. What have I to do with your wicked
empress, or your conspiracies? I serve the emperor."

The Patriarch rose from his seat, his tall figure trembling. For a little space he could not speak, but he mastered
himself by a strong effort.

"You are an honest fool!" he said sternly. "You have
heard the empress make a false confession, dictated by the

Eunuch John. Had she not spoken as she did, the tyrant would have thrust fresh indignities upon her; perhaps murdered her. If you must be convinced, I will convince you."

At his signal his ancient steward entered.

"Fetch me Zodatas, or Maria," he commanded. "Maria, if she be not too closely watched."

The domestic bowed himself out.

"Bide here but half an hour," the Patriarch declared, "and you shall learn the truth concerning the emperor's murder. There is a secret way which the Eunuch knows not of. Swear that, whether you believe what you shall hear or not, you will not betray this secret."

"Since you reveal this to me of your own accord," Harald assented, "I will not betray you."

The Patriarch's set lips relaxed. "The father of the empress, the late Emperor Basil, of holy memory, desired long life. Therefore he had two tunnels made beneath the palace: one serves as a sewer, the other was built as if for a sewer. This second tunnel was made to collapse when nearly finished, and was closed. But secretly the emperor had it reopened, to provide a hidden means of escape in case of revolt. One entrance, cunningly screened, lies under a trapdoor in the empress's chamber, the other opens into the vaults below my kitchens."

"Why does she not escape by it, then, if she is so abused?"

"It would do no good. So closely is my house watched that she could not leave it. Her absence would set John on the track; he would discover the secret way, and we should all be lost."

"You say," Harald objected, "this house is watched; that

none enters or leaves it save by John's will; that you are a prisoner. Lies, or fancies! I have entered to-night without hindrance, nor did I see any watching. John has told me that you are free to come and go."

The Patriarch's eyes grew mournful. "My son, my son! If you entered tonight unchallenged, it was because John wished you to think me a liar, or mad. Have you so soon forgot how his ruffians fell upon you and Cyra?"

"They were not his," Harald answered. "They were hired by the Syrian Demetrios, to slay me."

"You shall see."

The Patriarch assumed a listening attitude as to some sound from outside the room. Harald's ears caught the tap of slow, very light steps beyond the door. A soft triple knock; the Patriarch clapped his hands. The door swung open; in the dim rays from a tarnished lamp stood a slender figure, muffled in the white robes of a palace eunuch.

"Zodatas?" the old man inquired.

"Zodatas could not come, father; and I was free. The voice was musical and clear, like the low tones of a flute.

"Maria! Come hither, my daughter."

The graceful figure approached, casting aside its wrapping. It was the beautiful girl who had guided Harald in Zoe's garden. She bowed low before the Patriarch, and then turned to Harald. Her eyes were far from somber now: there was laughter in them; and her cheeks were lightly flushed.

"Said I not," she spoke softly, "that we should see each other again?"

10

TRUTH

HARALD COULD NOT hide his pleasure in her beauty. He had no defense against it; in the stormy war-filled years of his life he had known few women. He had no experience to place him on his guard.

Maria understood, and her eyes softened. The Patriarch also understood, and watched them both, wondering how he could use them for his will.

"My child," he said gently, "this all too honorable youth believes your mistress's confession. You must tell him the truth."

Maria turned her fine eyes full on Harald, so that he must look into them. They were clear and candid as the eyes of a child; but in their depths lurked all the woman's wisdom of the East. In her very loveliness there was a silent eloquence; when she spoke, the beauty of her voice itself persuaded.

"My mistress lied," she said. "Before you came, Northman, she received a letter from John bidding her tell you—what she told you, and commanding her to tell the story so that you must needs believe it, under penalty of enforced seclusion in St. Helena's convent."

Harald felt the spell of her witchery, and strove against it.

"Show me the letter," he demanded.

"John compelled her to burn it. Yet it sometimes happens that a burned letter is not wholly destroyed. See!"

She held out a sandalwood box, small enough to lie hidden in the folds of her sleeve. Snatching it, Harald tore it open, and bore it to the lamp. Within lay a charred fragment of parchment, on which blackened Greek letters could still be traced.

"I cannot read this," he confessed gloomily. "Tell me what it says."

"I have it by heart," Maria answered. "It reads: '—in such words that he may surely believe; else will I—' That is all that we could preserve."

"Little enough," Harald retorted. "And how am I to know that that little is as you say?"

"I will tell you the whole truth, Prefect," the girl said seriously, "and you must believe. John and Michael strangled the old emperor in his bath, compelled the empress to marry Michael, and then gave out that she had slain her husband. This I know, having been in the household at the time. John has made you believe his lies, lest you turn against him."

"If she was innocent," Harald persisted, "why did she not refuse to marry the murderer? She has no honor? She should have died first!"

Maria sighed. "My poor mistress, though no murderess, is weak and vain when she loves. She loved Michael. She sinned, truly; but have not others sinned for love?"

With Maria's loveliness before his eyes, Harald saw too clearly how easily one might err for love; and that knowledge made him cautious.

"You and John tell different tales," he said, "and John's tale is confirmed out of the empress's own mouth. Why should I believe you instead of her? If I could but read that writing!"

Maria laid her hand on his arm, and the light touch of her fingers moved him strangely.

"How could she tell the truth?" she cried. "A servant of John's stood by and watched, to report to the Eunuch what she said and how you took her story. Had she disobeyed, or failed to convince you as John wished, she would have spent the rest of her days in the cloister."

A servant of John's! Maria's words recalled the graceful figure leaning against a tree, just within earshot of the empress's raised voice; the figure which had passed into the palace, bearing a fine emerald on one finger. And in a flash he recalled that just such an emerald had been on the finger of Constantine when he had met the young man at John's dinner.

"It is enough," said Harald thickly. "I believe. But that an empress should consent to this! Could she not have told me the truth and risked the cloister?"

Maria smiled. "You know not what a living death the cloister means for her. My mistress—is in love again."

These words but increased Harald's contempt. "What women and what men do ye breed here in Constantinople!" he exclaimed. "The men lie and betray; the woman who should be an example to you all passes from a murdered husband into the arms of another, and longs for yet a third! Why should I do anything for such folk?"

THE PATRIARCH DREW himself to his full height, his old cheeks flaming.

"What matters it to you what manner of woman the empress is, so long as she is the empress? Your duty is to the throne, whose rightful occupant she is. You will place the empress on the throne, and so serve God! Do this, and I bless you; refuse, and I will lay the curse of holy church upon you as an abettor of regicide!"

Harald, thoroughly angered, took one step toward the flaming old man.

"Hark ye, priest!" he cried. "I am of the faith of Rome, not of your Greek heresy. There is nothing to be got from me by threats; the curse of your church is but so much wasted breath. I follow my own will and my own honor. This much I will promise you, and no more:

"When I have done, and done faithfully, the commands John has laid on me for the war in Sicily, I will return. If it then seems to me that your empress is less evil a ruler than John, then will I put her on the throne, and so punish John that this land will remember his fate till its walls crumble to dust.

"He has deceived me, and for that he must pay. But I will first keep faith with him in what I have sworn to perform for him. If your mistress would have my aid afterward, let her look to it that her life be less weak and vain than it has been; else she need not expect help from me."

He turned away, but Maria held him back. She looked piteously into his eyes, her hands clinging. Despite his wrath and his aversion to the woman she served, his arm trembled under her clasp.

"It is enough," she breathed, "but first, I pray you see the empress before you sail. Hear from her own lips how vilely she has been used."

Harald steeled his heart, and would have freed himself from her grasp. Swiftly Maria's hands slid down his arm and clasped his fingers tightly. She lifted them caressingly to her cheek, then kissed them. Swept with sudden emotion, he bent over her.

"I will do what you ask," he said huskily, "if you will speak with me alone, after I have seen Zoe."

Maria hesitated, her fine black lashes veiling her eyes. At last she bent her head in assent.

"Come hither the night before you sail," she whispered. "I will be here to guide you to her."

Harald strode out, angry, bewildered, and bound against his will by the Greek girl's beauty. That he knew the spell which bound him only made him struggle against it the harder; and wrath at his own weakness became wrath against her as he confessed to himself how deeply she had moved him.

When he had departed, the Patriarch spoke softly to Maria:

"He is ours, child. He loves you. If you but manage him cunningly he will be your slave."

"That may well be," she answered, with a little sigh. "Yet it will be hard to make him a slave, even to love, if I read him right. And I do not like his leaving the city. Georgios hates him, and Georgios—is terrible."

"This barbarian," the Patriarch spoke grimly, "is more terrible than Georgios. He will return, but how he acts on his return depends on you. What did you mean when you told him that the empress is in love?"

A tinkle of laughter parted Maria's lips. "The empress loves him!"

"What? Loves that barbarian?" The fierce old man bent over Maria, his long, white fingers shaking her.

"He is very handsome," she protested. "The sea on a sparkling day is not bluer than his eyes."

"Zoe loves him? And he loves you!" As the Patriarch studied the girl's face, wearing its half mischievous smile, his fingers loosened and he chuckled, but the chuckle was grim. "Why then, girl, the game is ours! We shall let the fool make himself emperor!"

Maria's eyes flashed. "Aye, father, so we will; but ye will not make me an emperor's mistress. I play for Zoe, and am true to her."

The fanatic priest frowned. "Take care! Play shrewdly, then, or ye lose the game!"

11

CONQUEROR'S RETURN

HARALD STOOD IN a group of his trusted officers, in the Strategium.

"We are leaving my galleys here," he directed. "The Greek ships are swifter, and equipped with fire-tubes. Aldhelm will bide here, in command of the division that guards the city."

Aldhelm surveyed his superior coolly. "What wrong have I done you, that you treat me so?" he asked. "Am I a coward?"

Harald wrung the Englishman's hand. "It is because you are a very brave man, and a shrewd one, that I bid you bide behind," he answered. "There may be trouble here; and moreover, I may need a stanch friend in the city against my return."

"What of us?" Eilif asked, glancing at the others.

"Ye all go with me. You, Eilif, shall be chief of my house-carles as before; for I shall take my own five hundred as the heart of my force. Ye others shall all have command of themes. Now go, and bid your men be ready to sail on an hour's notice."

Four days passed—days and nights of almost ceaseless toil. Two hundred swift ships, and two huge, slow-moving dromonds, were brought from the imperial yards on the Bosporus into the Sea of Marmora, where their tall masts and slanting yards forested the four ports. Shipwrights and chandlers swarmed like ants about them; the smell of tar and cordage mingled with the salt air.

Greek rowers were shipped, to free Harald's own men for fighting, and because the natives better understood the sweep and stroke for these light, fast ships. As John had agreed, crews for the fire-tubes were provided from the royal fleet; but, unwilling to be dependent altogether on them, Harald made them give such instruction as they could in so short a time to his fighting men.

The fourth day after Harald's interview with John, a horseman rode in from the Adrianople road with news that Georgios was in sight. In preparation for his coming, Harald had on the walls the division he meant to leave behind with Aldhelm, all save two themes held on police duty.

Every catapult and ballista was ready, its mule-gut cables renewed, piles of stones and heavy javelins laid by. Lead was always hot in kettles on the inner battlements.

There was a law that any general returning from foreign service must encamp his force in the broad open space between the inner and the outer wall, till he should receive permission from the emperor to bring them in. This was to prevent the sudden seizure of the city by discontented or ambitious commanders. Harald meant to enforce the rule on Georgios.

That afternoon a vast cloud arose far up the Adrianople road, till its dense haze blotted out the red ball of the sinking sun. The earth pulsated with the distant pound of marching feet. Drums rumbled like far-off thunder; cymbals clashed, the hoarse roar of Greek trumpets, tore through the quivering air. Suddenly, through the orchards and scattered suburbs beyond the walls burst a sudden sheet of flame—the emergence of thirty thousand armored men from their mantle of dust.

They came in an endless column, foot and horse. Before them a little knot of officers, mounted on splendid chargers, put their tired beasts to the gallop; and at the head of his hosts Georgios, conqueror of Bulgaria, spurred to the Adrianople gate. Even as the guards challenged, and the bull voice of Maniakes roared in answer, the vast column surged up, quivered, and halted with the precision of perfect discipline. As they came to a stop, their shields clanged hollow on mailed backs; and every man raised sword or lance in the salute to the emperor, given always at the wall by returning armies.

The brazen gates swung wide and the triumphant Georgios, making his horse caracole, rode in. His scarlet mantle was thrown back to reveal his shimmering gilded mail. He sat erect, wide shoulders thrown back, arrogant brow lifted exultantly.

A trumpet pealed from the gate; and down from the battlements came the officer of the watch, Aldhelm, to do the victor honor, and to transmit the emperor's commands.

Georgios bent stern eyes on the man who had replaced him as Prefect of the city; but he saluted, as every officer, even the highest strategos in the empire must salute the Officer of the Outer Watch, who represents the dignity of the emperor. Aldhelm's sword flashed instantly in the

Varangian salute to a superior; and even the grim Georgios smiled at the courtesy.

"Well done, Englishman!" he approved. "My orders?"

Aldhelm suppressed a smile, and spoke: "In the name of the emperor, Augustus, Blessed of Heaven, I greet the victorious Georgios, and thank him for his valiant deeds. It is the emperor's will that you hold your men outside the inner wall till his further commands reach you. The Orphanotrophos sends his submissive good wishes, and desires you to attend on him at once."

EARLY THE NEXT day Georgios, black with wrath, led his men out through the Golden Gate into the open country, and thence down to the Propontine shore. No drums beat now; the trumpets alone pealed commands; the men marched in silence, gloomy, embittered.

After their hard campaign in the Bulgarian forests they had expected the freedom of the city as soon as they had turned in their arms; but now orders had come to embark for Sicily. None knew what had been said in the short interview between the commander and John; but all guessed that the Orphanotrophos had paid some heavy price to recompense Georgios for this sudden change in the general's plans.

Georgios went about his work like a whirlwind: black-browed, furious, scattering destruction among all who obeyed him too tardily. His men, who feared as much as they worshiped him, moved about in trembling apprehension, eager to escape his eye, but just as eager to fulfill his orders to the letter.

That afternoon came John himself to the Port of the Golden Stairs, where the two leaders of the Italian expedition waited. The Eunuch was attired in glittering cloth of gold, with the royal eagles flying above his ivory chariot, and an escort of fifty Varangians and fifty Immortals.

As the procession came to a halt, he set one foot on the step of his vehicle, but made no further move to descend. He was the mouthpiece of empire, and the servants of the crown must come to him.

They came: Harald calm, inscrutable; Georgios like a thundercloud about to hurl its lightnings. The Eunuch gave each a glance, and signed to a clerk mounted on a mule beside the chariot.

Dismounting, the clerk threw himself at his superior's feet, bent his head thrice to the dust, and then, rising, proffered John a jeweled box. From this the Eunuch drew two golden chains, each bearing a round medallion set with rubies. At his signal Georgios fell on one unwilling knee, and bent his head. Throwing the chain about the bent neck, John cried:

"Herewith, by the supreme order, I proclaim thee Strategos of the Italian theme, Commander of all land forces, First General of the Empire!"

As Maniakes rose, fingering the emblem of his new dignities, he cast a glance of triumph at the waiting Harald. But the triumph died from his eyes as John rolled out, in unctuous tones, while he held the second jewel above Harald's head:

"By command of the mighty Augustus, I proclaim thee Grand Heteriarch, Commander of all Varangians within the Empire, and First Strategos of the Fleet!"

Then, less pompously, and in tones that held imperious dignity, he addressed them both:

"Ye two have joint and equal authority, each within his province. When ye operate on land, Georgios shall have the final word; when engaged on the sea, Harald shall prevail. Let there be no conflict between you. Each shall obey the orders transmitted to him. Bring back victory, and ye shall receive honor. Be ready to sail on the flood tide to-morrow."

Harald glanced at Georgios, who nodded curtly.

"My men are ready," he said.

"And mine," said Harald; "and the ships."

John waved his hand; the charioteer cracked his whip, and wheeled the four gold-bedizened horses. As soon as John's back was turned on them, Georgios laid a heavy hand on his rival's shoulder.

"I had not thought to make peace with you, Northman!" he growled. "Yet I shall obey my orders respecting you. When we return, there shall be a settlement between us."

Harald, remembering John's secret orders concerning this man who coveted empire, answered simply:

"The settlement will come in its time. Till then, we are comrades. Give me your hand." But Georgios turned on his heel.

As he strode off, Harald beckoned Thiodolf.

"Take charge here," he ordered. "I have private business."

"It will not be long?" the Skald asked, glancing at Georgios.

"Nay; and it is not what you think. I return by midnight, and sleep on board."

He stalked to the gate after Georgios, but paused as he saw the Greek in earnest conversation with a young man in rich attire. Constantine again!

"Constantine," he mused. "He whom John means to make emperor. What can Constantine want of Georgios, who intends to be emperor himself?"

12

THE HEART OF ZOE

TRUE TO HIS promise, Harald hastened to the Patriarch's palace on the last night before departure. Some distance behind him, unmailed, clad in the long robe of a simple citizen, an armed Varangian watched to see that none spied on his lord.

The Patriarch was not visible. His aged servant led Harald through the dusty rooms into a low, vaulted kitchen. At a touch of the finger, the servant released a hidden spring that swung back a great utensil cabinet from the wall, revealing a black, yawning arch that sent a breath of dank, musty air into Harald's face.

Harald hesitated. "The girl?" he asked.

The old man pointed within the arch. Harald bowed his head, slipped the thong that held his ax till he could feel its haft, and stepped within the archway. A flight of steps, slippery with moisture, led him down into the pitch-black bowels of the earth. A warm hand glided into his, even as the creak of the cabinet sliding into place cut off his retreat.

"It is I, Maria." Harald recognized her soft, rich voice, and his pulses quickened.

Lighting a candle, she led the way through a narrow tunnel, straight as an arrow, little higher than a man's head.

Its vaulted roof was supported at the sides by squat stone pillars, unadorned. The two moved forward silently, in no mood for speech. Harald was torn between his impatience at having given a promise to interview Zoe, a pledge that bound him to leave his preparations on the eve of sailing—and his very real longing for a few moments with Maria.

They came at last to a sheer wall that blocked the tunnel off short. A ladder leaned against this wall, and near by a metal tube curved down from the roof. To this Maria put her lips, and spoke softly, listening for an answer.

"In a moment they will admit us," she whispered to Harald.

After a short silence, in which Harald could hear his own heart beat, a parallelogram of light opened in the roof above them. As he gazed at it, it grew wider and wider. A square, thin slab of stone in the roof had moved aside, leaving a hole wide enough for a large man to clamber through.

"Place the ladder," Maria commanded, and Harald obeyed.

He found himself in a spacious, brilliantly lighted chamber, hung with tapestries of the finest, softest weave. The air was heavy with perfume. As he drew away from the tunnel entrance a white-robed eunuch replaced the stone. Maria whispered:

"It is Zodastas; he is faithful to the empress. John pays him to spy, but he reports only what we bid him."

Harald stood staring about him, breathing as short as he could, for the perfume sickened him. It came from a bronze vessel set above a brazier, about which strange implements—retorts, crucibles, and flasks—stood on a marble table. Boxes of colored pastes lay open among them, exhaling fragrance.

"What is that?" he asked, but Maria had disappeared. The eunuch grinned.

"It is the empress's beauty," he replied softly. "She is a famous chemist, and has all the secrets that make a waning complexion young again."

"Faugh!" grunted Harald; and the eunuch, frightened at the effect of his jest, turned pallid.

A light step behind him made the Northman wheel. The empress stood before him.

The sight of her would have ravished most men's eyes; indeed her smile, as she gave Harald her hand, betrayed that she wished his admiration; that she had done her utmost to be enchanting in his sight. Her beauty was even more radiant than it had been in the garden; the perfumed lamps shed a rosy glow that made her fine cheeks richer, and sparkled in her eyes.

Her supple figure was clad in a close-fitting robe that showed its lithe lines artfully; its open neck revealed the sculptured perfection of her throat. Her lashes, long and silken, were darkened with kohl, after the Moorish fashion. She swept superbly to a divan, and arranged herself gracefully in a cushioned corner, waving Harald to a carven chair opposite.

HARALD'S ADMIRATION, UNWILLING though it was, showed in his eyes; and Zoe accepted the tribute with a smile. Even the rash words of the humorous Zodatas, and the reek of the unguent boxes, were overbalanced by her charm.

"Lord Prefect," she began, soft music in her voice, "you

know the truth now. Will you not help a wretched woman? Can you, a king's son, see a queen oppressed?" Her kohl-rimmed eyes glanced at him in piteous appeal.

Harald was no courtier, but he had learned when to mask his feelings.

"I have told your woman," he answered, "that on my return from Italy I will weigh all things well; and, if I deem you a better ruler than John, will do all in my power to win you back your throne. And in any case I shall punish John for deceiving me. But till I have done his errand, I am faithful to him."

Zoe's large eyes flashed, and the robe over her bosom lifted with the quickened pulse of her heart.

"You will punish him? Ah, that is good! Cruelly, vilely, has he treated me. I, born in the purple, daughter of a hundred emperors, am no more than the slave of this base-born eunuch!

"You will promise to help me—now?" she pleaded. "You can do it—ah, so easily. Your troops command the city; there are but a handful of Immortals within the palace. If you need more aid—and you do not—the townsfolk will rise in arms if you bid them rescue their empress. They, at least, love me. They have loved all our house."

He could see that they would love her, who saw only her beauty, her exquisite grace, and had besides the tradition of loyalty to her family. Yet he frowned.

"I have given my answer," he said firmly. "Though I had but to raise my hand to topple John from power, and place you on the throne, I can do nothing till I have kept my promise to him, and ended the war in Italy. You should not ask me to abandon that task: the Moslems are this moment overrunning your own lands. If you are fit to rule, you should be the first to bid me crush to earth your country's foes."

"Is not John my country's foe?" she asked warmly.

"It may be," Harald shrugged. "There is also my honor to be considered. Never have I had to remind men of it so often as in this city of yours. Having pledged my word to John, I must keep it. If you wish my help, wait for my return."

She bit her lips: her tiny teeth, white and even, set prettily in the red flesh. For a little she was silent, thinking; then—

"Tell me something of your own land," she commanded. "Is it great? Is it fair?"

The sudden change made Harald smile. "It is not so great as this," he answered. "It has not one soldier where you have twenty; not one ship where you have five. This one room alone, with the treasures it contains, would buy all the wealth of Norway. It has few stone buildings, no castles, no walls but of earth and wood. Nay, it is a poor land, rough and bleak; yet I love it."

Her cool glance surveyed him, from blue eyes to heavy boots, measuring him without and within. "If I read you right, you would not be content to pass your life as king over so little, having seen our greatness and our splendor."

"Nay, I would not!" Harald's eyes flashed proudly; he drew himself up. "I mean to rule over more than Norway ere I die."

THIS PLEASED HER. She reached out, caught his hand, and drew him down beside her; made him sit close to her.

Her eyes searched his. Her cheeks flushed as daintily lovely as the soft fires within the pearl.

"You may easily rule more than Norway," she said; and her soft voice shook with half-hidden feeling. Her eyes were eager. "You are not as other men: you are strong, and there is a spirit within you which will not let you rest while there are lands to be conquered or glory to be won. I have known great men—earth's greatest—and never have I known a man more surely born to majesty."

Her words stirred him powerfully; they touched the hidden strings of his ambition, to which his soul had vibrated since his hands had clutched at the first toy sword of his childhood. Her real meaning did not reach him, so filled was his soul with its dreams of glory—glory to be won by deeds alone, not by intrigue and favor.

Her words called back a memory of his early days: when his brother, already a soldier and a king, had offered the five-year-old Harald and his boy cousin a gift, the cousin had replied: "Give me a farm and many thralls to work it!" But Harald had cried, in an ecstasy of baby ambition:

"Give me a long ship, and three score vikings to man it, and I will conquer England!"

He told her about it—this woman, this queen, who understood his dream. They laughed, forgetting their present wrongs and trials. It brought their spirits close to one another. Harald sat enthralled, not by her beauty, but by the visions of greatness her words evoked. And Zoe, easily misunderstanding, laid her hand on his.

"Cast my enemy down!" she whispered, her breath fanning his cheek. "Give him to the torturers! In return

I will give you a throne, an empress to wife. You shall be emperor, master of Constantinople, the heart of the world!"

Her words smote him. To his dismay, he felt her arms about his neck. The cunning with which she had tempted him made him suddenly angry. He put her arms aside and scowled into her wondering eyes. His ambition was not such that either her beauty or the vastness of the power she offered stirred it.

"Your pardon," he spoke brusquely. "I crave greatness, but greatness with honor. Nor do I see much honor in marriage with a woman who makes marriages so easily."

Zoe rose, withdrew a few steps, and stared down at him imperiously. Her eyes were proud, but there was hurt in them too. Two little lines etched themselves between her brows.

"You mean—" She broke off, her cheeks hot.

"I mean," he said the thing yet more bluntly, "that when I take a wife it will be one whom my heart loves and my mind honors."

She sprang at him, her small fists clenched.

"Barbarian!" she screamed. "Northern beast! Go hence!" But in the very flame of her anger her mood changed. To Harald's dismay, she cast herself to the floor, sobbing.

Alarmed by her cries, Maria ran from the adjoining chamber. After a quick glance at Harald, she knelt beside the prostrate empress, and tried to comfort her.

Harald touched the girl's shoulder. "I must go," he said. "You have made me a promise." He paid no further heed to Zoe; nor did she, immersed in her passionate tears, give heed to him, nor to Maria.

Maria sprang up, her eyes flashing reproach. Then, as if

remembering tender things, they softened. A little smile dimpled her cheeks, and was gone. She whispered: "Come!"

HER SLENDER FINGER touched a brilliant bit of mosaic in the wall, an innocent-seeming bit of mosaic that moved under the pressure she put upon it. The stone slab at her feet slid noiselessly to one side.

Together they descended into the tunnel, where Maria again lighted her candle. Walking with him a little way in silence, she at last bade him stop. But her thoughts in that short walk had gone back to Zoe. As she faced Harald, her manner was aloofness itself.

"Now," she asked coldly, "what have you done to her?"

Harald stood awkward and speechless. This girl's swift changes bewildered him. He could not betray the mistress's secret to the maid. He knew not what to say. But Maria understood.

"So you have rejected greatness and a queen," she said. "Such a chance comes not twice to any man. And you have broken a woman's heart. That may mean nothing to you, but you throw away an empire merely because you deceive yourself into thinking you could not love Zoe."

"Well you know why," he answered, and suddenly snatched her to him. She dropped the candle to the stone floor, where it sputtered in its own grease, but continued to burn. "Not that I would have such a woman for all the splendors of earth."

She struggled to free herself from his arms, and, ashamed, he released her. She bent over and straightened the candle in its sconce.

"We had to have light," she said, but in an unsteady voice that somehow thrilled him. He saw her clasp her robe closer about her to hide the trembling of her hands. How it happened he did not know, but in a breath of time her arms were about his neck, she was crying softly against his shoulder, his face was buried in her hair, and he held her tenderly close.

"I will be your wife—on one condition," she breathed, lifting her face and taking his bearded cheeks between her gentle hands. "As soon—as you come back—will you kill John and give Zoe the crown?" she concluded in a rush.

"By the glory of God, I will!" he cried. The words had no sooner left his lips, however, than he would have bitten them back. He stood fighting for composure, for words that might persuade her to give back the promise that sudden joy had wrung from him. All the time he was holding Maria in his arms, and she was murmuring in a low voice:

"She has been so wronged. You cannot understand as I do, you have not seen it. She has suffered so much, and will suffer more." A heavy sigh heaved her bosom. "I love her—almost as much as I love you."

She was pressing the candle into his hand, the next moment gliding swiftly from him. "I must get back to Zoe before she misses me," she smiled over her shoulder.

Familiar with the ground, she was soon out of sight in the distant darkness of the tunnel before he realized she was gone.

"Come back!" he cried. Did his voice reach her? Her very footfalls had ceased to sound. He ran back after her, only to see the square of light at the tunnel's end darken as her form passed upward into Zoe's chamber, and the stone slid shut again.

For a moment he stood, gazing stupidly at the lighted candle in his hand. He was bitterly angry with himself for his moment of weakness. At last he said to himself ruefully:

"I promised Zoe to punish John on my return and to make her supreme once more if she proves to be better than he. I pray that she will, for my honor's sake."

As he neared the tunnel's farther end, he was thinking:

"Women are not to be understood. How can a woman like Maria love a woman like Zoe?"

He beat with his ax upon the closed archway: softly, thrice. The Patriarch's servant let him through.

MARIA FOUND HER mistress quite recovered, dry-eyed, but with two hot patches of wholly natural color on her cheeks. The girl would have laid her arm about her mistress's neck, but Zoe thrust her off.

"He loves another woman," she said, bitterly. "Could I but find her! The barbarian! What matters it to him that he tortures me?"

"His love. Is that so much to you, my lady?" Maria's voice was sweet with affection, and remorse that her own happiness was the queen's pain troubled her deeply. "He has sworn to kill John when he returns from Italy. If you are patient the rest will follow."

How soft she had been! She would change Harald's heart. She would be cruel, make him incline to Zoe. What a traitor she had been, knowing Zoe loved Harald! "No man can resist your beauty to the end," trying to believe what she said. "You have but to be patient, and hereafter avoid angering him."

Zoe turned smoldering eyes upon her. "You are wise,

Maria. I will do as you say. But first I must find her. The woman he loves!"

Her face became suddenly savage, all its beauty lost. "I know who she is!" she cried.

Maria paled and felt her knees giving way beneath her.

"I know who she is!" the Empress repeated. "It is the dancing girl, Cyra! Have you not told me how he saved her from the Moslems?"

Maria did not dare undeceive her. In Zoe's present mood it would be dangerous. The Empress's cunning with retort and alembic was not confined to the making of cosmetics.

Zoe fell to calculating, her lips set in a rigid smile.

"Bring me a reed, parchment, and ink," she ordered. Her eyes had narrowed to cruel slits. "When I have written, wake Cyra, and send her to me."

Zoe sat long over the writing, weighing each word. Presently Cyra, in her white bedrobes, stood before her lady at the distance prescribed by court rule. As the Empress looked up she fell to one knee.

"Dress," Zoe commanded, "and take this letter to the great cypress at the south end of the gardens. Give it to the Prefect Harald, whom you will find waiting there. Be very careful, lest the guards see you—it is death to be caught with this. Keep in the shadows."

Cyra departed. Zoe summoned Zodatas.

"Speed to the Eunuch John," she said. "Bid him watch the great cypress in the gardens."

Maria sat silent, pity gnawing at her heart, her face a mask. Oh, this life at court! This hard, cruel life at court! Almost she hated Zoe.

"It will cut two ways," smiled Zoe, glitteringly.

13

THE EBONY COFFER

CYRA STOLE OUT into the soft night, slipping through the fragrant, silent garden like a ghost. Her heart beat so, what with fright and the secrecy of her mission, that she thought the guards must hear it from their stations. From bush to bush, from hedge to tree, she crept, soundless, casting timid glances all about, lest some white-robed eunuch or mail-clad man-at-arms surprise her.

She knew what risk she ran if she were caught. But she bore a message from the Empress—a message to the brave Northman who had thrice saved her from slavery; and the longing to show her gratitude to him, even by the simplest service, was stronger than her fear.

Now she could hear the breeze from off the Bosporus soughing through the trees, could smell its salty tang. The great cypress stood by the south wall of the palace grounds, scarce a stone's throw from the high, square lighthouse and the curving beach. She shuddered: it would be light there. It was a strange place for Harald to wait. But perhaps he had rowed up from the shipyards, and had a boat waiting for his escape, and hers.

Cowering close to the nearer leafy wall, she tiptoed on, her feet drenched with the heavy dew. At last she saw the black outline of the cypress, separated from her by a stretch of sand, swept by the searching eye of the beacon. Then, in one sudden, fear-winged rush, she ran across the sand, and pressed her slim, dark-robed figure against the trunk of the tree, scarcely adding to its bulk. Harald was not there.

As she waited, her body close against the rough bark, she was afraid, horribly afraid. Why did the Northman not come?

Then, at last, she heard him: heard the measured pace of his feet, the rhythmic clash of his mail, the clatter of his scabbard. She turned toward him, freed from all tension by his nearness, holding out the Empress's message. He took it from her; then, even as she raised her eyes to look upon him, two rough hands caught her by the shoulder.

Cyra screamed, falling on her knees. It was not Harald— it was an Immortal. And beside him, silent as a snake, stood Constantine.

The young man smiled, a smile that twisted his soft lips. "Let one man take her to the Orphanotrophos," he commanded. "Are the others well hidden? Good. Let not this Varangian escape, or it will go ill with you!"

JOHN GLANCED FROM the sealed scroll in his hand to the terrified girl before him. His eyes were rimmed with red, for he had drunk heavily, but their smoldering glow was steady. Cyra, her hands bound behind her, stood like a wounded bird in the fowler's net, quivering in the extremity of fright.

Ripping the seal, John unfolded the scroll. His brother Constantine peered to read over his shoulder. Smiling at his eagerness, John read aloud:

" 'To the illustrious Prince Harald, Prefect of Varangians. From the Serene Porphyrogenita, Augusta, Empress, greetings:

" 'Believing you to be a true man, and no creature of him who oppresses us, we appeal to you for justice. The confession which you heard from our lips is false. If you would know the truth, follow her who bears this letter.

" 'Zoe.' "

The two brothers exchanged glances. Constantine licked his lips.

"Plain enough," he said silkily. "She means to use him to crush us both. If she succeeds in reaching him, we may bid farewell to our hopes. He has enough Varangians in the city to—"

"You forget Georgios and his Immortals," John interrupted. "I do not think the Northman is mad enough to strike now, even if Zoe gets word to him. And we have intercepted her messenger. No; there is something in this that I do not understand."

"Question the girl."

"I have questioned her already—not with words. It is plain from her eyes that she knows nothing. Think you Zoe would take a dancer into her confidence? Nay, she is but a tool."

John thought so long, and in such deep silence, that Constantine grew restless. But John brooded on; the great brown eyes seemed lost in philosophic contemplation; the lines of the flaccid, worn face deepened.

And still Cyra stood, in mortal fear and very weary, half-supported by the burly soldier who guarded her. Now and again she stole a furtive look at John, her judge—John, whom all the city feared. The bitterness of death was in her heart; her flesh grew very cold.

Some one tapped on the door. A servant entered, followed by a soldier, much out of breath, who saluted. "The Prefect of Varangians is aboard his ship, Most Serene Orphanotrophos. I myself saw him inspecting the weapon-chests. His men say he has not been ashore for the last hour."

"Good. Go!"

John turned to his brother. "You heard? There is something strange in this; but it is clear that Harald knows nothing of it."

"But the letter?"

John laughed, quietly. "You are so shrewd, little brother; yet you cannot see trickery in this! If the empress wished to get word to Harald, why should she write a letter? It were much easier, and safer, to give the girl a vocal message. Letters are dangerous to the sender, and Zoe is none such a fool that she does not know it. Then this letter is written in Greek, and Harald cannot read Greek. But it might be that Zoe does not know that."

"But why then," Constantine insisted, "knowing it was foolish, did she write?"

"For those that do read Greek," John answered blandly.

Constantine in his turn fell into silent thought, trying to solve the riddle. John motioned to the guard.

"Put her in the dungeon!"

WHEN SHE WAS gone, Constantine lifted a puzzled face. "What does it mean?" he demanded.

"It means that Zoe, for some reason of her own, wishes us to think that she is in communication with the Northman. Perhaps she hopes to make me lose faith in him, and so to stir up trouble on the very eve of our operations against the Saracens. That would be a shrewd stroke. If she could make me depose him, or throw him in prison, the Varangians would rebel. If they won, they might slay us; if they lost, there would be none to resist Georgios, who would make himself emperor at once. But Zoe is a fool if she thinks Georgios would restore her to power."

"But in either case we should lose," Constantine observed.

"We should die," John said emphatically. "And it may be that Zoe so desires my death that she is willing to let the crown fall to Georgios. The woman is desperate; and this scheme of hers is the shrewdest she has yet devised against me."

"It were well," Constantine said, "to make an example of her messenger, and so let her know she cannot play such games with safety."

John laid a hand on the young man's arm. "You are not yet wise enough to be an emperor," he rebuked. "Harald has warned me that his honor is concerned in the dancer's safety. If a hair of her head is harmed, and he comes back from Sicily alive, he will avenge her terribly."

"You fear this Northman too much." Constantine's dainty lip curled. "Moreover, he needs to be chastened. Have you, who are so wise, never understood that he means to be emperor himself?"

John sat up straight in his chair, his eyes flashing.

"He? Emperor? A barbarian?"

"I have seen it in his eyes," Constantine resumed earnestly. "I tell you he is mad for power. You must frighten him, teach him a stern lesson, or he will turn on you and crush you."

John looked long into his brother's eyes. "I believe you think your words true," he said slowly. "But you never were farther from the truth. In the first place, this Northman has the loyalty of his race; in the second, neither you nor I can frighten him. To try it would be but to loose his wrath upon us; and I warn you he can be terrible.

"Nay; leave Harald and this girl alone, lest Zoe get her wish—that he shall destroy us. I have plans for him that will yield us far more fruit than you dream of.

"Now hear me, my brother, and take my words to heart. I have watched you long; I have held high hopes for you. One day I shall make you emperor, if you keep faith with me.

"But of late there have been signs that you grow too proud. Think not to rise to power without me; I still rule this land. You are young, and chafe at the thought that you may be but a puppet king in my hands; perhaps you have even dreamed of plotting against me, that you may rule alone. Cast such thoughts from your heart—or you shall never rule at all!"

Constantine could not meet his brother's hot eyes; he sat with bowed head, sullenly.

"I have not plotted against you," he mumbled. "But you should trust me more. You think me a child, a fool! It is you who are the fool, to trust that barbarian. He will destroy us both. In what is he different from the barbarians who overthrew Rome? Having seen the riches of this city, think you he will rest till they are all his?

"If you were as wise as you think yourself, you would

crush him; not crudely, so as to arouse his men against you; but cunningly, so that none would know from whom the blow came. I could do the thing myself. I think age and drink have made you mad!"

John turned on him with such hot fury that the young man cringed. Fondly the Eunuch thought his secret vice of the wine cup unknown. That his brother and pupil, of all men, should discover it, drove him to frenzy.

"You have heard my will!" he stormed. "See to it that you do not interfere! Lay one finger on my plan, and the crown I have destined for you shall never rest on your head. As for this girl, she shall spend one night in the dungeon, that she may learn to be less bold; and in the morning she shall go free."

IT WAS NEAR morning when Constantine crept down to the dungeons. His face was pale, and his fingers twitched; but his lips were thin with cruel resolution. The jailer came forward at his summons.

"Which is her cell?"

"The third, master."

"Open it, by order of the Orphanotrophos!"

The jailer set his huge key in the lock, and the door grated open. Constantine pushed past him, while the fellow raised his torch high, that Constantine might the better see the prisoner.

Cyra lay huddled on her narrow couch in one corner of the cell, her frightened eyes blinking in the sudden light. Constantine smiled his cruel, leering smile at her, as he addressed the jailer:

"You have the boiling oil, as I commanded?"

Cyra screamed.

"It is here, master. But—the Orphanotrophos—"

"It is his order. Be silent, and obey."

The jailer carefully carried a steaming kettle across the floor to the side of Cyra's couch. The girl lay still and white; she had lost consciousness.

"There are bandages, master?"

"Aye. Here. Bring the light nearer. So!"

He seized the girl's hands roughly, drew them to the light. Scanning them, he smiled again.

"It will do," he said softly. "Now the blade!"

JOHN AWOKE LATE, his head throbbing with the fumes of wine. At his summons a servant came running.

"I order the release of the girl Cyra!" spoke the Orphanotrophos. The servant bowed, and withdrew. He was back within the quarter of an hour, pale and trembling.

"Most bountiful one!" he wailed. "Most serene!"

John leaped from his bed, a vision of ludicrous fury in the wrinkled night-robe that fluttered about his thin shanks and showed the round eminence of his belly.

"Speak, fool!"

"Most excellent, the girl is dead!"

Seizing the man's shoulder, John shook him savagely.

"Dead, knave? How? By whose order?"

"I—indeed, I know not! I found her in her cell, stone-cold, the bandages torn from her arms."

"Bandages? What bandages?"

"Most magnificent—her hands, which had been cut off by your order—"

John screamed with rage. "Fetch me Constantine. At once!"

The servant ran like a frightened deer down the long

*Straightaway each Norseman became
galvanized into a fighting demon*

corridor, down the grand staircase, not knowing whither he
went. John himself, fighting for self-control, shot back the
panel that gave into Constantine's chamber. It was empty.
The room was a welter of disorder.

John stared at the chaos before him: at the garments
strewn about the floor, the scattered books, the broken
alembic.

"Has he fled?" he muttered. "The serpent! The beast!
The fool!"

He returned to his own apartment. Fumbling in his
cabinet, he drew out a cup and a flask of wine. He was
about to break the seal when he stopped thoughtfully, and
held the flask to the light.

"It looks untouched," he whispered, "yet there was a nick
in the seal, and this is unscarred."

He broke the seal, poured out a cupful, which he left

untasted, and waited. It was not long before the servant returned.

"I have given order that the palace be searched, most glorious," he faltered.

"You did not find him?"

The frightened man crept back toward the door. "He—indeed I do not know—"

Forcing a smile, John beckoned him nearer.

"I did not mean to frighten you," he said, in gentler tones. "You are weary with running. Drink!"

The servant thrust out a shaking hand, took the cup, and raised it to his lips. One moment he hesitated, glancing anxiously at his master.

"Drink, drink!" John repeated. "I give you permission."

The man gulped down the wine at a draught. John watched him narrowly. At first the servant stood as before, the color stealing back into his cheeks as the alcohol warmed his veins; but after a little he gave a violent start. His eyeballs grew rigid, contracted, and stuck out. With a howl of pain he clutched at his stomach.

John sat, his lips drawn thin in an evil smile.

"So I thought," he spoke aloud. "I knew that seal."

The servant quivered once, all over, and fell to the floor.

John, rising, paced up and down, paying no more heed to the wretch stiffening before him.

"The dog!" he muttered. "The ungrateful viper! When I lay my hands on him—"

He burst into an agony of tears.

"How I loved him!" he groaned. "How I loved him!"

DAY AFTER DAY the weather held fair, with a following wind. The great fleet held on its course for Sicily, its eagle-flaunting banners stiff in the breeze, its hundreds of sails patching the blue Mediterranean.

For greater safety, the expedition passed the hostile straits of Crete at night, all lights out. Even so, as morning saw the western shores of that Moslem island a mere blur behind the rearguard, a tiny flutter of white to the south of the huge flotilla revealed the vigilance of the heathen outposts. No use to send even the swiftest pamphylian after the distant sail: the lean, rakish Arab galleys were no less swift than the Greeks.

Harald, by the steering oar, watched the tiny patch of white dim out against the azure sea.

"So many ships cannot pass unseen," he spoke. "Even the sea birds would betray it; and the Saracens have as keen eyes as they."

Harald turned away, and fell to pacing the poop deck. In the four days of the voyage he had had his first leisure to think calmly of those things which had befallen, from his interview with Zoe in the gardens to the last feverish preparations for war.

As he gazed back over the warm blue water, sprinkled with the flashing sails of his fleet, and felt the power which he commanded, he realized more than ever the true might of Constantinople. Here was a flotilla such as he had never dreamed of, going forth at the command of John to crush the heathen—and intrusted to him, Harald, who but a few short months before had been an unknown adventurer.

He felt a sudden warmth as he recalled how much, how constantly, John had trusted him. Aye, he had had trust, despite the army of spies John set on all within the walls, even on Harald himself. And at this thought Harald was struck with a sense of John's own greatness. Aye; upstart and rascal as he undoubtedly was, the Eunuch was yet a leader of men: one who ruled them well and strongly.

"And I have promised to slay him!" Harald thought, with sudden remorse.

"I have promised to slay him—because a girl gave me her lips! Because an empress unfit to wear a crown hates him! Is this a deed worthy a man?" The more he thought on it, the less manly it seemed.

A promise bound Harald to kill him; his promise to John bound Harald to be true to him. In vain the Northman reproached himself, in vain sought an escape from his dilemma. He had pledged his word both ways. The words of his sainted brother, Olaf, before his last battle, came back to him:

"I am called a hard man, yet have I never oppressed the weak, nor been false to my word. If I die now, I die with clean hands, hard though they be."

Staring moodily at the creaming wake of his flagship, Harald pondered these words. How could he make them true of himself?

At the companionway he stopped, confronted by Thiodolf. The skald bore in one hand a small, richly carved ebony coffer.

"What is that?" asked Harald.

Thiodolf handed over his burden. "From John the Eunuch. Constantine, his brother, gave it me before we sailed. I was not to deliver it, nor speak of it, till we left Crete behind. I have obeyed."

"Some secret order," Harald guessed, thinking of his

commission to arrest Maniakes. He broke the sealed silk that bound the box, and raised the lid.

THIODOLF, WAITING, SPRANG forward at sight of the frightful change that came over his leader's face. Harald's eyes glared; a cry so terrible broke from his lips that the very house-carles rushed aft, thinking some treachery had befallen.

In the coffer lay a woman's hands, severed at the wrists. Small hands they were—very small and very beautiful. On one right forefinger was a little mole.

Harald stared long at them, unable to look away. At last he flung the coffer into the sea and, turning, faced toward the east. In one swift motion he stripped the ax Hell from his shoulder, shook it aloft, and cried:

"Thanks, Eunuch, for breaking the covenant between us! Thou hast made the way before me plain!"

Thiodolf wheeled on the house-carles. "Get forward!" he ordered.

As they trooped away he approached the stricken Harald and laid a hand on his arm.

"It was Cyra," he guessed. "None other had such hands. But why?"

"Speak not of it," Harald said in a smothered voice. "But, by my brother's soul, I will repay!"

The skald smiled frostily. "It takes no longer to sail back than it took to come thus far. We can come about after dark and slip past Georgios in the night."

Harald grasped his friend's hand.

"That is my will, comrade, but not my way. If I turn back now, have I the right to ask these Varangians to follow me? They have taken the rich wages of the Eunuch so long, have worn the emblem of the Greek emperors so proudly! They are athirst for the war and loot of Sicily; how can I deny them? Nay, first I must lead them in battle, must shed my blood with theirs, that they may know me and I them. Then will I pay my debt to John, and may God send me evil if I pay him not in full!"

Thiodolf went below, and was by himself for many hours. The stars were out when he came on deck again, and the moon revealed the rocky shore of Zante far to starboard. The skald leaned over the rail, watching the phosphorescent water washing the side. He was humming lightly to himself, his right hand striking the rail in rhythmic cadence.

After a little he straightened, and the skald's great voice boomed out in the first song he had made since he had worn the Emperor's coat:

> "Keen is my king's ax,
> Keener his hatred.
> Hard does it bite, when
> His heavy hand swings it;
> But harder and deeper
> And deadlier it cleaveth
> When held by the severed
> Hands of a woman!"

14

WAR

THE MOON FILTERED from under a low cloud-bank and silvered the whispering reeds. The stench of stagnant salt water poisoned the night, so that the troops pouring ashore from the first beached pamphylians drew their breaths short. This, then, was Sicily the Beautiful, this land of muddy lagoons and sickening stinks!

As fast as they disembarked Harald drew up his men in companies on the low shore, advancing his ranks little by little to make room for those behind. By command of Georgios, supreme on land, Harald emptied each pamphylian, save for an anchor watch of twenty men and the crews.

"It is madness, leaving the fleet undermanned," Harald protested. "We are near a great port, perhaps filled with Moslem galleys. It were best to leave a theme to guard the ships."

"Know you not that yonder mountains may swarm with men, too many for us to deal with?" Georgios barked. "We must first break a way through, ere we can spare good troops to stand idle by the shore."

"What if the Saracens have a fleet in Messina Harbor?" Harald suggested calmly.

Georgios laughed, and not politely. "Why, so they have!

We shall march from here on Messina, seize the town, and destroy the ships. We are now behind the town. There is no danger till they know we are here."

"What if they know already?"

Georgios, never too patient, glowered at Harald's insistence.

"If you dare not face them," he sputtered, "I will let you take your mailed maidens and watch the ships till we return with the spoils."

Harald stiffened. "Lead on!" he answered. "I will go as far as any Greek that ever bore sword."

In a foolish hope of attaining a surprise, the drums were silent, the trumpets mute, orders being passed from mouth to mouth along the host. Up, and ever up, skirting ravines, swarming through orchards, clambering over rocks, they made their way painfully eastward toward the walls of Messina.

As they debouched through three defiles into the peak-surrounded valley of Rametta the watchfires of a great army sprang into view below them.

"The Saracens! The Saracens!"

The cry ran all along the lines. Rank after rank swung into the plain, took order, formed in a long line facing the hostile camp. In the Saracen lines, long aware of their advance, men cried aloud, horses neighed, armor and nakirs rattled, commands rang out in guttural Arabic.

But neither side dared to strike in the dark. Dimly the Christians could see their foes forming.

Dawn came at last, and with it pandemonium in both camps. The drums burst into roll on roll; the trumpets sang like an army of embattled cocks; ranks were closed.

Then, slowly at first, with short, sharp cries of exultation, the Saracens advanced.

Their cavalry led the assault, and at its vastness Harald marveled. They rode neither in column nor in line, but in a great conglomerate swarm, shaking lances, tossing turbaned helmets, their nakirs throbbing incessantly. At long arrow-range they burst into tumultuous cries:

"Allah-il-Allah! Allah-il-Allah! Allah-hu! Allah Akhbar!"

The Christians had their backs against the bulwarks of the hills, with the three defiles behind as a means of retreat. In default of cavalry, Georgios had stationed the Varangians, in their favorite wedge formation, in the center; and held his Immortals in lines five deep on either wing.

Knowing the total number of the Greeks—counting out those left with the ships—less than thirty thousand, Harald wondered at this seeming recklessness of Georgios. That vast army of Arabs, strung out along the entire eastern rim of the valley, must be at least fifty thousand strong; their cavalry alone was well-nigh half that number.

It was almost on the Varangians now, its front expanding till it outflanked the Greek line; the lean horses galloped belly to earth, the riders leaning far over their saddles, yelling and whooping wildly.

HARALD BELLOWED A last command:

"Stand fast! Shields up! Hold, though ye die!"

His shout was drowned by the clamor of the Arabs. With one final yell they bounded in to close quarters, and the storm burst; but not as Harald thought. A sudden hail of darts and arrows smashed into the unmoving Christian

ranks. The horsemen wheeled, almost in the very faces of
their foes, and darted back to their waiting infantry.

This was astounding to Harald. The great Greek strate-
gists, whose works he had studied so diligently, had never
faced Arab cavalry, and so had given him no preparation
for such tactics. He had expected a charge that would roll
over his lines, or at best break after cutting half through
them. No time was given him to scan the effects of their
onslaught; from the right wing came the peal of Georgios's
trumpet, sounding a counter charge.

The Greeks sprang into instant action, leaving their
dead strewn as they lay. Closing the many gaps left by
the Moslem shafts, they came on in a dense phalanx, too
narrow by far, but deep and strong. And in the center, all
his Northern ferocity unleashed by the ring of Georgios's
trumpet, Harald led his Varangians in the terrible Northern wedge.

He saw the Arab cavalry divide and ride away through a
score of lanes opened for it through the Moslem infantry.
Then, with short, deep shouts, the whole Moslem infantry
host moved forward to meet its foe.

Suddenly the Northmen were lost in the thick of a forest
of spears, which thrust, lifted, and thrust again. Scimitars
flashed, blades rang on shields.

The Varangian wedge hit something that felt like an
iron wall, save that it held, gave before them, gathered,
held like masonry, and gave again. Then all was a welter of
flashing steel.

Manfully the Arab infantry stood against the onslaught,
though where their center stood the brunt of the Varangian
charge they stood not long. The heavy Northern axes bit

through mail and bone, lopped hands, divided arms from shoulders; the fearful wedge of huge bodies and mighty limbs gored them in one fierce forward surge after another. Wherever those axes fell, all gave way before them.

The Saracen center melted like mist before the sun. Harald found himself faced by nothing but the plain, strewn with corpses and dotted with fugitives; beyond, the hills and the sun-washed walls of a city far in the distance—while a swarm of desperate men, lean, lashing out with reddened scimitars, hung on his flanks.

But now the Saracen cavalry came on again at the gallop, determined to force the issue. As before, they hurled a volley of darts, then followed it with a headlong charge.

Now it was the Immortals who held best. Their fivefold line, hedged and bristling with long lances, flung the light Arab horses back.

Georgios sounded his trumpet, and on both wings the Immortals gave pursuit.

The Varangians, ranked but two deep, had been hurled aside by the shock of the fiery horsemen. If they had had spears, they could have held; but their axes were all too short to reach the riders ere the impact of meeting broke their nakirs. With loud cries of triumph the Arabs rode round and through their ranks, thrusting with slender lances, hacking with curved blades.

THEN THE ARABS found out what it meant to come to close grips with Northmen. Though thrice outnumbered, and on foot, Harald's men fought to better advantage half surrounded than against the sheer shock of the mass charge that had just broken them.

Each man, at most groups of two or three together,

lashed out desperately with two-faced axes and long, heavy swords. Their big bodies, long limbs, and great strength told heavily against the lighter, weaker frames and thinner mail of their foes. One Norseman against four Arabs was but the odds Varangians liked.

The fight in the center resolved itself into a thousand swirling groups, half-hidden by dust, from which the flash of ax and scimitar gleamed like lightning.

And for every slice of a scimitar through Varangian armor the Northern ax bit thrice through mail and bone and life.

Neither Northman nor Saracen heeded the outcome of combat on the wings. The flying dust-clouds shut them off, obscured their vision, filled their nostrils; the fury of fight gave them not time nor chance to see more than the flash of stroke and parry. Each man cut and stabbed at the foe before him, nor could any have done otherwise and yet saved his life.

But it could not last. The weight of their armor and the continual stroke and parry wore the Northmen down at last. Faster they fell, giving ground foot by foot. Harald sounded his horn again, four long blasts.

This was a signal to his own house-carles. Though less used to discipline than those who had served longer under the Emperor, they had fought under Harald in three countries, and understood his ways.

Straightway each became galvanized into a fighting demon, smashing down all before him, fighting with every ounce of strength to do that which his leader ordered. Slowly at first, one at a time; then faster, by twos and threes, they shook off their clinging foes and battered their way to the center of the reddened field.

As fast as they reached the spot where Harald fought, they grouped about him. Man by man and group by group, they formed the shield wall. When all were together, a little hollow square that faced four ways, a great voice rose in a song that outdinned the very din of battle, and made battle-mad those who heard it:

> "Our prince has gone hunting,
> And harries the heathen:
> 'Hell' waits them, 'Hell' bites them,
> They cringe from his hatred.
> The raven flaps o'er us,
> The ravening wolf howls;
> Their thirst Harald sateth
> With Saracen corpse flesh!"

Once, twice, and again the song roared forth; and the house-carles took it up, slashing in time to its thrumming beat. On all four sides the Moslems clung to them; but before the mighty, terrible joy of that song and the redoubled strokes it inspired, their resistance weakened.

The singing grew till all the Varangian host heard and took heart. Wherever Harald's men fought, they took up the song, chanting in pulsing rhythm, their swelling hearts sending new strength to tired limbs.

Suddenly panic rose in the Arab ranks. New sounds hummed in their ears, a diapason to the chanted song: the beat of Greek drums. The plain shook beneath advancing feet; new shouts rang above the clash of blade on mail.

Here and there a Moslem officer looked behind him, and shouted frightened orders. All at once, as vultures rise when frightened from carrion, the Moslem horse scattered.

THE VARANGIANS DID not follow. Each man kept his stance, chests heaving, sweat rolling from reddened faces. A few breathed sobbingly, drawing in the air in great gulps. The song ceased. Not a man had breath or strength for pursuit.

Having hurled back and crushed his own assailants on either wing, Georgios had fallen back to the original field, and then caught sight of Harald's plight. It was his drums, the tramp of his themes, that had frightened the tattered remnants of Harald's foes back to their rocky nest across the plain. Not a living Moslem held his ground! All, save the dead, were in the thick of the vast dust cloud that fled, as before a storm, toward the walls of Messina.

Georgios rode up on his third horse of the day, man and beast fairly sobbing with fatigue. The charger's head drooped almost to its knees; but Georgios held his chin high, and his dark eyes glared fiercely. His shield, shot full of arrows, hung on his left arm; his right hand still clutched his drawn sword, broken almost at the hilt. Blood welled from one shoulder; both hands and arms were crimson.

Straight to the Varangian ranks he rode, and almost fell from his horse at Harald's feet. Harald, waiting, could barely hold himself erect. His helmet was gone, his mail slashed to ribbons, the ax Hell dull and streaming.

Proudly Georgios straightened his exhausted body; as proudly Harald stood before him. He shifted his ax into his left hand, and held out his right.

Georgios ignored it. His mad eyes rolled in his back-flung head.

"I like you not!" he panted. "But, by the sacred blood, you and yours are men!"

Harald surveyed the bleeding, battered figure.

"You are as good as any, Greek," he answered.

They stood confronted thus, while, each behind its leader, the masses of Varangians and Immortals, as exhausted as their commanders, stared at each other. The Northmen, still as the fight had left them, were in ragged companies, each man standing as weariness and his own will bade him; while the Immortals, coming fatigued from a stricken field, held themselves by sheer force of will in perfect alignment.

Here and there looks of admiration, or weary grins, were exchanged. In this first desperate battle they had been welded into one army—comrades, as long as their leaders kept peace together.

Harald turned to his house-carles.

"Who made the song?" he asked.

From the company on his right, Halldor the Icelander thrust himself forward, his green eyes flashing.

"It was Thiodolf!" he cried. "Thiodolf, your brother's skald, who to-day opened his lips in battle for the first time since Olaf's last fight."

Looking about him, Harald caught sight of the skald in the center of the right flank of house-carles.

"Well done!" he applauded. "When we return you shall have a gold shield for that."

Georgios laid a hand on his shoulder. "Rest your men an hour," he ordered, "then speed back to the ships, and watch the coast."

"And you?" Harald returned coldly. He liked neither the command nor the tone in which it was uttered.

"I press on to take the town. The fugitives from this fight, mayhap the entire garrison, will take ship at once for Palermo. You are to cut them off. When you have them, join me at Messina."

Harald understood. Georgios meant to have entirely for himself the glory of taking the first Sicilian city. He had to obey: on land Georgios outranked him.

"We will take our rest on shipboard," he answered. "Turn, lads! To the ships!"

HARALD REACHED THE reed-grown lagoon just as the setting sun was staining the water a red as deep as that of the field of battle. But the ships were no longer anchored by the shore, or drawn up on the shelving beach. Their masts rose, like a forest, from the deeper water, crowding the throat of the Straits.

At his hail a pamphylian put in. She shot into the lagoon like a bird winging to its nest. As she beached, Rotlieb the Frank thrust his red mane over the rail. His eyes were furtive.

"Too late, Prefect!" he bawled. "The Moslem fleet came past us ere we could thrust out. We followed, but they outdistanced us; wherefore we returned here to wait word from you."

Harald was astonished and angry. "Ye had no lookouts?" he questioned. "Not one keel on the water?"

Rotlieb shook his head. "What if we had?" he retorted. "We have but an anchor watch aboard, not enough to meet them in battle. It was safest to lie ashore and let them pass."

"But ye followed?"

"Aye, hoping to reach them from the rear with our fire-tubes."

Harald's eyes became twin points of flame. "Could ye not have met them on the water, barred their way, and swept them with the fire tubes ere they passed?"

"We are too weak," Rotlieb insisted stubbornly. "It would have meant the loss of the fleet; and how then would ye have reached Constantinople again?"

"While you skulked, your comrades have been dying," Harald answered bitterly. "It was ill for me that I left you in command. Henceforth, you fight in the ranks. Bring the ships in!"

Rotlieb scowled, and withdrew. Slowly the fleet moved toward shore: one by one the tall prows beached, and the Varangians embarked. There was nothing to do now but rest, and lay to till morning; then make for Messina Harbor, a dash of a few miles. The great chance to take all that was left of the first Sicilian army was lost.

Rest was sorely needed. The Varangians dropped on the decks and slept where they fell. In the morning there would be more fighting.

At dawn they bore down on Messina, the doomed water gate of Sicily. The sun was just paling from rose to lilac as they worked into the sickle-shaped bay. Swiftly the pamphylians thrust their prows into the shingle, and the troops poured overside.

High above them, crowning the cliffs that closed in the low sands, frowned the battlements of the Moslem citadel. To right and left of the bulwarks crowded the pink and white and yellow houses of the town.

The cliffs rose too high for the fire-tubes to reach; but there was a way round at one extremity of the harbor.

Before advancing, Harald provided the men with spears out of the reserve stores of the Immortals. He had learned his lesson of the day before. Georgios would rage when he knew of the requisition; but Harald was within his rights as fleet commander.

Since the battle of the previous day had been waged on the landward side, Georgios must now be beleaguering the city from the rear. Marshaling his men on the sands, Harald left Halldor with three ships' crews to cover the advance. As he waited for the fire-tubes to come into action, he was intently forming his plan of attack.

HALLDOR WASTED NO time. At his command the compressed-air tanks were opened with a hissing roar: the blended sulphur, phosphorus, and naphtha, readily ignited at low temperature, burst into flame with the heat of friction, and poured from the lean muzzles of the fire-tubes. Tilted to high elevation, the bronze mouths spewed forth their glowing load in streams that, at first slow and drooping, gained force till they shot straight out and fell across the battlemented ramp by which alone the Moslem defenders could make their way to the beach.

Six tongues of fire from the bow and port tubes of three ships, played steadily across the ramp; and though they could not ignite the stone, the flames clung and blazed wherever they struck with a long-lived tenacity that was appalling. "March!" Harald commanded; and his house-carles led the advance straight over the low neck of land. The few missiles hurled at them from catapults fell short.

Nakirs were beating the alarm within the citadel; but

from the other side of the tableland on which it perched came the clash of steel and the shouts of many men.

"Georgios attacks!" exclaimed Harald. "Come! We will strike here while he engages them in the rear."

Forming hastily, the Varangians left their scarce-begun trenches behind and scrambled up the hill. As they came on, watchful eyes saw them. Fresh alarms sounded within the town: stones and heavy darts flung from catapults began to hurtle among the ascending column. Here and there a man, transfixed, spread wide his arms and crashed to earth, rolling among the loose stones; little groups, blotted out in one destruction by a crashing rock, lay smashed and bleeding. But the column wound on and on, determined, thirsting for fight and loot.

Now they were within arrow flight, and the barbed Moslem shafts flickered in. Casting a rapid glance at the ramparts, Harald noted that the javelins and arrows came thinly, though the masses of rock hurled by the engines were as frequent as so strong a fortress justified.

"They have enough men to handle the catapults," he concluded, "but all too few to meet an assault with hand-arms on two sides at once."

The storm of stones grew thicker, the slender stream of arrows wrought more deadly havoc, as the Varangians swept closer. There was but one way to pass that too high and massive wall—through the gate, stout and barred as it was. If Georgios kept up his assault on the other side, it was possible; but possible only because the defense lacked strength. Harald guessed that the garrison was only a determined rearguard, left behind to work what damage it could, while the main Saracen army, beaten on the plain the day before, fled for Palermo.

Into his mind flashed a trick, one of those his Greek clerks in Constantinople had read to him from the imperial works on siege craft. It was a simple thing, such as an army without engines might use against a place not too strong. **"THE TORTOISE!" HE** bellowed through cupped hands; and his captains relayed the command. Immediately his men charged for the base of the wall, increasing their pace to get under the arc of the catapults the sooner. It was a costly maneuver; but it had been far costlier to bide where they were, in full range.

A hundred men were smashed to pulp on the white hillside ere they gained the brink. Once there, they formed under volley on volley of arrows; formed in a compact group of solid squares, each man crouching, shield raised above his head, the rim of one man's shield overlapping his neighbor's. Thus they were protected against arrows by a solid shell like that of the creature whose name their formation bore.

"Archers to the rear!" shouted Harald. The only archers he possessed were two hundred of his own house-carles, for the Varangian carried no bow. Swiftly the Norwegian bowmen ranged themselves behind the serried group of tortoises, in open order, loosing arrows as fast as they could to cover the advance of the shielded phalanxes.

Their work was well done. The archers on the wall were more numerous; but the light Arab bow was no match for the long, tough elm staves and three-foot shafts of their foes. Though the Saracens clung stubbornly to their posts, they were driven back till scarce one dared show his head between the merlons.

"Now!" shouted Harald; and one of the tortoises surged forward, cumbrously, but gaining force as it advanced. A tree trunk grasped in a dozen pairs of mighty arms thrust the blunt snout ahead of the tortoise and, impelled by all the weight of the phalanx, smashed against the stout gate. Having delivered the blow, the tortoise retreated, stepped aside, and made way for another, which repeated its tactics.

The gate was of massive olive wood beams, bound together with iron bands, and studded with thick plates of iron. Strongly it held; but at each repeated blow it quivered more and more. Bands gave, hinges groaned and tore away. At the sixth assault it gave, and the phalanx that struck the final blow, unable to check its impetus, surged in above the fallen framework. At once Harald drove one phalanx after the other through the breach, urging them on so fast that there was scarce a gap between. On the heels of the last came the bowmen, eager to be in at the death.

As more and more of the Northmen poured in through the ravished gate, the Moslems, outnumbered and driven against the house-lined sides of the narrow streets, fell back farther and farther.

Then Harald himself, his troops in full cry behind him, made down the main thoroughfare to a wide plaza or parade ground in the very center of the town, turned, and sped for the landward gate. Seeing his purpose, the foremost of his men raised a thunderous yell, and rank after rank, company on company, sped at his heels.

Caught between walls of stone and walls of steel, the

Saracens struggled for one brief, fierce moment; then, borne down by sheer weight, gave way.

The gate burst open, and the Immortals rushed in like a river in spate.

THIS TIME HARALD did not wait for Georgios. His work was done. Amid a knot of house-carles, he ascended to the battlements over the newly forced gate.

On the parapet, gazing out upon the moat below, the slope beyond, the fields reaching to the distant hills, he exclaimed in dismay. The earth was strewn thick with the bodies of Immortals.

It had cost the Greek not less than a fifth of his host to reach that gate; and even then he had not won it till cooler heads and stronger arms came to his relief. Harald was astounded at this revelation of his colleague's headlong fury. In the battle of the day before, Georgios had fought with skill as well as heroism; but here, confronted with a foe infinitely weaker, he had thrown away lives in a mad frontal attack, not against an already beleaguered city, but on sheer walls and an unpreoccupied enemy. The truth was that Georgios, cunning against odds, was recklessly contemptuous of a force lesser than his own.

So appalled was Harald at the slaughter below him that it was some time before the tumult raging in the city caught his attention. He sprang down the stone stairs to the city streets, to find a massacre in progress. The last of the garrison, herded like sheep between hedges of Greek spearmen, were being struck down without pity.

Georgios, once more mounted, towered above his men, urging them on with bellowed oaths. Harald found himself wedged in by the mailed backs of the slaughter-mad

Greeks, unable to reach the frantic figure on horseback. Not till the last Saracen was down did the ranks make way.

His blood seething at this butchery of surrendered men, men who had fought heroically against hopeless odds, Harald pushed through the crowded warriors to confront the Greek. When he had won clear, and only the reddened pavement stretched between them, Georgios saw him. With a roar he spurred his horse forward.

Before the whole host, or such as had not scattered to loot, Georgios reined his horse back almost in Harald's face, and sprang quickly from the saddle.

"The ships?" he boomed. "Did you intercept them?"

Varangian and Immortal alike stood by, riveted by the tension in the air. All sensed that a conflict was impending: a conflict between generals. Silence settled over them, amid which the distant shouts of the looters rang sharp and clear.

Harald shook his head. "They had passed before I came up," he answered. "Rotlieb deemed his force too weak to challenge them."

"Dog!" Georgios blared, his eyes fairly starting from his head. "You let them go!"

Harald's own wrath, already stirred by the massacre, flamed hot at this injustice.

"Not I," he began; but got no further. Georgios, smarting under the losses his own rashness had brought upon him, was the less able to control his hate for Harald, which mounted on the instant into ungovernable rage. His heavy right hand shot out, the knotted fist striking the Northman full in the mouth.

As Harald fell, a mighty howl of rage rose from the Varangians, and an equally mighty jeer from the Greeks.

One moment each side stood glaring at the other; then the Norse surged forward, steel out and flashing. The next instant the two corps would have been at one another's throats; but even as they rushed Harald picked himself up and ran between, flinging out his arms.

"STAND, FOOLS!" HARALD shouted at the oncoming Varangians.

They recoiled, but came on again. Snatching out his dagger, Harald placed it against his own breast.

"Back, or I slay myself!" he threatened.

The Northmen fell back in earnest this time, puzzled and enraged. Why should their leader balk them of the vengeance they meant to take for him? They stood irresolute, waiting.

Harald whirled to address the Immortals. "My men are in hand now," he said, and his eyes drew theirs to him. "See to it that ye provoke them not again. Ye have suffered heavily to-day: so heavily that ye no longer outnumber the Varangians. If ye anger them, most of you will never see your homes again. This quarrel is between your commander and me: leave it to us to settle."

A murmur rose from the ranks; but they stood, and sheathed their weapons. Harald stepped up to Georgios.

"It was due to your own folly that we did not intercept the Saracen fleet," he said coldly. "Had ye left behind a force strong enough to man the ships, as I advised, not a galley would have won past them. To-day you have shown yourself a fool again, in seeking to storm these walls before I could join you. Your thirst for glory has cost the lives of four thousand men. You have murdered prisoners, who had yielded themselves. Now you dare to strike the man who has won this stronghold for you.

"The feud between us has gone so far that it must go to its finish. Draw sword, and put an end to it!"

Georgios stood poised on the balls of his feet, his right hand fingering his hilt, his face crimson with rage; and the muscles on his huge bare arms rippled and swelled for action. Yet he spoke not, and he did not draw his weapon.

Incredulously Harald stared at his foe. He knew Georgios was a brave man; yet, challenged before his troops, he shamefully hesitated. If he did not draw he would be shamed in the presence of his troops—the troops who idolized him. Instinctively Harald knew it was not fear that held Georgios back.

Harald's face was stinging with the pain of the blow; but his soul hurt worse. Unless Georgios would fight, there was no way to remove the shame the Greek had put on him. He knew not, for the moment, how to act to avenge the insult.

At last anger triumphed. Swinging his ax across his shoulders, out of his way, he drove his open hands, one after the other, into the Greek's face. The blows came mightily, with all the force of his strong arms and shoulders behind them, and cracked resoundingly against Georgios's crimsoned cheeks.

Reeling, the Greek fell back, recovered, and again only glared at his enemy.

Harald could not understand it. What force, in all the world, could restrain Georgios from trying to wipe out the insult in blood? Instead, the Greek only gritted his teeth till the gums bled, turned on his heel, and walked away.

The Varangians raised a frantic cheer. Their leader's

honor was clean again, his enemy cowed. But Harald knew Georgios was not cowed: for some mighty reason of his own, he had refrained from that duel to the death for which his soul longed. Light dawned on Harald slowly, but it came at last. He stood where his foe had left him; and Eilif, Thiodolf, and Halldor came to him.

At last his face cleared; he met their eyes, his own twinkling.

"It has come to my memory," he said softly, "that Georgios desires to be emperor. A man may easily get his death wound in a duel, and a dead man cannot wear a crown."

"H-m!" grunted the skald. "There are things I would not give to be emperor."

Halldor thrust his keen face forward. "Aye; but a Greek knows the way to be emperor, and to take revenge afterward. Or perhaps before, if revenge comes safely. Henceforth we shall stay closer, by you, Harald, lest you leave your back unguarded."

"Two strokes for one! Hard measure, that!" Eilif chuckled; and ever after that Harald was known as "Harald Hard-measure."

15

TREACHERY

THE SPOIL OF Messina was not great, the Moslems having themselves taken and looted it too recently. The army was discontented. The general gloom fed the jealousies and strifes already fomented by the quarrel between the leaders.

Both commanders saw that, unless sharp measures were taken, the expedition would be shattered ere it was well begun. It was Harald, anxious as he was to return and take vengeance on John, who took the first step toward reconciliation. He visited Georgios in his tent, and offered his hand. Whatever the Greek's feelings, he was too much the soldier this time to refuse. Next day the whole camp knew that the generals had officially buried their quarrels.

Georgios summoned Harald to him on the eve of departure.

"Such is the rancor between my men and yours," he said, "that it were best to move separately. I will march overland, while you take the fleet south by sea. Occupy the greater harbor of Syracuse, and inflict what losses you can on the Moslems till I arrive. Then you shall lay siege to Ortygia, while I invest the western or landward wall."

So Georgios led his Immortals across the Pelormitan Mountains, past the wide-flung flanks of smoldering Etna,

over a countryside once as rich as any in the world, now
bare and deserted after centuries of fire and sword.

And now the ill fed Immortals learned to draw their
gilded belts tighter; for nowhere in the four-day march
did they find food or wine of decent quality or sufficient
to appease their hunger.

The Varangians fared better, since each ship carried
ample provisions for her crew and fighting men; and they
had but a two days' sail along the coast.

Near noon of the second day they raised the Thapsian
shore, passed the outsweep of a bold promontory, and
sighted the first of the outer defenses of Syracuse. This
was a great wall, set all along the coastal bluffs of Achradina, commanding beach and anchorage.

For one entire league that frowning wall, shimmering
with spears and the crests of turbaned helmets, smoking
with caldrons of oil, pitch, or molten lead, lowered at them
from the shore. At last it receded in a long reentrant angle,
its battlements rising higher, its parapets resounding with
the fevered clash of cymbals and the shrill of horns.

"Syracuse!" the pilot called. "The little harbor!"

Harald cast one glance at the narrow port, its converg-
ing walls swarming with warriors, the arms of its catapults
dipping from sight as the garrison turned the creaking
windlasses—and gave the order to sail on. Well, he knew
he could not force an entry. The ramparts were too high
for his fire-tubes, and commanded his decks with their
fearful engines.

As soon as the island no longer cut them off from sight
of the port, they saw a sight that set their pulses hammer-
ing. In the northern arm of the harbor, protected by a pali-

sade of piles sunk in the shallow water near shore, lay three
score Moslem galleys. From every masthead fluttered brilliant silken streamers. Every slanting yard was decked with
pennants; but no man moved on their decks and no sound
came from them. They had done their work, and their
masters had no more need of them.

The Greek pilot fairly danced up to Harald, his
sea-tanned face working with rage.

"Africans!" he screamed. "Those are Tunisian ships; I can
see by their rig! They have poured reenforcements into the
city. Burn them! Burn them!"

HARALD SMILED THINLY, concealing the anger that
suddenly flamed within him. The Aghlabite Emir of Tunis,
vassal of the Egyptian Caliph and nominal overlord of
Sicily, had sent those galleys to save the garrison; and this
he had done because Cyra had been denied him by Harald,
when Yusuf ben Mirza went to claim her. Cyra! Harald
remembered two tiny severed hands; and because his
tortured heart must have relief, he poured forth his wrath
on the empty Moslem ships.

His flagship backed water, veered to starboard, and, out
of range of the walls, trained her fire-tubes on the single
narrow opening in the palisade. A hiss, a sulphurous breath,
and streams of fire shot across the water. Down on the stern
of the nearest galley the roaring naphtha poured, and a
sheet of smoke-shot flame rose from the Moslem decks.
The tubes rose, and at a higher angle raked the galleys on
either side. Soon the whole Arab fleet was one crackling,
seething conflagration.

Screams of anger rose from the walls; but no missiles
answered the fire. The heat from those vast sheets of flame

was so terrible that the defenders ran from the wall, leaving catapult-gut and the wooden arms of the engines to smoulder as they would. The Varangians might almost have stormed the battlements, had not the very flames they had kindled shut them off.

But one thing they could do—land. The low coast south and west of the harbor was unguarded, even unwalled, for there the Greeks had left no walls that their conquerors might restore. Into a cove, the Bay of Daskon, Harald sent his prows.

Beaching, he ordered seven thousand men ashore, with food, planks, tools, and fifty light siege-catapults. The remainder of his force he distributed among the ships, leaving Eilif in command of the fleet, with orders to cruise off Ortygia and Achradina, lest fresh succor come from Africa for the besieged.

Marching northwest along the strip of firm land west of the swamp, the Varangians threw a plank bridge across the thirty-foot wide river, and crossed.

On the other side they camped. South of them was the river, too rapid to ford, accessible only by such a bridge as they had built, and dominated by their missiles in case of attack. Northward lay the swamp, draining into the bay, whose waters, under the guardian fire-tubes of the fleet, protected them on the east.

Only on the west lay open country, and from this direction no attack was to be anticipated. Nevertheless Harald ordered entrenchments thrown up all along the west side, across the road, and dominating the bridge-head.

On the night of the fourth day, the camp was alarmed by the sight of myriad points of light twinkling from the hills to the northwest. The Varangians scurried to line their trenches, posted guards along the river and the rim of the swamp, and prepared for whatever might be in store. Yet in truth there was little chance that the distant camp fires were those of Moslems. Whatever doubt Harald had vanished at midnight, when a blue flare shot up from the hills. Georgios had come.

The signal was answered, once from the Varangian camp, and once from the fleet. The latter revealed the position of the ships as off the south coast of Achradina, just above the city. The investment was almost complete.

At dawn a mounted Greek dashed into Harald's camp, with a written message from Georgios, which Thiodolf the Skald read to his commander:

"Attack the mole at noon, from land and sea at once. I will storm the west gate."

Harald frowned, remembering Georgios's futile assault on Messina.

"Bid your Strategos send me a force strong enough to escort to him half of my siege-engines," he instructed the messenger. "Otherwise he will waste many men on that gate. I will attack at noon as he orders."

Before he could obey, he must get word to the fleet, and time for that was short. A single company made all haste back to Daskon, where they had landed, and sent out one of the galleys moored there with orders for Eilif. The Saracens, their own ships burned, could not intercept the swift pamphylian; but she must make speed if Eilif were to bring the fleet around in time to cooperate in the attack.

HARALD DID NOT like the plan at all. The mole, an artificial tongue of land connecting Ortygia with the mainland, was fortified with a wall on both sides; and from the Great Harbor, Harald had seen the towers of a higher wall to the north, shutting off the entire mole from Achradina. His ships were ill fitted to approach those catapult-lined ramparts. There were two possible directions of attack for the fleet: it might either risk the perilous Little Harbor, thus menacing the east side of the mole; or it might return to the Great Harbor and assail the southwestern side.

The first alternative would expose the ships to missiles from the walls on three sides, and so bring about their certain destruction. The second involved less danger, since the only wall confronting them would then be on the northeast; and on the east the fleet could make contact with Harald's own position. His orders to Eilif were to attack on this side.

Harald marched three hours, reaching his assigned position before noon, so that he might have time to throw up rough entrenchments in case his intended assault were beaten back.

He saw with a frown of amazement the point where Georgios meant him to attack. It was a bad position, well-nigh untenable. He must camp in the ancient grass-grown stone-paved marketplace, where he had just halted.

He was fronted directly by the angle in the wall where the defenses of the mole joined the main rampart of Achradina, the latter bending sharp northwest at this point. This might have been a weak point in the Moslem line but for a second great reentrant angle a quarter mile beyond, where the Achradina wall made a salient that threatened the whole north side of the Varangian position.

South and southwest of him lay the swamp, effectually

cutting off his retreat save for a narrow space between swamp and wall to the west. This was so narrow that an effective sally from the salient might throw the Northmen into the swamp before they could make good their escape.

Georgios had not yet sent for the catapults, and the morning was passing. Harald wandered about the camp, scrambling over heaps of tumbled ruins, surveying the menacing walls for any signs of weakness. There were none. The parapets were thick with helmets and spears; the engines of war thrust their arms above the battlements almost as close together as they could possibly be set. There was even a sally-port in the salient, as he had feared, guarded by a double bastion.

Returning, he set his men to work, just out of catapult range, collecting the fragments of stone from the ancient ruined temples. With these they hastily threw up one line of wall connecting two temples, which were to guard their rear; and another at the extreme limit of range from the wall, to serve as front-line entrenchment. As these were rising, a trumpet pealed; the distant clank of mailed feet rang out: and down from the heights of Epipolae tramped three companies of Immortals.

As they drew nearer, Georgios himself spurred out, surveyed Harald's preparations, and approved sullenly.

"Well planned," he grunted. "How many engines can you spare me?"

"A score," Harald answered tersely. "My position here is so perilous that I need thirty for myself."

"There were more on the ships," Georgios scowled.

"Aye, a hundred and fifty more; every one needed to

protect the fleet against the engines on the wall. If more
could be spared, I would have had them."

Georgios showed symptoms of breaking into a rage;
but of a sudden his eyes slewed round to the salient in the
Achradina wall, and he smiled.

"I will take the twenty," he decided. "I see your men have
armed themselves with my reserve of spears from the ships.
I am glad that in some things Varangians will take a lesson
from Greeks."

WHILE THE CATAPULTS were being transferred, Harald
let the Immortals do all the work, keeping his own men
relentlessly busy running a line of wall between the temples
in his rear and the salient, which threatened his left. He
succeeded in raising the rampart to a height of four feet
all the way, joining it to the wall in his front, before the
Immortals marched off with their twenty engines. Georgios lingered as his ranks formed about the catapults.

"Why the rampart in front?" he asked. "You cannot
advance easily over that."

"I shall not advance—yet," Harald answered. "I shall
need all the protection I have to save myself from attack.
Look yonder, how the heathen gather on the wall!"

"By St. Nicodemus! They do indeed!" Georgios
exclaimed. Setting spurs to his horse, he rode back, his
escort advancing at the double. The rumble of the wheeled
platforms bearing their catapults sounded like the march
of a mighty army; the limestone dust rose about them in
clouds.

Straightaway Harald saw to the emplacement of his own
thirty catapults behind his new-made ramparts; ten against
the salient, ten facing the line of wall connecting salient

with mole, ten more concentrated on the angle formed by the lap of mole wall with land wall. The short space south of that would be dominated by his ships.

Harald scaled to the portico of the nearer temple, and looked out over the harbor for his fleet. Soon around the point of Ortygia shot the first pamphylian, bending northward for the final dash to the mole. Behind her came another and another. He sighed his satisfaction with Eilif—the ships were on time.

But others saw the same sight. From the Moslem embattlements came a great shout, the clatter of kettle-drums and the shrill of flutes. A trumpet pealed, and the clash of arms arose.

Making his way with all speed to his counter-walls, which even now were pitifully low, Harald marshaled his men to meet the expected attack. Well he knew it would be folly to obey Georgios and undertake the attack himself. Better save his men than waste them in a vain dash against the towering Moslem ramparts, defended by thousands on thousands of men and scores of siege engines.

His own house-carles, whom he trusted even more than the best of the other Varangians, he stationed in the center of his north wall, facing the salient; their bowmen he concentrated in groups between the engines. From the other companies he set a second line behind these, both to feed the engines and to support the archers. A third line formed a reserve.

On the other sides, where he had less reason for fear, he stationed double lines. In the midst of the square thus inclosed he held a thousand men in reserve, ready to reinforce any point of danger. Only the side nearest the swamp was unwalled and unmanned; for on this side none could approach him. It was also the side most easily supported by the fleet.

As he finished this task, two things happened with almost perfect unison. The fleet, its oarsmen slacking pace to avoid crowding and fouling, drew up off the mole and the shore beyond; and the gate in the salient opened.

The entrenched Varangians had no time to observe the movement of their ships. They knew nothing of the mutual storm of missiles from deck and wall, of the shouts of the fighters and groans of the wounded. They no longer heeded the vanishing dust-cloud behind the departing Georgios. All their energies were centered on adjusting the screws of the catapults, loading the pans with stones, fitting arrow to string, lapping shield with shield. Then, with the instant fury of the thunderbolt, the salient disgorged a mass of Arab infantry.

THEY ADVANCED, NOT with the wild, reckless charge of the desert tribes; but in serried ranks, disciplined and firm. One glance at them, and Harald guessed them for what they were—the Berber guardsmen of the Tunisian Emir.

"They know the Varangians!" Thiodolf bellowed in Harald's ear. "They save the weaker island Arabs for the Immortals!"

As the Moslems rolled forward, catapults from the wall showered down rocks into the market place; but after a few volleys they desisted. Every stone fell between the advancing infantry and the low Varangian ramparts, doing no harm. Then the Berbers, increasing their pace to the charge, closed in.

"Loose!" ordered Harald. His voice was drowned by the

twang of mule-gut; then blocks of limestone tore through the dense Moslem front, plowing red gaps. Grimly the ranks closed, and advanced again.

"Arrows!" And, while the catapults were being rebent by the windlasses Harald's house-carles fell to work with their long elm bows. At such range, against such a target, not a shaft could miss; but the Berbers never paused.

So many they were, so fired with fanatic fury, that a hundred wounds at once could no more stop them than so many pin-pricks. So swift was their onrush that the engines could discharge but one more volley before the heathen reached the wall. This time the jaggard stones, tearing into their front at close range, broke three whole ranks, but they merely flowed around on either side, and came on.

"They fight silent," Thiodolf muttered. "Never before have I known the heathen to do so."

He had no sooner spoken than the whole Moslem column broke into a united yell; "Allah Akhbar!" And with the words on their lips they flung themselves against the wall.

The first brunt struck the house-carles, who were accordingly hardest pressed; but behind the head of the column the other Moslem ranks deployed, spreading all along the north wall and lapping round the angle of the eastern rampart. This was not merely the effect of their greater numbers making room for action: it was a deliberate plan.

Behind them, protected by them, there opened a port in the mole wall, and from it sallied a second Arab horde. At close grips with the Berbers, the Varangians could not man the first three of their catapults on that side, so that only seven could be brought into action against the newcomers.

But these newcomers were Sicilian Moors, neither so strong nor so fierce as the Africans; they advanced with caution after the first volley had smitten them. Their slowness gave time for a second volley, and a third, ere they mustered courage to close.

This gave the Varangian reserve time to pour in to the rescue. With long spears the house-carles thrust and thrust from the wall till their points were clogged or broken, and the Berber swords flashed in their faces; then they dropped pikes, and seized swords and axes.

The other Varangians leaped to the rampart, making fierce play with their two-faced axes, thrusting the Moslems down with heavy blade and heavy arm. There was no breathing space, no end to the wave on wave of flesh and steel that washed up against them, until the Saracens were scaling the low walls upon the horrible incline of their own heaped-up slain.

The Northmen fought on, drenched with blood and panting for air; their blades rose and fell as fast as they could strike; yet still the torrent broke against the wall; and they were slowly pressed back by sheer weight of numbers. The reserve was now dwindling, only three hundred holding back, because they had orders not to strike save to cover a retreat; and the attack on the mole side, though not so sharp, still held every Northman there engaged.

THEN CAME A little relief. One after another, a series of mighty crashes drowned out the din of steel on steel and the shouts and grunts of the combatants. The assault from the mole weakened, broke, scattered. From the Varangians who had faced it rose a cheer, as they rushed to reenforce their battered comrades fighting the Berbers.

Eilif, from the harbor, had seen the plight of his fellows ashore; and after losing six ships, had given up his hopeless fight against walls that overtopped him twenty feet, to urge his ships west along the swamp-fringed shore.

Now out of range from the walls, he poured in volley after volley from his deck-catapults into the massed Sicilians attacking from the mole. He brought twenty engines to bear; and the Sicilians, unable to withstand or meet the storm, rushed back through the gate into the city.

But the Berbers held on. At them Eilif dared loose no stones, for his own comrades stood between. They were over the wall now, and still coming on. Drawing closer together as man after man was dragged down, the Varangians gave back foot by foot, their heavy axes and savage strength contesting every inch. Only in the center, where the Norse house-carles flanked Harald and the ax Hell, did the defense still hold the wall; and even here they must soon give way to keep contact with their comrades.

Now Harald played the stroke he held in reserve. A word to Halldor, who was viciously thrusting over his Prefect's shoulder; and the big Icelander squirmed like an eel out of the press. Leaping back from the rear rank, he shouted an order to the meager reserve, and ran at top speed for the temples.

He was fleet as a deer, and well for him, for a dozen Moslem shafts sped after him. Bounding up the broken temple stair, he ran to the rear portico, down the steps there, and so to the broken ground behind, where a horse was tethered. Springing to the saddle, he galloped away from the fighting, straight north to the camp of Georgios.

Having thus dispatched an appeal for help, Harald threw all his strength into a determined attempt to make room for his retreat. Back and back the Varangians pressed, giving way stubbornly, ever holding formation, with lapped shields, opposing the Moslem scimitars. As they gave way they were forced to extend their line, lest the Berbers outflank and surround them in their own walls. The last reserve now came into play, flinging itself against the assault, striving to make their fresh strength tell against numbers till the main force could win clear and make good its retreat.

They succeeded. Backed by those who had held the moleward wall, they drove into the Berber line, ragged and broken as it poured over the wall, and bit deep into it ere the Africans could form again. The distraction was brief, yet it saved the main force. With utmost difficulty, fighting for every inch, the reserve joined ranks with their outworn comrades, and together they withdrew.

The Berbers followed them up with savage joy. Still bearing the brunt, Harald's rearguard fought as even Varangians had never fought before. While they held off pursuit, the others formed the wall of shields, rims lapping on all four sides, points out.

The shield wall opened in the rear for the briefest instant, allowing the rearguard to pour through, then closed again. Slowly, a man here and a man there, they who had thus entered the shield wall edged themselves into its face and took up the fight again, till every man was in formation.

The retreat had now brought them to the very temple

steps; and up these the shield wall rushed, with every last ounce of its strength. All but a few made the top step safely, and backed into the portico. Instantly Harald rushed half his men to the rear portico, by which the Moslems might try to force an entrance if they thought of it; the rest formed where they stood.

Commanding both stairways, the Varangians could hold out almost indefinitely. Man for man they were stronger than their foes, and in their present position they could not be outflanked. In readiness for just this emergency, Harald had piled the stores he had brought with him, including casks of wine and water, within the temple sanctuary.

THE BERBERS PRESSED the attack with the fury of madmen; and now Harald could laugh at their blind ruthlessness. For, while he held the temple against them, Georgios could come to the rescue—and the gate or the salient was open. If Georgios had half the skill men imputed to him, he could have the city for the taking.

In their very blood-lust, the Berbers did not at once think of the temples having two entrances. Before they remembered, Halldor had galloped back from his errand, and was safe within the rear portico. But the beat of his horse's hoofs had sent some of them scurrying around.

Halldor came panting up to Harald.

"Georgios refuses!" he cried. "His word is: 'Tell him that, in disobeying my order to attack, he wrecked my plan for taking the city. Let him take the consequences. I must save my men for an assault on the main gate. Should I lose Syracuse to save an insubordinate officer?'"

Snatching out his sword, the angry Icelander rushed into the fight.

For a space Harald stood motionless. Georgios refused! Refused to aid his own colleague in the midst of a desperate action, in spite of an urgent appeal! When, too, he might have forced the salient gate and captured the city.

But Harald had no time to be overwhelmed for long by the Greek's stupendous animosity, for the fight was too furious. Between blows, however, it haunted him, lent strength to every thrust he made. It was as well, for his weapon was blunt with overmuch striking. As he fought on, clearing the stair again and again, fuller realization of the meaning of Georgios's message came to him. This was his answer for the two blows in the face.

The Greek's intent was clear. Harald and his Varangians should die. If any survived to report in Constantinople that Georgios had deserted them in battle, Georgios could answer that he had to choose between rescuing men who had disobeyed orders and keeping his Immortals intact for another action.

He would lay all the responsibility for failure to take the city on Harald; and dead men, or discredited men, could not effectively defend themselves. His rival out of the way, he could easily send to the city for more Immortals to prosecute the war; and ultimate victory would cleanse him of any suspicion of guilt. To Georgios, Harald's death meant vastly more than an easy victory before Syracuse.

He would probably have his wish. Chanting their confession of faith the Berbers came on and on; nor, though the Varangians held out for days, could they hope to escape. For, if Georgios would not give aid, ten thousand fresh heathen might sally on the little garrison, and keep up the assault till every Northman fell.

Of a sudden the enemy's onslaught received an unexpected impetus. Where before they had clambered breath-
lessly up the stair, they now were flung sprawling up it in
one violent surge. The Northmen, astonished, met them
with cut and thrust and forced them back again. Once
more they dashed up, like the outflung crest of a wave, but
this time their dead were borne with them.

Then the Northmen saw the reason, and raised a mighty
cheer. They had been so hard pressed, so blind with the
madness of fighting, that they could have eyes only for the
oncoming front of the foe; but now they looked beyond.
Long axes playing, lips chanting the song of Thiodolf, a
thousand fresh Varangians had struck the Moslem rear and
flung the whole column headlong up the stair. A second
detachment was even now working its way round to the
farther entrance.

It was Eilif from the ships, come to the rescue barely
in time.

16

THE COUNTERSTROKE

INSTANTLY HARALD DISPATCHED orders to Thiodolf, commanding at the rear portico; and at the blast of his trumpet the Varangians who had themselves been beleaguered, now counter-attacked down the stone stairs. The descent broke their shield wall, but it gave their impact greater weight; and the Berbers were caught simultaneously in front and rear.

The Northmen's onrush carried them deep into the swirling mass; and Harald's sudden thrust held them, prevented them from forming to meet Eilif. The Moslems crowded back. For a little longer they bore the attack; then, wherever they could, they broke free and fled.

Nor were they saved even then. Pursuing as fast as their laboring lungs permitted, the Varangians drove them past the inclosed market place, and under the very walls of the city. But it was the Moslem garrison that struck the final blow.

Panic-stricken at the defeat of the terrible Berbers, afraid lest the fearful Varangian axes should follow up their victims into the city, the Syracusans closed the gate in the very faces of their beaten comrades. Having thus assured their own safety, they did what they dared to check the pursuit, lobbing great rocks from their catapults into the Varangian ranks.

Instantly Harald ordered a company of his engineers back to man his own engines. From their lesser height, the Varangian catapults made poor play against the towering ramparts, most of the stones falling short. Harald was forced to recall the pursuit, lest it cost more than it was worth. But his engines played on, their stones smiting down the rearmost Berbers, who huddled as close as they could to their own walls, beating at the gate for admittance.

They were doomed. The Varangian engines were advanced just far enough to bear on the gate itself and shattered the Berbers as they clamored to their fellows to let them in. The defenders dared not open the gate, so terrible was the hail of rock that hurtled against it, and so great their fear of the Northern axes.

Just out of range Harald held his infantry, waiting for the Saracens to open. But the Arabs, at sight of them, were all the more determined to keep it closed, preferring to sacrifice the three thousand battered, beaten men without rather than risk the city.

From the north came the crash of drums, and the pelting of running feet. A river of men flowed down from the broken wall of Epipolae!

The Greeks had come at last. Harald laughed stridently as he recognized them, and sounded the call for his own men to retire. Now that the Northmen were safe in spite of him, Georgios had been forced to give over his pretended demonstration against the main gate, both to save his face and to reap the fruits of Varangian valor.

Swerving to the edge of Harald's wall, Georgios brought

his column past it and to the verge of the stone-range from the battlements. Halting them there, he realigned them, gave them a moment's rest, then drove them full at what was left of the wretched Berbers, who huddled like sheep at the foot of the city wall. If the garrison had not dared open the gate before, they had even less courage now.

Caught between the wall and the advancing Greeks, the remaining Berbers were blotted out in one ghastly moment.

Withdrawing as promptly as they had struck, the Immortals marched straight back to their safe position on the hills. From the stricken city rose a bitter wailing, and the thin sound of flutes, mourning the slain. Well they might mourn, for of ten thousand Berber infantry, the pride of Africa, not one that had sallied forth so confidently returned within the walls.

"THE SYRACUSANS WILL be too weak to risk another stroke," Harald decided. "Send orders to the ships, Eilif, bidding them withdraw half a mile, and lie off the swamp. I can use your lads here."

Then Harald, summoning his captains, had them dispatch a fourth of the host to gather up the slain and dump them into the bay, since there was no time to bury them. The rest were divided into two divisions, the first of which was ordered to collect all the scattered stones still left in the marketplace and extend the wall, while the second stood guard in case of another attack from the town.

Eilif surveyed Harald's bloody ramparts with a grim smile.

"A small thing to set up against yonder battlements," he said, "but well did you defend it."

"Not well enough, had it not been for you," Harald replied. "I shall have it built higher, and extended parallel with the town wall, to the very shore. Thus it will both shelter us while we invest the city, and protect the fleet from a sally. But I think the heathen have had enough, and are willing now to hide themselves behind their walls till we run out of food or patience."

"That need not be soon," Eilif answered. "The marsh is full of fowl and fish, and though the river is a mile away, water can be brought from it without danger from the heathen. But what ailed Georgios that he did not come to your aid till the fight was done?"

"I sent for help, and he refused," Harald explained. "When you had saved us, he was forced to strike for very shame, to snatch some credit from a plight that else would have brought him only dishonor."

Eilif scowled. "Now he will say, when he returns to Mikligard, that he saved us all," he growled.

Ulf Uspaksson came up to them, wiping the red face of his ax.

"You talk of Georgios?" his eyes flashed. "He meant us to die, Harald."

"That I know as well as you."

"Aye, but I know more. He stationed us here and ordered us to attack for no other purpose than that the heathen might sally and wipe us out. He has not forgot the shame you put upon him at Messina."

"All that I know too," Harald answered.

"There is more," said Ulf darkly.

"What more?"

"Why this: when you were quarreling with him at Messina, I was talking with Rotlieb the Frank. I drew next him, quietly, and thrusting my knife against his ribs under his cloak, so that none might see, I whispered to him. This was our talk:

" 'You are no coward,' I said to him. 'Why, then, did you let the Moslem ship escape last night?' He would not speak at first, but my knife nestled so close to his flesh that he saw I meant to know or have his life. So he confessed that Georgios had bribed him, ere we ever landed on the island, to let the Moslem ships slip past, that Georgios might have a pretext to lay the blame on you.

"Georgios planned to let the matter drop till he could lay complaint against you in Constantinople; but his losses at Messina, and your victory, so enraged him that he lost his head and struck you. Your two blows made him resolve you should die, since he could not master you."

Harald glanced at Eilif. "A pretty plot, and a pretty comrade-in-arms," he said bitterly. "He shall pay me for this, and for my good lads who fell today.

"I can plot myself; I should have learned how in Constantinople, if not before. And I shall so plot!" he said with emphasis, "that not Georgios, but I shall take this town as well as Messina."

Ulf laughed loud. "Well crowed, master! But this is ten times the town Messina was."

"It will not be," Harald rejoined, "if you will help your men in extending that wall."

DAY AFTER DAY passed, and the wailing within the walls of Syracuse scarce abated. The Arab sentinels paced the

"This is no deed of mine!" John declared contemptuously

ramparts day and night, watching against surprise; but the
kind of surprise they expected was what Harald planned.
His men labored on, always well guarded, extending their
rampart to the bay and raising it, course by course. It could
never equal, either in height or in thickness, the ponderous
defenses of Ortygia; but it served.

The men worked like beavers, jesting as they toiled, for
none of them could understand what so fragile a roof was
good for. But for all their rude fun-making, Harald said
nothing of his purpose till his flimsy roof was up; then,
summoning his captains, he sketched lines in the earth.

"We cannot force the gate," he went on, "but we can dig
under the walls." He smiled at the flash of comprehension
that lit up their faces. "Set your men to work!"

The men dug in shifts, and, understanding the object
of their work, they dug lustily. The dirt came out in reed
baskets, which were piled on the wheeled platforms that

had been used to transport the catapults, and so trundled to the marsh and dumped.

Days and weeks passed, the tunnel growing fast; and the men, whose appetites grew with the hard labor, took much feeding. Whole companies were sent out to hunt, to fish, or to bring salt meat from the ships.

The Immortals seemed as busy as the Varangians. They were constructing a wall something after the pattern of Harald's, using the stones of the old Greek walls. Neither Harald nor Georgios vouchsafed his plans to the other, but the Northman made a shrewd guess.

"By St. Olaf!" Harald exclaimed to Eilif. "He means to make a counterwall as high as the battlements!"

And this Georgios did. Within a month he had erected a vast salient of his own, matching the city walls in height, though far outflanked by them. Then his envoys came to Harald, demanding more catapults. Harald sent them to the ships, bidding them take what they needed. Reports came from the fleet that Georgios had taken more than catapults: sealed tanks of naphtha, sulphur, tar, ropes, pulleys, copper kettles.

"Can the fool be meaning to make Greek fire?" Eilif growled. "No fire-tubes will carry that far, nor has he taken any tubes."

"Then you go to the ships and leave order that he take no tubes, and that no more naphtha be given him," Harald commanded. "The tunnel is now well-nigh under the wall, and I have use for the Greek fire myself."

The next noon Ulf, in charge of the day shift in the tunnel, came hurrying to Harald.

"We are under the wall!" he exulted. "We have struck the foundation of a great house."

"Leave off digging and shore up," Harald ordered. And calling Eilif, he directed:

"To-night at dark move your ships to the southwestern side of Ortygia. At midnight bring them as close to the wall as ye dare, without being discovered. When ye hear my trumpet to the north, run your ships against the walls, set up ladders, and storm!"

As soon as Eilif was gone, Harald sent off a messenger to Georgios, with these words:

"If ye take not the wall opposite you by midnight, I will be first in the town!"

"IT WOULD BE a brave end, if the earth should cave in and smother us!"

An officer dug his elbow into the growling house-carle's ribs.

"Keep your mouth closed," he rebuked, "and no earth will enter it."

The column filled the tunnel almost from wall to wall; and with the torches smoking, there was none too much air for so many to breathe. Yet Harald would not permit them to advance fast, lest the clash of their mail and weapons give the alarm. He himself, with a score of men armed with iron picks and shovels, led the advance.

Carefully he scanned the exposed surface of stone at the tunnel's end. The diggers had done their work well; they had struck the bottom of a stone floor, followed it for perhaps thirty-feet, and scraped it clear of earth. The floor proved to be of tiles: not set in cement after the modern fashion, but held by the mortar between them and supported by beams set fairly close together.

The engineers set to work on the beams with knives, while spiked poles, each driven upward by two men, smashed into the flooring. The supporting beams once severed, the tiles were put to great strain, which was increased at every stroke of the poles. Whenever the pikes loosened a bit of mortar, the tiles sagged lower and lower. One dropped, another; then a whole mass, still cleaving together.

"Up!" commanded Harald.

Climbing on each other's shoulders, the engineers broke away more and more, till they had cleared a space large enough to pass six men through at once. Quickly, yet warily, lest their armor clash against the stone, the warriors swarmed up by threes and fours, each man, as soon as he was up, forming line with those who had preceded him.

They found themselves in a large, almost unfurnished building. It was coldly, but richly beautiful. Harald's torch gleamed on Arabic inscriptions in letters of gold, on richly molded capitals and bright mosaic.

"A Greek church, made into a mosque," Thiodolf whispered. "This is not the hour of prayer, else we should have found greeting from the worshipers."

From some unseen room or passage came the shuffle of slippered feet, and the querulous whine of an old man disturbed. A light glowed from a pierced bronze lantern, and a bearded, turbaned ancient came into view around a column. At sight of the Northmen, their mail and bare weapons glinting in the torchlight, their fierce faces and hot eyes shining, he gave a sudden shrill cry, and turned to flee.

Thiodolf leaped forward, his long ax shooting out; and the old man dropped. He lay quite still, his white beard stained with dark blood. Thiodolf bent over him, fumbled at his girdle, and held up a pair of heavy keys.

"The custodian of the mosque," he said to Harald. "He is doubtless the only one here."

The Varangians were streaming up from the tunnel like an army of giant ants, till they filled the mosque; and there were more to come. Flinging wide the doors, they flooded out into the narrow street.

Here all was dark and silent, for the hour was late. Only here and there lights burned in the houses; and on the battlements, marking the line of the walls, iron cressets filled with blazing-wood gave light to the Moslem garrison.

It was Harald's purpose to make his way into the heart of the city, if possible, before his entry should be discovered. Then the defenders would be forced to leave the parapet and assail him on level ground. A direct attempt to storm the walls from within would be too costly.

Through the streets the Varangians poured, shields up, blades flashing in the occasional beams of light. Of a sudden, at an intersection, they came full on a group of white-clad citizens, squatting around a brazier before a brightly lighted coffee-shop. The Arabs sprang to their feet with cries of alarm, breaking into flight like startled rats. Instantly the Varangians were upon them, striking out in haste to silence their shouts. From the wall came answering cries, as the alert sentinels heard and understood the shouts of the frightened men:

"Help, oh, Moslems! The *Nasrini* are upon us!"

The alarm was taken up through the whole quarter. Lights flashed in house after house; the shrill screams of women rang on the night; in the distance trampling hoofs thundered. Horns blared and drums rattled: somewhere a great bell pealed in a one-time Christian belfry. Horses neighed, a cock crowed. Men cursed and women whimpered behind pierced gratings.

Into an arcaded square the Varangians rushed. A small crowd, that had gathered to learn the cause of the turmoil, fled howling for shelter. There came the shuffle of many feet, the pound-pound-pound of spurred mounts, and a troop of Arab horsemen burst from the mouth of a wide street.

HOPELESS NOW TO attempt surprise. The city garrison would be pouring troops from the walls at any moment. It was imperative that Harald summon aid from Eflif before the whole Syracusan army was upon him. He sounded his trumpet, once and again, till its peal rang back from wall to wall.

The roll of drums grew to a frenzied din. From down one long, straight street, a knife-slash in the close-built city, the Northmen could see a swarm of armed turbaned figures clambering down the stairways that led to the parapets.

The Moslems, falling into array, pressed forward. From every side street other Arabs were hastening up, some fumbling with the lashings of their mail as they ran. Harald brought his men to a halt, that they might catch breath before closing.

"Charge!" Harald then roared, determined to dispose of the enemy before him ere others should come up.

The Northmen surged forward like a living batter-ing-ram. The head of their column swept the Moslems back, broke them into a formless crowd, and jammed them against the inner side of the wall. But fresh numbers from the parapets constantly trickled down to their aid, and the fighting grew furious.

Harald burst through a press of foes to come face to face with the Moslem officer in command. But the Arab did not fight; instead, shouting a command to his men, he pulled frantically at the reins, trying to force his horse away from the vicinity of his foe. The ax Hell licked in, and he fell.

The Saracen rout was so sudden, so complete, that the Varangians stood a moment bewildered. The cressets on the battlements shone down on dead and dying, on the clustered Northmen, and on the backs of the fleeing Arabs. Then, as Harald gave the order for pursuit, a long, wailing peal came from the southward.

"Eilif!" Thiodolf shouted. The sounds of fighting came, faint and distant, across the city; the cries of alarm redou-bled. Then the Northmen understood what they had supposed to be a panic-stricken retreat of their foes: the heathen had not fled; they had been summoned to relieve Eilif's pressure on the south wall of the island.

Without more loss of time, Harald drove his men after the running garrison, detaching a thousand to scale the now depleted parapets and harass the defenders there.

Down twisting, narrow streets the column rushed, unchallenged. It was strange that the hurrying Varang-ians met no more opposition. Not all the garrison could have concentrated on Ortygia to repel Eilif's attack. Then the riddle was solved. From the north came the bitter tang of smoke, the glint of flame, and the outcries of many men in mortal fight.

And Harald knew that Georgios had come. He saw the meaning of those catapults now, and the inflammables Georgios had taken from the fleet. On his tall angle of wall the Greek had mounted siege-engines, and from them he had hurled balls of tar and twine, soaked with blazing naphtha. The north end of the city was on fire; and under cover of the fire, Georgios was storming!

The streets rang with the hoofs of mounted Moslem messengers, sent pell-mell from north to south, from south to north, from both quarters to the eastern wall, each portion of the menaced city imploring the others for help.

The fire suddenly became a roaring conflagration: for in the whole north quarter, where the poorer suburbs lay, the roofs were of dry thatch.

ONLY THE STERN Varangian discipline enabled Harald to keep his blood-maddened, loot-hungry men in check; else they would have scattered down a dozen by-ways and fallen to plundering. Holding them in firm array, he marched them toward the southern wall, where Eilif was hard pressed. At last they found the rearward ranks of a whole Saracen division, and hurled themselves on its back like wolves. Ere the Arabs could face about, the bright axes were biting deep, breaking their ranks, flinging the whole army into confusion. The defenders broke, and sought safety down every street and alley.

Flinging the scattered remnants aside, the Varangians spread out into a long open space between the town and the western wall. From the opposite side came a sudden rush: against the Varangian shields crashed a column of Arab horse. How many they were no man could see, for the distant fire, though rolling ever nearer, was masked by intervening buildings, and the scattered lights cast but a vague, confusing glow here and there. But the Moslems drove in with a weight that spoke of mighty numbers. The whole front of the Varangian column was driven in, throwing those behind into disarray.

"Hold fast!" boomed Harald's voice, and the captains repeated the order. The axes swung and bit, swung again, while the rear ranks fought for space to wield their weapons better. Thiodolf, fighting with both hands, lifted his bull voice in the song he had made at Rametta:

> "Our prince has gone hunting.
> And harries the heathen:
> 'Hell' waits them, 'Hell' bites them,
> They cringe from his hatred.
> The raven flaps o'er us,
> The ravening wolf—"

He paused, grinding his teeth, for a scimitar had shorn into his right shoulder. A moment he fought with compressed lips; then, as his blade found the skull of the man who had smitten him, he burst into full song again:

> "—thirst Harald sateth
> With Saracen corpse-flesh!"

With flashing ax Harald was proving the song true. Heartened by the fury of his strokes, his whole front rank struck as he did—not so much at the Moslem horsemen as at the legs and breasts of their mounts. Beast after beast went down, choking the mouth of the street whence their attack had come, till the Varangians won space to realign behind a rampart of dead horses that checked the riders behind.

But these men were picked troopers, commanded by a famous leader. Unable to leap their horses over the heap of mangled men and animals, they slipped from the saddle and scaled the rampart afoot. Though they went down in whole ranks, they pressed on; and one in the van, falling out with a huge scimitar that smote swift and hard as lightning, led them forward. Leaping the barricade, he fronted the shieldwall before all his men; and these, following with exultant yells, cried loudly:

"Abulafar! Abulafar!"

Harald sprang to meet him. "Draw your men back!" he shouted above the din. "I command here, as you command the Arabs. Let us fight it out man to man!"

The giant Saracen lashed out with his scimitar with such speed that Harald had to fling himself aside to escape the steel. Thiodolf came to his rescue, and Ulf Uspaksson. Three or four Moslems pressed to their chief's side. Instantly both forces were embroiled again. But Harald, thrusting friend and foe aside, closed once more with the Moslem leader.

Sword and ax clashed, steel striking fire from steel. Once and again the Saracen thrust; cut after cut he drove in with the edge at head and shoulders. Harald warded with the shortened haft, holding the defensive, waiting for an opening. He struck, and Hell knocked the helmet from the Moslem's head. Had it not turned, the duel would have ended then.

The scimitar played like a living flame, rising and falling, slashing at a dozen angles, giving Harald scant time to parry. His wrist tired, his shoulders ached. At last, goaded to fury, he thrust the horn that flared beyond Hell's head full at the Arab's throat. The scimitar rose to guard, but the sharp-edged horn tore away two fingers, broke the grip of the maimed hand, and tore the curved blade from its owner's grasp.

Unwilling to slay a disarmed foe, Harald waited for him to raise his weapon with the left hand; but the Moslem staggered back and fell crashing. A stream of blood welled from his throat. Even as the ax-horn had severed his fingers, its blade, driven on by the desperate fury behind the stroke had torn through his mailed neck.

The Saracens raised cries of grief and fear over their fallen comrades. They fought now with doubtful valor, and at length broke, fleeing like wounded deer, with the Northmen in full cry after them.

"Who was—yon heathen—you slew?" Thiodolf panted, as he fumbled at his wound with a strip of his tunic.

"Abulafar, Emir of Sicily," Harald answered calmly. "He has paid his share of the price of Cyra's hands."

THE CONFLAGRATION SET by Georgios's tar balls and fire bombs—copper kettles filled with naphtha and sealed with clay—raged as far as the narrow mole between Ortygia and Achradina; and there the heroic efforts of the Moslems stopped it. The whole northern half of the city was laid waste, but the walled island, the heart and citadel, was almost unscathed.

But, under cover of that fire, Georgios had battered down the gate opposite his camp; and on its ravening red heels he had marched unopposed through the inner gate that gave entry to the wall across the mole. Only beyond the wide devastated area did the Moslems succeed in gathering their forces to oppose him; and for three hours they held him there without gain.

In vain the Immortals battered at the Saracen front; ranged across the narrow neck of artificial land back of their own fire-ruined wall, the defenders of Syracuse could neither be outflanked nor driven in. They fought for life itself; and they fought with the strength of despair.

The news of Abulafar's fall did not spread thither, for Harald's Varangians stood between that battle front and any Moslem messengers that tried to win through. But south of the great square the city learned of it speedily; into every quarter the fleeing Moslems fled, bearing the grievous word that the Emir of Sicily was slain. Where this news, and the report of the terrible fury of the Varangians, spread resistance died in mortal fear. The city was taken, save for the last heroic resistance to Georgios.

"North!" Harald commanded. "The Greeks are hard pressed, or we should have heard from them."

Back through the city the Varangians marched, weary, but exultant, their blood-splashed faces lifted in the joy of victory.

They smote the gallant Moslem defense in the rear, drove its outflung flanks into the sea, and rolled the center up against the long spears of the Immortals. Heartened by the timely relief, the Greeks broke through, overcame the last resistance, and then, drunk with joy at the reconquest of the great Greek city, fell on the necks of the Varangians.

Only Georgios held aloof, tasting for the third time in one campaign the bitterness of jealousy at his rival's triumph. To him Harald stalked, a grim figure in slashed and bloody mail.

"My men took the town, while you were held at bay," he boasted with the open, unashamed pride of the Northman. "Therefore we have the plundering of the town. You may take the loot from that part which you have conquered." And he pointed disdainfully at the desolate field of ashes and tumbled walls where the fire had raged.

Georgios stood immobile with anger.

Harald was merciless. "You would have had me die at a Moslem point rather than rescue me," he charged boldly. "To-night, in spite of that, I have rescued you; and if your share of the plunder does not please you, remember I have given you life. If you accept, say so; if not, draw sword and settle the matter with steel. There has been so much bad blood between us that it will be best for all if that blood be drawn."

Georgios gripped his dripping sword, and his eyes burned savagely; but the sight of that grim figure with the lifted ax was enough. Harald had beaten him once, man to man; nor had the Greek since then been able to break down his secret fear of the barbarian, his fear that if they came to death grips not Harald, but he would yield up his life.

"Well," demanded Harald, "do we agree, or fight?" He took one step forward, balancing Hell as if to strike.

Georgios drew back. "I—I agree," he mumbled.

17

THE MIRACLE

"**THIS NEWS MUST** be kept from the emperor."

The Eunuch John let his smoldering eyes rest on the dust-stained soldier before him, and went on:

"It were best to say naught of it within the palace, lest it come to his ears. He lies in the extremity of fever. To learn now that one of his noblest cities, the Eye of Mesopotamia, has fallen to the Moslems, might bring on a crisis that would kill him. You understand."

Left alone, John strode up and down the room, frowning. His flaccid face was lined with anxiety. Finally he summoned a servant.

"No news from Sicily?" he asked.

"None, Most Mighty, since the Bari merchantman brought word of the fall of Messina."

"No trace of—my brother?"

"None, Magnificent."

"Help me change my robes. I go to the Emperor."

The servant flung open a coffer of cedar, and drew out a long white garment, fringed with gold.

The Emperor lay, prone and unmoving, on an ivory bed. The room was half dark, heavy damask curtains shutting out the sun that else would have poured in from the gardens. His face, wasted and shrunken, bore yet an air of majesty.

John stepped lightly to his brother's side, and laid a hand on the hot forehead. Its touch burned him.

"Why does he not stir, when such a fever racks him?" he whispered to the physician.

The doctor bowed, hands crossed.

"He has not yet worn off the sleeping draft I gave him. If he wakes too soon he may die."

John started. "Is it so soon?"

"Only a miracle can save him, Mighty One. If the fever could be made to break, if he could perspire—"

"You have tried everything?"

"Everything known to science, lord. Crushed pearls in an elixir of wine and balsam. Everything. In vain."

A eunuch crept into the room, and caught John's eye.

"There is a soldier in the Chalke, Magnificence," he whispered, "from the Mestopotamian theme."

"His news?" asked John sharply.

"Edessa has fallen!" In his excitement the eunuch spoke too loudly.

John stepped toward him with a silent, tigerish stride. "That I know," he hissed. "Be quiet. Go!"

The eunuch cringed, and vanished. Turning back to the bedside, John saw that his brother's eyes had opened.

The Emperor lay rigid, his features drawn together painfully. He moved one hand convulsively, and before John or the physician could aid him, he had flung himself from the bed. His face turned a deep red; beads of perspiration started out. Almost on the instant his cheeks and chin were bathed in sweat.

"The Father in Heaven be praised!" the physician murmured. "The fever is broken!"

John caught his brother about the shoulders and tried to force him back to the pillow. The sick man struggled, a half insane strength coming to his wasted, but once powerful frame. He tore himself from John's arms, shook off the covers, and struggled upright, his bare feet on the marble floor. His eyes glittered with a light half angry, half mad.

"Edessa! Edessa fallen!" he panted. "Edessa, the jewel of the East. This has come upon me for my sins!" He spoke with mournful vehemence. "For my most black and awful sins! Because I slew him who trusted me, because—"

In a flash John clamped one hand across his brother's lips, praying that the doctor might not understand. With unexpected strength Michael thrust John's arm away.

"I will atone, O God!" he cried, in a vibrant voice. "I will take back my fair city from the heathen, and plant Thy cross on its towers again! Aid me, give me life and strength to keep my vow, and I will take the cowl of monkhood!"

Sweat was streaming down his limbs, making his night robe cleave to him. His lips worked as in desperate prayer. John, shaken to the soul, tried to quiet him. The terrified physician, fearing that he had already heard too much to live long, cast furtive looks from one to the other, telling his beads with trembling fingers.

"BRING ME MY armor!" the Emperor suddenly demanded, in a voice like the ring of a trumpet. From the surrounding chambers came the squeak and scurry of frightened eunuchs, none of whom dared enter.

"Arm me! Saddle my horse!" the Emperor shouted. "My sword! My guards! Beat the alarm!"

"Be still! Be still!" John urged. "You are sick. Your generals—"

Michael's fingers bit suddenly into the Eunuch's soft shoulder.

"Am I Emperor, or a slave," he cried in a royal rage, "that a slave dares dispute me? By the three Holy Names, I march on Edessa this day!"

Seeing his fury rising higher and higher, John knew force would not move Michael from his mad desire; therefore he tried humoring him. A eunuch was summoned to fetch the imperial armor, and lead a saddled horse to the palace.

With trembling hands, expecting every moment to see the Emperor collapse, John himself dressed his brother in the imperial robes of silk and cloth of gold, set the crested helmet on his head, buckled the jeweled, gold-inlaid corselet about him. Shaking off all aid, the Emperor walked, without a supporting arm, to the Chalke.

Eunuchs and slaves prostrated themselves before him, panic-stricken; and when he had passed them, ran scuttering through the great palace, whispering the news. The palace buzzed. The great double-headed eagle on the imperial banner was raised above the Chalke gate, to proclaim to all the world that a miracle had raised the well-nigh dead Augustus to life and strength.

It was indeed almost a miracle. The sudden access of health, like the fevered torpor preceding it, was one of the little-understood turns that advanced epilepsy may take. As delusive as the prostration of earlier stages, it meant no real return to health, nor postponed the day of death one hour. But not even the physicians understood the disease well enough to know this.

The city broke into open rejoicing. The loss of Edessa was as nothing; the Emperor, whom none had seen since his illness had grown acute, would win it back. The Emperor was cured: God had vouchsafed a miracle. Bells rang in the cathedral, echoed from every church in Constantinople. The people thronged the streets in their gayest robes.

Nor was it because the Emperor was loved. Neither he nor any of his lowborn house held the affection of his subjects. But he was Emperor, successor to Justinian and Heraclius; he was well, and he would win back their lost honor from the scimitars of Islam.

At the end of the second week messengers dashed through the gates with news that the provincial troops, whom Michael was to lead into Mesopotamia were approaching. Without further delay Michael, followed by half a troop of Immortals, spurred through that gate to join his armies.

The next day men whispered that John the Eunuch, not daring to leave his brother unattended on the perils of a campaign, fearing lest he die on the way, had followed him to Mesopotamia.

The report was true. John was too much the skeptic to trust so dramatic a miracle; he knew it had come too late to check for long the ravages of his brother's disease. None perceived so well as he that, if Michael should die on the campaign, the strongest and most ambitious among his generals would proclaim himself Emperor, and march on Constantinople at the head of that very army destined for the relief of Edessa. If Michael's sickness returned, only the presence of the feared Eunuch himself could keep the troops in hand and save the Empire from revolution. True, Zoe would seize the occasion of John's absence to intrigue; and Constantine had not been found. But John had taken his precautions against Zoe ere he left; and he trusted Aldhelm's Varangians to hold Constantine in hand.

The news of John's departure left the folk dazed at first, and somewhat frightened; then a great relief flooded the hearts of all. The Emperor was God's Anointed, but John was a tyrant. He was gone, and men might now do as they pleased. So they thought, till Aldhelm and his police put a bloody end to several intoxicated riots. Then it was understood that, though the tyrant was gone, the swords of the Varangians remained.

Zoe, too, learned that John had left his shadow behind him. It was her maid, the lovely Maria, who rushed breathless into her apartments with word that John had gone with Michael. Pausing but to put on her royal robes and coronet, and adorn her face with cosmetics, Zoe advanced regally toward the throne room. But she never crossed the threshold of her quarters.

A eunuch and a guard of Immortals barred her way; nor would they let her pass for all her threats and cajolings. John still ruled the city; it was only his brother, the Emperor, whom he no longer ruled.

18

REVOLT

THE PATRIARCH OF Constantinople glanced inquiringly at the cloaked and muffled figure admitted to his presence.

"Your business with me?" he asked. "Few dare seek me in these evil days."

His visitor cast off cloak and hood. He was young and supple; and at first sight of his features the Patriarch started forward in his high seat. He stared a moment, intently; then he fell back, shaking his head.

"You are like one I know too well," he muttered.

The young man smiled, frankly and winningly. "Perhaps there is reason for the likeness," he answered. "I am Constantine, youngest brother of the Emperor."

The Patriarch leaped to his feet, his whole frame quaking with rage.

"What do you here, son of an evil brood?"

Constantine met his fury with composure. "Your Holiness thinks evil of me?" he asked innocently. "It is not my fault that I was born brother to a tyrant. May I explain to Your Holiness that I am now a fugitive, with a price set on my head by that same loving brother John?"

"Nay, I have heard no wrong of you," the Patriarch frowned. "I did not so much as know of your presence in this city. But you come of a house that has brought shame on our land, murdered its rightful ruler, and held captive her who should bear the imperial crown. Therefore my roof is no fit shelter for you. Your errand? Speak, that I may be rid of you!"

Constantine crossed his hands on his breast, the picture of just humility.

"It has been my wretched fate," he spoke sadly, "to look on at the crimes of my brother John, helpless to prevent them. He took me secretly from my home, where I lived an innocent youth, meaning to make me his secretary and so bend me to his will, and make me the tool of his wicked deeds.

"I fled from court, resolved to live a fugitive or die at his hands, rather than be thought an accomplice of his baseness. For months I have lurked in dark and perilous hiding places, fed and aided by a few friends, waiting only a chance to escape, so that I might come to you and place in your hands the means to undo the wrongs he has committed. That chance has come, now that he has left the city."

The Patriarch eyed him with suspicion. "It had come to my ears that John had set a price on the head of one Constantine, a Paphlagonian; and the description given of the fugitive fits you well enough. But how can you, a mere youth, sought by the police, overturn that vast fabric of evil which your mighty brother has taken years to build? And, even if you could, how might I trust you, who are of his flesh and blood?"

Constantine appeared to hesitate. "I shall be safe in your hands?" he temporized. "You would not betray me when I have given you my confidence?"

"Speak, speak! No man can say I have betrayed him; nor do I harm those who would undo the evil wrought by the tyrant."

Constantine's words came with a rush. "Get me speech with the Empress!" he implored. "I know, for John has told me that in some way you maintain communication with her. Let me but have a few words with her, and I will show her how to win back her throne."

The Patriarch's eyes kindled with a fanatic hope, with which distrust was blended.

"You would do this?" the Patriarch panted, aflame but distrustful. "What surety have I that, if you succeed, you will not merely take his place as her oppressor?"

Constantine sighed, as one bitterly misjudged.

"This rebuke is one our house has deserved," he said. "Yet there is one way to convince you of my honesty, my single-minded desire to serve the Empress. From the moment when Zoe is proclaimed free and sovereign once more, you, Holy Father, shall be her chief minister. I will step aside, asking but to live a safe and retired life as a private citizen."

Like most weak men, the Patriarch was confident of his strength. Let him but regain his freedom and his grasp of state affairs, and he was sure he could dominate all the mighty empire. In no other way could Constantine have appealed more surely to his trust. Yet he was not convinced: he could not bring himself wholly to believe a brother of John.

"You shall see the Augusta within the hour," he promised, "but your eyes shall be blindfolded, that you may not know by what way I lead you to her. We cannot go openly to the palace, lest John's hirelings, seize us." He called his servant.

Patiently Constantine allowed the two old men to bind his eyes.

CONSTANTINE STOOD AT last in the Empress's bower; but not alone. The grim-visaged Patriarch kept by his side, determined to prevent any possible treachery. Though Constantine had spoken well and convincingly, he remained the brother of John.

In the same heavily perfumed chamber where Zoe had declared her love to Harald, Zoe now, attended by the girl Maria, awaited Constantine. She bade him approach; and most humbly Constantine kissed the polished marble at her feet.

"The hour has struck," he said softly. "John has left the city, not to return for many weeks, perhaps months. Now the mighty Augusta may resume her majesty."

Zoe smiled contemptuously. "If this is all your news, your breath is wasted," she answered. "I have tried to enter the Daphne, but John's Immortals barred the way. I am no more Empress now than before."

"But those Immortals are a handful," the young man insinuated, "before the thousands on thousands of Varangian police."

"The Varangians!" Zoe rose from her divan, her kohl-rimmed eyes wide. "The Varangians? Whom John left behind to guard the city for him!"

"They do not recognize his authority," Constantine reminded her. "They swore adherence only to the Crown, not to him. The barbarian Harald held them in restraint by their loyalty to him, but they have only to be convinced that John means treachery to Harald, and they will obey any order you give them."

"How convince the Varangians that John is Harald's enemy?" she asked, veiling her emotion behind lowered lids.

"I have the copy of an order given to Georgios to murder Harald in Sicily," Constantine made answer.

Watching her closely, he could see her features set, and the convulsive coiling and uncoiling of her fingers. Ignorant of the interview she had had with Harald in that very chamber, he could not read her emotion aright.

"John gave that order?" she cried hoarsely.

Eager to convince her of his devotion to her cause, Constantine made his first mistake. "Nay, divine Augusta. I gave the order, signing John's name and sealing it with his seal, that I might later use it against my wicked brother.

"Moreover, ever mindful of your welfare, I spoke with Georgios just before he sailed, urging him to see to it that the barbarian never returned alive. It was plain to me, though hidden from John, that the Northman had designs on the throne."

Zoe's eyes smiled dreamily; she was amused at his error. But the smile grew hard as she remembered Harald's disdain.

"So you expect the Varangians, when they see that order, to cast aside all obedience to John," she mused. "And since their allegiance is to the Crown, they will obey me. If that is so, then you have indeed done me a great service. But for that forged order"—the sudden coldness of her voice did not penetrate to Constantine's intrigue-hot brain—

"but for that forged order, which will bring about Harald's death, they might have hesitated to listen to my appeal."

"It is true, Augusta. I have done this that you might regain your right."

"You shall be appropriately rewarded."

Now the Patriarch bent his gray brows on Constantine, watching him for the least sign of undue ambition. But Constantine, bowing humbly, answered:

"I ask no reward, Augusta. You have suffered much at my brother's hands. Give me only the joy of knowing that it was I who made your triumph possible."

Brilliantly Zoe smiled upon him.

"Give me pen and parchment, Maria," she commanded. When they were brought, she wrote:

> To THE PREFECT ALDHELM, Commanding the Forces Within the City. From the Empress Zoe, Porphyrogenita, Augusta, Greeting:
>
> Be it known to thee that John the Paphlagonian, who so long usurped our powers, has left our domains. Having asserted our right to resume the throne, we have been denied by his servants, who hold us imprisoned in our chambers. We command thee, on thy allegiance to the Empire, to march forth with on the palace and proclaim us Empress, with undivided rule. The order which the hearer of these our commands will bring thee will release thee from any further duties to the usurper.
>
> Zoe, Augusta.

SHE HELD THE parchment out to Constantine, but withdrew it from his very grasp, asking: "How shall you get this safely to the Prefect, you on whose head there rests a price?"

Constantine smiled, vain of his cunning.

"That was John's order, and John is gone," he answered. "Moreover, I have powerful friends. The Syrian Demetrios, whom Harald persecuted, is back in the city. He nurses a grudge against John, who dared not protect him; but he is my man, for I have promised him much wealth in recompense for his wrongs.

"One thing more: It would be well to command the Varangians to post guards at every gate, forbidding any man to leave the city till John returns. Otherwise the tyrant will learn of what we do, and may contrive a plan to overthrow you."

"Wisely counseled!" Zoe commended, and wrote the order into the letter. Handing him the scroll, she gave him the gesture of dismissal, and bade Maria lead him, blindfolded, back through the tunnel. The Patriarch remained behind.

"Do you trust him?" the Empress asked.

The priest considered. "He has asked for no reward," he said.

"The more reason to doubt him. He has told one lie: Harald does not covet the throne. I offered it to him— with my hand."

She turned, challenge in her manner, to the old man; but the Patriarch nodded sage approval.

"A wise offer, Augusta. In truth, I do not believe the barbarian covets aught but honor; nor could there be a man more fitted to share your throne. It was ill done of

Constantine to plot against his life; but that is the nature of his breed."

Zoe laughed silently. "Nay, I trust him not; but he cannot harm us till the empire is in our hands again. He depends on my power for any hidden design he meditates. Now do you return to your dwelling."

After closing the tunnel entrance behind the priest, she cast herself on the divan and waited for Maria. It was but a little while ere the girl's voice sounded through the well-concealed tube. Springing to her feet like a girl, the Empress touched the spring that controlled the stone. Maria clambered out and quenched her light.

"To the balcony!" Zoe ordered; and the two women hastened to the stone balustrade that commanded the Augusteion and the senate house. From it a stone stairway led up to the battlements, and, seizing Maria's hand, Zoe drew her up the stair.

An Immortal halted them at the top. "You are confined to your chambers, Augusta," he warned her.

Zoe smiled on him flatteringly.

"I wish but to enjoy the clear air and the sight of the city," she protested. "I will go no farther than the stair there. I will not stir from your sight."

The soldier grew thoughtful. John was away; and the Empress at hand. No man knew what might happen in the easily disturbed city. It might be as well to grant a favor that could cost him nothing.

"If you will abide where I can watch you, Augusta."

"Have I not promised?" she asked, with queenly condescension.

She crossed the topmost step, and walked slowly to the merlons, the Immortal anxiously following beside Maria. **DOWN THE LONG** Mese Zoe's eyes roved, intently scanning the streets. The sun dipped lower and lower, till it glared level into her eyes. She shielded her soft complexion with one hand, but she did not move, save now and then to ease her position.

Then, far off toward the Forum of Constantine, something gleamed. The gleam grew, spread, became a flowing river of light. Zoe leaned forward, so suddenly and eagerly that Maria ran to her in alarm, fearing her mistress would fall from the battlements. From the distance came the blast of a horn, the shouts of many folk; the river of gleaming steel grew and grew.

From the direction of the Strategium flowed another, advancing to join the first; smaller columns moved in every quarter of the city. The excited shouts mounted to a many-tongued roar. The two rivers of steel joined, and their united flood streamed toward the palace.

The Immortal, roused by the mounting tumult, came to Zoe's side, and peered out over the city. He thought the police had mustered to put down one of those sudden mobs which sometimes sprang up out of nothing in the city; but Zoe's excited glances woke his suspicion.

At the same moment he perceived that the shouting townsfolk were not confronting, but following, the Varangians. Instantly forgetful of the two women, he ran along the battlements to the first tower, shouting the alarm.

Zoe, exultant, drew Maria down the stair. Returning to her apartments, she commanded:

"My royal robes! My crown!"

Smiling happily, the girl stripped off the robe of fine tissue which her mistress wore, replacing it with the long coronation robes, heavy with gold and jewels, and set on Zoe's head the triple tiara of the Empire.

The palace garrison was not fitted for resistance. Stripped to a mere handful by the needs of the wars, too few even to man the Chalke alone, it was good for no more than a guard for Zoe and her household. The Varangian column swept to the very gates; and there, ax-blades fronting the bronze bars, they drew up in perfect order.

"What do you here?" the captain of the guard asked angrily.

Aldhelm the Englishman stepped from the shieldwall.

"Open!" he commanded. "We are thousands; ye but a few score. If ye deny us, we will break the gates and slay you all; if ye let us pass, ye may march out in peace. Choose!"

The garrison chose as they must. The great gates creaked open, and the Varangians surged in. They came in good order, harming no man; but their eyes burned with rage, for it had been told them that John had given secret orders for the murder of their Prefect in Sicily. Had any man resisted them, he would have been cut in pieces.

They found Zoe seated stately on the imperial throne.

THE MARCH OF the Varangians on the palace revealed to the people what was in the wind. Lovers of the old dynasty, they flocked into the Augusteion, yelling their joy, tossing their wide-brimmed hats into the air, singing songs of triumph at the very gates of the Chalke. Wherever a Varangian appeared on the walls, he was wildly cheered. The streets rang with the name of the Empress.

But it was Constantine who enjoyed the greatest

triumph. The Empress, grateful despite all her doubt of
him, had given out word that it was he who had restored
her to her throne.

When he appeared on the battlements to make official
proclamation of her restoration, the applause that greeted
him from a hundred thousand throats was heard across the
straits in Asia. It was half an hour ere he could make his
voice heard; and he knew better than to speak long. In a
few words he poured into the ears of the folk the message
he wished them to believe:

"I have given you back your rightful Empress. Henceforth I shall see to it that none deprives her of her throne
and power. Ye may trust me, citizens, to protect your
Augusta."

Thus he won the adherence of the people, and their
powerful if fickle support. That he had as yet no authority
did not trouble him; he knew how to gain it. He was too
shrewd to ask Zoe for anything; he would merely wait till
she had need of him. The time would soon come.

The strength of Constantine's position lay in his will-
ingness to work, and in that familiarity with the cares of
state which he had acquired under John's tutelage. Well he
knew that he who performs the actual labor of administra-
tion, who shrinks not from its drudgery, wields its power.
Zoe was hopelessly ill-fitted to rule, and the Patriarch was
little better.

In all her life Zoe had never known the need to work.
Her conception of an empress's duties was to pose upon
the throne, to accept homage, to receive the flattery of men.
This flattery Constantine gave her, delicately and with
the sure touch of an artist. He waited on her ceaselessly,

performed her every wish with humility and eagerness. She had but to express a desire, and he hastened to perform it. Slowly, inevitably, she came to rely upon him.

For a time the Patriarch diligently strove to perform his new duties as minister, bustling about the palace, receiving envoys, listening to reports. But the old priest, cloistered since youth, and for years a prisoner in his own house, knew nothing of the Empire, nor even of the city. The boundless red tape of business, the intricacy of politics, were beyond his comprehension.

Since the city must be governed, Aldhelm and his police governed it, and well; but the network of commerce and statecraft that bound the capital to its provinces became hopelessly ensnarled. At length the Patriarch, at the end of his patience and strength, implored Zoe to relieve him of his responsibilities. An honest zealot, weak and ignorant, he had tasted the tragedy of his own incompetence.

This was Constantine's moment. Precisely because he had never asked anything for himself, but had stood ever at her beck and call, Zoe turned to him. At first she gave him nothing more than the chance to work, and the title of minister of the household.

This was enough. He flung himself into the snarl of affairs abandoned by the Patriarch, and with all the talent born in him and so long fostered by his brother, reduced all to smooth-running order. Taxes once more flooded into the treasury, trade revived, the provincial armies received their supplies, and the very palace ceremonial recovered all its grandeur.

Zoe's indolent, selfish heart was delighted. Insensibly she came more and more to lean on her able minister.

So he waited, with cunning patience, till he had become indispensable to her; nor did he even then ask anything for himself. Received in private audience, he reiterated his concern for her.

"Divine Augusta, you are not safe. The folk love you; the Varangians will defend you to the last drop of blood. But, when John returns, with what can you oppose him? He has thrice as many troops as you."

"The Varangians are worth ten times their weight of Greeks," the empress answered contemptuously. "And they hold the walls."

"But when Georgios comes back from Sicily," Constantine urged, "he will join with John. Does he not hate the Northmen, and covet the crown?"

IN SPITE OF her newborn greatness Zoe was frightened. The name of Georgios was terrible from one end of the empire to the other.

"What do you advise?" she asked.

"Recruit fresh troops from the Bythinian theme. Bythinia was ever devoted to your house. With two themes, and the Varangians, you will be safe."

Zoe was silent, unwilling; Constantine understood her reluctance.

"They need not be brought into the city," he argued gently. "Let them camp outside the wall until word comes of John's advance, or of Georgios's return. Then they can be admitted to defend you."

"I will take counsel of the Patriarch," Zoe temporized.

Constantine risked all on one bold stroke.

"The Patriarch is in correspondence with Georgios," he

whispered. "I have intercepted a swift pamphylian bound for Sicily, carrying letters from him."

He handed the empress a scroll, sealed with the staff and cross of the Patriarch. With a cry of dismay Zoe read the superscription:

"To the noble Patrician and Caesar, Georgios Maniakes."

"Caesar!" she gasped.

None was called Caesar save the heir to the throne. To Zoe's morbidly suspicious mind the term was enough to prove that even the Patriarch conspired against her. The old priest's fanatic devotion to her suddenly counted for nothing; she had endured captivity and scorn so long that the least breath of treason found ready entrance into her anxious mind. She was as ready to be convinced of unfaith in others as to be untrue herself.

"He shall be imprisoned!" she stormed pettishly. But this was not what Constantine wanted.

"To lay a hand on the Patriarch now were to offend the people," he objected. "Have you forgotten, Augusta, how his ill treatment at my brother's hands roused them against John? Nay, let him go free, but watch him; and do not trust his counsel. Yet I fear he may have got some word to Georgios before my suspicions were roused. Let me, then, recruit the new troops, lest Georgios come before they are ready to meet him."

"Do as you think best," Zoe agreed.

Not till the Bythinians were encamped without the walls did Constantine deal his next stroke. None told the empress, for none but Constantine knew that the new themes were not Bythinian, but Paphlagonians from Constantine's own province. Their officers kept close tongues, and the troops in their camp were out of contact with the people. They moved through their drill with the awkwardness of recruits; but a skilled eye might have seen that the awkwardness was artificial.

Then John came. The first word of him was a messenger on a blown horse; and him the Varangians on guard admitted directly to the empress.

"The host returns!" the messenger panted.

"And John?" demanded Zoe.

"He commands them."

"He? But the emperor?"

"The Divine Augustus died of a sudden fever, a fortnight after his troops had stormed Edessa."

Zoe closed her eyes, recalling the days when the stricken Michael had been dear to her. A little pain touched her heart, as she thought of his beauty and his strong youth. He had been a mighty soldier, and he had loved her. That was before John had seduced him to murder, and so brought on him the awful remorse that wasted his strength and paved the way for his long sickness. He had turned from her then, thinking his epilepsy a judgment from God.

"How—how near is John?" she faltered.

"A day's march, Augusta."

Signing to an attendant eunuch, she sent for Constantine, and made the messenger repeat his news. Constantine started back, and seemed much disturbed. Nothing in his manner betrayed that he had already heard the news.

"We must admit the Bythinians, Augusta," he said. "And since you, though wiser and mightier than any other monarch, are yet a woman, it were well to appoint a man to command them."

"The Prefect Aldhelm—" she began; but Constantine was now bold enough to interrupt her.

"The Bythinians would not obey him."

ZOE HESITATED; BUT her fear of John overpowered her. "Then, do you take command, Constantine."

"For your sake, Augusta, I will. But with what title?"

In her need Zoe yielded the point. Only one office justified the assumption of military command within the city by a minister.

"With the title of Grand Strategos, and Protector of the Realm."

Constantine was satisfied; nor could she have done less if he were to have authority over Varangians as well as over the pretended Bythinians. Bowing to the pavement, he went out to order the gates opened.

Zoe relaxed helplessly on the throne, a prey to dire misgivings.

John's vanguard approached the Kaligaria Gate at noon of the next day: John himself riding in a litter, just behind the black-draped wagon bearing the embalmed body of the dead emperor. As was usual, the returned troops were challenged from the wall. On John's formally announcing himself, and the death of Michael, the gates swung open to admit him into the fields between the inner and outer walls.

But once he had entered, with the funeral wagon and his chief officers, the gate was immediately closed in the faces of his advancing column. The outer wall erupted armed men, bows drawn to the head; catapults and creaking ballistae thrust out their lean arms; cranes poised with tilted caldrons of molten lead; fire tubes thrust their smoky mouths toward the astonished army.

"What means this?" John asked calmly, though he perceived at once that there had been some sort of revolution.

Constantine advanced to meet him, clad in the scarlet cloak and embossed armor of a Strategos; and at sight of him John smiled a sour smile.

"I see," he observed quietly. "I am under arrest?"

"You are condemned to death for treason!" his brother declared pompously. "Away with him, guards! Ho, there! Hold the wall!"

A pair of burly Paphlagonians laid hands on the deposed tyrant; but ere they could lead him away, Aldhelm, the Englishman, strode forward.

"I ask a gift, Lord Protector," he said to Constantine; and his blazing eyes traveled to the Eunuch's face. "It is deserved, for we Varangians have served you well. Give us this John! He has betrayed our Prefect to death: let us punish him!"

The Varangians on the fighting platforms raised their voices in a howl of approval. Constantine hesitated; but the grim look on Aldhelm's face convinced him that John would never escape Varangian vengeance. He knew, too, that not even his hatred could devise a punishment more cruel than the Northmen would inflict. Therefore he delivered his brother into the hands of the Varangians!

19

THE NEW TYRANT

AS THE VARANGIANS led John away, Constantine beckoned imperiously to his brother's staff officers, who stood irresolute, penned in between the gate and the massed ranks of Paphlagonians.

"Which do ye prefer," he asked haughtily, "life or crucifixion?"

The officers paled, and stammered out a prayer for mercy.

"Mercy ye shall have, if ye do as I bid," the Grand Strategos promised. "Ye see that we are well-nigh as strong as you in men, stronger far in siege engines and fortifications. Lead back your troops to their provinces, otherwise ye shall be beaten and crucified."

He paused, giving the dismayed Strategoi time to consider the situation. They glanced at one another, nodding confirmation of his words, and conferred in short, low-pitched sentences. They could neither starve out nor storm this garrisoned city. There was nothing to do but acquiesce.

"We obey," said the senior Strategos at last. "Yet, in consideration of our services to the empire—for we have taken Edessa—give us money to pay our troops."

"It shall be done," Constantine agreed. "Now go, and wait without the wall."

Constantine, on a splendid African charger, led his Paphlagonians in a triumphal march to the Forum of the ancient Emperor his namesake; and there, surrounded by the excited people, he announced that the army which had redeemed Edessa was on its way to its home stations.

The cheers of the citizens changed to lamentation as the black catafalque bearing the dead Emperor's body paraded behind the garrison. Gravely smiling, greeted with applause, Constantine made his horse caracole over the flower-strewn streets toward the palace, acknowledging the homage of the folk like a Caesar.

FAR DIFFERENT WAS John's welcome. With hands behind his back, escorted by a thousand mailed Varangians, the deposed dictator was led to the prefecture of police. Seeing in him only the oppressor of their Empress, the townsfolk greeted him with catcalls and yells of derision. Stones and refuse pelted him; but as the foremost Varangians were hit as often as their captive, Aldhelm ordered a company forward to clear the way.

John had held up well, marching steadily, his face pale and drawn, but his great eyes glowing. But when he was brought into the court that served as Aldhelm's offices, fatigue and fear mastered him. He would have fallen had not the Prefect ordered a bench brought for him, unbound his hands, and given him wine. Then, every exit guarded, Aldhelm himself confronting him, the Eunuch was brought to trial.

He waited for no indictment. "What have I done to you," he cried, every vestige of his self-control vanished, "that I should be made a prisoner? Ere I left the city, ye obeyed my orders; why should ye now join with the traitor Constantine against me? By St. Justin, if I regain power—"

"That you are not likely to do," Aldhelm interrupted, grim with hate. "As for what we have against you, read this!" He cast before the prisoner the death order brought him by Constantine on the day of the rebellion.

John read, noting with widened eyes his own signature at the end, which authorized Georgios to slay, or have slain, the Grand Heteriarch Harald at the first opportunity. He straightened, regaining a shade of his former calmness.

"This is no deed of mine," he declared contemptuously. "It is a forgery."

Aldhelm smiled a thin-lipped smile. "I expected no other answer. No man confesses his crime while there is hope of escape. Know you how we Northmen avenge a slain lord?"

John's only answer was to stare at Aldhelm as at a well-meaning but bungling subordinate.

"They lay the murderer on a stone slab," Aldhelm went on, slowing his speech for emphasis, "and cut the bloody eagle on his back, severing ribs from spine. It is long ere the knife finds the heart, and so puts an end to the unbearable pain. To the Norwegians among us shall this be intrusted, that it be done slowly and well."

JOHN'S LIPS SET, but he gave no other sign of fear.

"I can prove that writing false," he answered. "There are those in the palace who know my signature. The seal is mine, but that is easily stolen. He who could enter my chamber at will, and put poison in my wine—" His speech trailed off.

"Who is that?" Aldhelm asked.

"My brother Constantine, whose orders ye obey."

Aldhelm's forehead wrinkled with the effort to think straight and fast. The soldiers on guard stood like statues, seeming lifeless save for their eyes, which shifted from Aldhelm to John and back again.

"What you say is doubtless false," Aldhelm decided. "But I will give you a fair chance to prove it. Who of those in the palace would most surely know your hand?"

"Any of the eunuchs," John replied, "but Zodatas, who guarded the Empress's apartments, received my written orders oftenest. Yet if he is still there, Constantine will scarce let him come."

"Ulfgar!" Aldhelm called to one of his officers. "Take two men, and bring the eunuch Zodatas from the palace. If ye find him not, ask the Grand Strategos to place him in our hands, that he may give evidence against the Orphano-trophos. Mark well my words: 'that he may give evidence *against* the Orphanotrophos.' Come not back without him."

When the men had gone, Aldhelm folded the forged order so that the signature alone was visible, and laid it on his desk. Then, taking from his cabinet a second parchment, the lower half of which was blank, he folded it similarly. It was old, and so no whiter than the order.

"Write your name here, even as it appears on the order," he commanded. John, taking a pen from the desk, obeyed.

Aldhelm passed the still wet parchment to a soldier. "Lay that close to a fire, that the ink may be dried and a little faded. Now bring the prisoner food, lest he grow faint."

It was close to midnight before Ulfgar returned, bringing with him a sleek eunuch, terrified almost to palsy. When he found himself confronted with John, Zodatas cringed and gabbled excitedly, praying for mercy.

"No harm shall come to you," Aldhelm assured him. "I ask of you but a small service, which shall be rewarded with gold." He passed over the two sheets of parchment, each showing nothing but John's signature.

"Are both true?" he asked. "Scan them well, and be sure of your answer. Nay, turn your back to the prisoner." For Zodatas had turned his head slightly, to catch some sign from his former master. But John himself had turned aside, confident of the outcome.

Zodatas, his hands still trembling, took the sheets. Aldhelm towered over him, ready to snatch them from him if he unfolded either. For only a moment the eunuch studied them; then, glancing up with an access of confidence, he said firmly:

"The thing is easy. Both look like the hand of the Orphanotrophos, but this in my left hand is forged. Both read 'Joannes,' not 'Johannes,' as others sign the name. Therefore he who forged this knew my master's ways, and so must have been familiar with the palace.

"But the curves here are faint on the downstroke, whereas my master's hand was the same on both strokes. More: my master being always free with wine—" He paused, and shot a frightened glance at John, but the prisoner showed no offense. "My master's hand was not so steady as this. This is clearly false."

Opening the parchment Zodatas had declared forged, Aldhelm saw that it was Harald's death order. He tossed a bag of gold to Zodatas, and bade Ulfgar see him safely back to the palace.

JOHN, CLEARED OF the chief charge against him, smiled with relief. "I am now free?" he asked. "I am under your protection?"

"Not so," Aldhelm replied. "You are but proved innocent of outright treachery. I am not yet sure you have played fair with my master. You shall remain under guard till the Sicilian troops return. Then, if Harald is safe, he will deal with you as he thinks fit; otherwise you will die as I have said."

All John's composure fell from him, leaving him shaken and pitiful.

"But my brother will have me crucified, or blinded, if I fall into his hands! Let me go, that I may flee; or take me under your protection!"

The grim Englishman felt a contemptuous pity for the strong man thus broken.

"He shall not touch you," he promised. "You will lie safe in a guarded chamber here; and there are no troops in the city that will dare face Varangian steel to take you hence. Moreover, for your comfort and my greater certainty, I will so deal that Constantine shall think you already dead. Asgrim!"

An underofficer strode to the desk.

"Go to the palace, and report to the Grand Strategos that the prisoner has been put to death. If he asks how, say that he was cut in pieces, slowly, and his limbs and head fed to the dogs of the street."

John's eyes lighted. "I thank you, Prefect," he said. "Now I must ask you one thing more, a thing you will admit should be granted. Let me send a message to Harald, telling him of the Emperor's death."

Aldhelm looked up, instantly suspicious. "Why that?" he asked. "Suppose Harald is already slain, the message then will fall into the hands of Georgios."

John smiled bleakly. "In which case, Georgios would at once sail for Constantinople, to make himself Emperor. He would deal harshly with Constantine."

Aldhelm shook his head. "You would make of me a tool for your vengeance on your brother. I will not do it. But this I will do: I will let you write a letter, at my dictation, addressed to Harald.

"It shall be borne to Sicily by a Varangian, with orders to deliver it to Harald if he lives; and, if he is dead—" Aldhelm's fist clenched—"it shall be given to one of his Norwegian officers. Thus the matter shall be kept between Varangians, whom I can trust. I will myself see that the message goes by a swift ship."

ASGRIM SAUNTERED THROUGH the brazen gate of the Chalke, wiping from his beard the wine with which his comrades still on duty there had regaled him. They had pumped him also, and knew as well as he did how Constantine had received the news of John's death with a crooked smile, saying:

"There will be rewards for those who serve the state so well."

The underofficer was pleased with himself. He had been on state business, and had some hope of his share in the promised rewards.

"Good days," he mumbled, "when the Guard is once more honored in the palace."

He quickened his pace as he emerged into the Augusteion; for it was getting late in the year, and a bleak wind blew from the Black Sea. Passing under the shadow of Santa Sophia, his eye caught a patch of black that stirred slightly against the lighter stone of the cathedral wall. In a spirit of mischief born of the wine, he leaped forward and pounced on the moving patch. Something gasped and writhed under his hands.

He drew it closer to him, and bore it, struggling fiercely, to a narrow aperture farther along the wall, where a square of light came from the study of some priest. It was a monk he had captured, face wrapped in the hood of a long, black gown.

Quickly Asgrim's merry mood slipped from him. It was an ill matter to jest with the Church.

"Forgive me, father!" he implored. "I have drunk much."

The hooded figure suddenly flung itself upon him, clasping him with arms too soft for a man's.

"Save me, Northman!" she begged. "Death waits for me!"

"A maid!" the Varangian exclaimed. "In a monk's cowl! Nay, this passes belief. Who art thou, sweetheart?"

Immediately the woman loosed her hold on him, and gathered her hood closer about her face.

"I am Maria, lady-in-waiting to the Empress," she whispered, her voice hardly audible. "The Empress has been seized. Take me to the Varangian Prefect, ere the Paphlagonians find me!"

"Why—what—" Asgrim stammered, but she cut him off.

"Be swift!" she cried. "The city is full of soldiers hunting me, to drag me to death. To your master, quickly!"

Some promptings of chivalry rose in the Northman's breast, confused by wine, but genuine. He reached for his ax.

"None shall harm thee under my care!" he boasted; and, tucking the girl's arm under his left elbow, he strode off through the gardens.

So swiftly that the girl could scarce keep pace with his long strides, he made his way down the long Mese to the Prefecture. Here and there soldiers passed them; but for every Paphlagonian there was a Varangian on duty, and none interfered. Only here and there a Northman called a greeting, or joked Asgrim for flocking with monks.

When they climbed the long marble stair to the brightly lighted Prefecture the girl reeled against the doorway, exhausted. Lightly Asgrim picked her up, and carried her straight to Aldhelm's quarters. Setting her down there, he kept one arm about her while he beat furiously on the prefect's door.

Aldhelm opened almost at once, sleepy-eyed, wrapped in his cloak.

"What now?" he asked inhospitably.

"A monk—nay, a woman garbed like a monk," Asgrim answered. The brisk walk and the excitement had driven the wine from his legs, but set it mounting higher in his head. "She says the empress is slain."

WITH A STARTLED exclamation, Aldhelm withdrew into his chamber, whence he shortly reappeared, clad in full mail, and with the cloak of his rank about him.

"Enter!" he commanded. "Hold the door, Asgrim! Let none enter. Now, girl, speak out."

Maria spoke, her voice dragging with fatigue, but sustained by her courage.

"Constantine came back to the palace and announced the capture of John," she said, beginning in the midst of things like one with no time to waste. "The empress poured out her joy, bidding him ask any reward he would. He begged her, seeing she was childless, to make him her heir; and she—having no idea of keeping the promise— consented. Straightway he received confirmation, under her seal, of his new rank, but he asked her to keep it secret for a time.

"Soon after, soldiers were admitted to the palace by the Watergate, lest the Varangians in the Chalke forbid their entrance. These men were Constantine's troops. They broke into the empress's apartments, seized her, and carried her away. I hid in a closet, and while they ranged through the gardens seeking me, I crept to a secret passage which leads to the Patriarch's palace. Even as I closed the entrance behind me I heard the shrieks of the other maids and the eunuchs, all of whom, by this time, are dead or in prison.

"Constantine's men must have discovered the tunnel, for they rushed after us into the Patriarch's palace. I fled, but the Patriarch was caught and borne away by the soldiers. I reached Santa Sophia, thinking to take sanctuary there, but there were soldiers in the porch. So I hid in the shadow of the wall, praying they might not find me. Then that man," she pointed toward Asgrim, "found me and brought me hither."

"And none knows what Constantine has done with the empress," Aldhelm said to himself, half in despair. "He would hardly dare kill her, though, as the girl says, he will doubtless spare none of her attendants. It is plain—he means to make himself emperor."

Maria laid her white hand on his shoulder. "You are right, Prefect. He will not dare slay Zoe outright, nor let any know she is not still safe in the palace. He will certainly have her carried to some nunnery and imprisoned there. When he has gathered enough power he will announce that the empress has taken the veil of her own free will, leaving him as her successor. Then, when the people have forgotten, she will grow ill, of slow poison, and die. That is how things are done in this realm."

Her tired eyes glittered, her breast heaved. Aldhelm tried to calm her, but she grew half hysterical. At last he seized her arm and spun her about, commanding:

"Peace! Gather thy wits, and tell me what nunnery he is most apt to place her in."

The girl calmed at once and twisted from his grasp, a little indignantly. "There is but one nunnery that would be safe," she replied. "The great cloister on Prinkipo, in the Sea of Marmora."

"Prinkipo Island," Aldhelm reflected. "It is but an hour's sail from the city. Constantine may have had a galley waiting at the Watergate."

"What will you do?" Maria demanded. "You must send ships there, at once, to bring her back! You must storm the palace, and bring the traitor to justice!"

Aldhelm shook his head. "Peace, child, not so fast. Constantine will have provided against both measures. Knowing you have escaped, he will patrol the coast and place all ships under guard. To force a fight now would plunge the city in bloodshed; and we might lose. If we got to Prinkipo, we might not find Zoe there.

"We must wait till we know more. Then, this is in part Harald's affair, since Constantine has plotted against him. Best to wait till his return, or till we have news of him. You will lodge in the prefecture, maiden. A guard will keep your door against all danger. Find her a chamber, Asgrim, and her safety on your head!"

20

THE WOLF BREAKS HIS BONDS

THE MOSLEMS OF Syracuse kept their houses, behind barred and muffled windows. The garrison had been rounded up, disarmed, and herded under strong guard in Casr, the Arab citadel, which once had been a temple to Minerva. Every nook and cranny in the city, already searched thrice over for loot, was ransacked for fugitives from the beaten host.

Late on the second day there rose from the very ground the strangest procession that Greeks or Northmen had ever seen. In the very faces of the troops that patrolled the suburbs, Achradina, Neapolis, and even the ridges of Epipolae where the Immortals had encamped, yawned great gulfs, curtained over by trees and bush-growths rooted in their rocky lips; and these the invading Christians had ignored, after reconnoitering their edges, thinking them groves and overgrown old gardens.

But now erupted from them hordes of ragged, emaciated folk, the men bearded to the waist, the women bent and broken things, the children almost skeletons. All were filthy, half naked, and white with an unearthly pallor.

The astounded troops at first raised the alarm, and drew together in ranks and companies. But as the weird host grew and advanced, it broke into song: shrill, feeble from individual lips, but overpowering in the mass of joyful voices. And the words were Greek—the words of the Christian litany, "Kyrie Eleison!"

Shambling forward with halting, eager steps, their limbs scarce holding them up, their heads bravely lifted, they held out their arms in thanksgiving for deliverance. And the soldiers, astounded, half afraid of these gray apparitions, stared.

As fast as the singing groups drew close to the soldiers, men, women, and children fell to their knees, still singing; and when the litany was done they still knelt, their lips moving in prayer. From somewhere came a voice, trembling, but still powerful:

"We thank Thee, O Lord, Who hast preserved us in our adversity, that we might see the day of blessed redemption. Pour Thy blessings on these Thy soldiers, who have set Thy people free!"

Down from the Casr rode a knot of Greek and Norse officers, on captured chargers. Dismounting before the kneeling horde, they poured out a flood of questions.

He who had prayed, a lean old bishop, clad in ragged, earth-fouled remnants of cassock and stole—and these of an age long past—made answer:

"We are the Christians of Syracuse, the few thousands spared by the Moslem sword, by sickness and hunger. For generations more than we know, we have lurked in the ancient quarries, emerging only by night to plunder the fields for seed corn and fowls, that we might plant and raise a meager fare. Thousands have died, but we remain, a faithful flock; and above us God caused His trees to grow, that we might be hidden. Praise to Him, who hath let us see this day of joy!"

To the credulous soldiers it was a miracle; therefore they doubted not that other miracles also might have been visited on these poor shreds of the once mighty Christian population.

"Art thou," an officer asked the aged spokesman, "art thou he who was bishop of this city when the Moors first came?" His voice was choked with awe. The old man looked down at the ruins of his outmodeled episcopal attire, and smiled.

"Not so, my son; that was more years ago than thrice my age could number. He who was then bishop fled with such of his folk as escaped the massacre, taking refuge by night in these well-hidden quarries. By him was my grandfather exalted as successor; my father by my grandsire, I by my father. And I ordained others as priests under me."

The soldiers broke into cries of wonder and praise. Then and there, while messengers rode to the walls to call forth all the host save those on watch, the ancient bishop made his rude preparations for a solemn mass of thanksgiving. The troops, Greek and Northman alike, gathered together to partake in the service.

WHEN THAT WAS done, they had time for their quarrels once more.

Trouble began over the loot, which Harald had ordered removed to the Varangian ships. Having won the city almost solely by the valor of his own Northmen, after Georgios had tried to contrive his death, he continued to insist that the plunder should go to them who had earned it.

The Greeks grumblingly assented, demanding as their own the booty of the next great city captured. For this reason Georgios gave orders that they should march on Palermo as soon as they could gather fresh supplies and ship the prisoners to the slave markets of Constantinople, where they would be sold by the State and the price received banked in the name of the two Christian corps that had captured them.

"Do you fight for plunder, or for the empire and the faith?" Harald taunted him.

" 'Twas you who looted first," Georgios retorted.

"Aye; treasure, not men."

"What would you do then, who are so wise?" Georgios jeered.

"Bide here with ten thousand men, sending the rest with the fleet to harry the coasts. Burn every shore town and destroy its fortifications. Meantime we have the material for fresh troops in the rescued Christians."

"Famished, enfeebled wretches, scarce able to scare the birds!"

"They will grow strong with food, and we can drill them," Harald clung to his point. "And others are coming in: sturdy country folk, whom the Moslems forced to work as slaves on their villas. By the week's end there will be thousands of them."

"They are not worth their keep!" Georgios asserted scornfully.

"They bring their keep. Have not those who have come in already risen against their masters at the first news of our success? Have they not brought in loads of grain and droves of cattle? They will be glad to bear arms against their oppressors. When we have enough, we can leave them here with arms and a stiffening of our own troops, and then advance, leaving everywhere behind us garrisons of liberated men."

Georgios rose, his black brows meeting over angry eyes.

"It is easy to talk so when your ships are heavy with loot. My men have no loot, and are ill content. If I do not lead them soon to booty there will be no holding them."

Harald settled back in his chair, and looked out between the columns of the Casr, down on the gutted city.

"You are mad," he said with infuriating calmness. "You dare not march without me, and I choose to bide here."

Georgios brought his hairy fist crashing on the table.

"It is time you and I came to a settlement!" he bellowed. "Are we not on shore? And do I not command on land?"

"You did," Harald replied, "till you sought to betray me to the enemy. Now, he commands who is the better man. If you wish to settle the matter, I am ready."

Georgios glared, but had no answer.

HARALD HAD SAID rightly that the Greeks dared not march inland alone; and while Harald commanded the fleet, they could not advance on Palermo by sea.

Some ships there were which never left the port: those which Harald had stripped of their Greek crews, filled with Northmen, and laden with the plunder his men had taken. These, their fire-tubes trained and ready, were prepared for any attempt Georgios might make to take for himself the rich booty of his rival. The Greek commander seemed to pay no heed to them; but Harald knew he coveted their precious freight, which would go far to satisfy the greed of his Immortals. But no Greek cared to try conclusions with the Varangian axes.

Six weeks passed, and Georgios fretted till he could bear no more. He stalked into Harald's quarters with a dozen officers at his back.

"The fleet has returned, and we can march," he began resolutely. "My men threaten revolt if they are not led against Palermo."

"Revolt?" Harald smiled. "It will gain them little. They cannot force me to do what I will not; nor can they conquer Palermo without my aid."

Georgios turned purple; his great teeth gnawed at his lips.

"Yet," Harald resumed quietly, "I am minded to satisfy them. The peasants are well enough trained to hold stout walls, with a few of our engineers to man the catapults for them. Bid your fellows break camp."

The Greek officers were much relieved; but Georgios withdrew with swelling chest and fiery eye. He understood that Harald, while apparently, yielding, had played with him. Harald had given him an order, and he must obey, or face the anger of his men. He had tried, many times, to assert his superiority over Harald, knowing that in such an army there must be but one commander. Now Harald had made himself that commander.

"Did your men break camp?" Georgios fumed with rage; but there was nothing he could do. His men were indeed on the verge of mutiny.

Harald summoned Ulf Uspaksson.

"We break up when Georgios is ready," he said. "Bid

Eilif bring the ships as close in as he can, and send the boats for supplies."

Ulf grinned. "Time enough for that, Harald. I have been on the sea wall, and have seen that which may need looking to first."

"And that?"

"A Greek ship has entered the port," Ulf explained. "Eilif went aboard her to learn her business, and has but now come off with her captain, and a Varangian from the city."

Eilif entered while Ulf spoke. With him were a tall Varangian and a Greek, both in rusty mail and brine-encrusted cloaks. The captain was a little man, very self-important; and for all the ravages a hard passage had made on him, he was fresh-shaven.

Harald could not keep back a smile at sight of him; it was the same coxcomb officer who had challenged him so insolently when he first sought to enter Constantinople. The fellow was humble now, and fawned before the man he had once insulted.

The Varangian stepped forward and gave Harald a case of oiled leather, stained with salt water, which had faded but not loosened the seal. Opening it, Harald drew out a parchment, which he passed to Eilif.

"You read Greek," he said.

The Gautlander studied the manuscript laboriously, and uttered a cry of astonishment. Catching the interested eye of the Greek captain, Stephanos, he said to Harald:

"It were well that I turn this into Norse." And in Norwegian he read, slowly, to be sure of his translation:

" 'The Emperor is dead. Signed, John, no longer Orphanotrophos.'"

But this time Harald was ready

The three Northmen stared at each other.

"No longer—" Harald echoed.

"The Emperor dead!" Ulf repeated.

"Let us question this fellow," Harald suggested.

"Wait!" Eilif broke in. "There is more: in Norse, and signed by Aldhelm."

The officer pricked up his ears at the name Aldhelm; John's name he had not taken in, for Eilif had rendered it by the Norse *Jon,* not by the Greek *Joannes.* Eilif handed the letter back to Harald, saying:

"Aye, Norse, though such as an Englishman might write. And in runes, by the ghost of Odin!"

"Wise man, that Englishman," Ulf grinned. "Well, he knew that things best hidden from Greek eyes are written in letters Greeks cannot read."

Harald nodded shortly, the while he read eagerly. Both Greek and Latin script were mysteries to him; but every

Northman of good blood knew runes. When he had finished:

"Take these men away," he ordered Ulf. "Give them food and gold; then give the Greek in close charge and come back."

WHEN ULF RETURNED alone, Harald held up the parchment.

"This is Aldhelm's word," he said, and read: " 'Giorgios has an order, signed with John's name, to cause your death. John has proved that Constantine forged that order. Constantine now rules the city; John, who swears he has kept faith with you, waits your pleasure in one of my cells. If this finds you alive, look to it!' "

Harald's eyes roved out over the city and the water, as if seeking a solution of the riddle.

"I call to mind," he said softly, "that just before we sailed, I saw Constantine in close talk with Georgios, by the quay. It was then the order was given; and under a false signature, that John might bear my anger if the trick failed."

"Also that Georgios might have guarantees for his own safety if John accused him of your murder," Ulf hazarded. "But Constantine may have acted on John's command; the Eunuch has thriven on treachery; why should he not prove false to you?"

Harald disagreed. "In that case John would have signed the order himself; and Aldhelm writes he has proved the act Constantine's. Constantine, then, is my foe, not John; and Constantine rules Mikligard."

All at once his face set like granite. "If Constantine, and not John, wished my death," his drawn lips scarce formed the words, "then it was Constantine who—"His voice died; he was thinking of the severed hands of Cyra.

Ulf looked at Eilif, and Eilif at Ulf, neither caring to speak. For a time Harald sat silent, seeming not to see them. Then, with a gesture as if to clear mists from his eyes, he rose.

"The Emperor is dead! And Georgios wishes to be Emperor. I have heard John say so. If John spoke truth, we shall know it when Georgios learns of Michael's death. Bring back Stephanos, and the Varangian!"

The Norse messenger and the Greek captain came in under guard, the Greek's little eyes turning every way in suspicious fear. Harald fixed him with a cold gaze.

"How did Constantine rise to power?" he asked.

Stephanos squirmed, reluctant to answer lest he displease somebody, somewhere.

"You have nothing to fear if you tell the truth," Harald assured him. "I will protect you. But if you speak not, or lie— Show him your knife, Ulf."

Ulf drew steel, all too obviously willing. The Greek paled, and stepped back, but two Varangians held him fast.

"Mercy, my lord!" he gasped. "I will tell!" And tell he did.

Harald turned to the Varangian who had brought the letters, and asked:

"Has the Greek spoken truth?"

"In all things," the Varangian answered, likewise in Norse, "save that John is not dead."

"Good. Now go, and hold yourself at my command. Take this Greek windbag away, and see that he gets no chance to speak with Georgios till I command it. Let none of you dare breathe a word of this."

Once more alone with his two officers, Harald asked Eilif:

"How soon can we sail?"

"For Palermo? To-morrow, if Georgios is ready. I have kept my ships provisioned. The crews are still aboard."

"Well done!" Harald approved. "But it depends on Georgios whether we sail for Palermo—or for Mikligard."

"What mean you?" Eilif questioned.

Ulf snorted. "Think you," he asked, "Georgios will waste time on Palermo, when a crown awaits him at home?"

"Not he!" Harald laughed. "Once he hears the throne is empty, save for a woman, he may forget Palermo, and risk all on a bigger stake. If he plans evil against us, we must know it in time to outwit him."

"You have a plan already!" Ulf exclaimed eagerly.

"Aye. To test his treachery, I must give him the means to show it. You, Eilif, will warp out the five treasure ships before sunset, and moor them in the Great Harbor with the rest of the fleet. Then bring ashore and beach the ten slowest pamphylians, and bid the crews make ready to scrape their hulls; but work slowly, so that the careening is not done before dark. At sunset leave them there in charge of their Greek crews. Have all other ships moored well out, with all boats inboard.

"You, Ulf, will go about at dusk among our men ashore, ordering thirty companies to withdraw as swiftly and silently as possible to as many of the swiftest ships. Send wine casks filled with water aboard those thirty galleys, and bid all on board them shout and carouse as if mad drunk—but see to it that they drink nothing. Command the captains, to watch for flares from the shore, and when they see them to put to sea in pursuit of any ships that seek to escape. At the third hour after nightfall I will permit the Greek Stephanos to go to Georgios, and you may be sure Georgios will get the news of Michael's death out of him. Have a boat ready for me at that hour."

Ulf licked his lips. "A good trap for traitors!" he chuckled.

THE WINTER NIGHT fell fast, bringing with it gusts of rain. The wind gathered from the southwest, kicking up choppy waves that the rain tried in vain to flatten. Aboard the fleet few lights shone, save at the outer fringe of the forest of masts, where thirty ships rang with maudlin shouts and drunken howls. The beach was black dark, blackest of all where a few hulls loomed in dim contrast with the white, wave-whipped sand.

In the lee of a heap of stones, the ruin of some ancient wharf, Ulf Uspaksson crouched, hiding something carefully under his heavy cloak. He shivered, chafing at his cold hands, for the wind off the hills was cutting. Suddenly he stiffened, every sense alert.

Above the whish of the wind and the drum of rain, he heard sand crunching under many feet, punctuated thinly by the restrained chink of mail. He could see nothing in the darkness; but the sounds drew closer, louder, between him and the city wall, where a few lights still glimmered like yellow blobs in the wet night. Hugging the stones that had him, Ulf waited, trying to keep his teeth from chattering.

He felt, rather than saw, a crowd of men draw in upon him, perhaps a bowshot away. Their footsteps were clear now, crushing the sand with little grating noises. Officers spoke in muffled tones.

Then came another sound, the hissing grate of keels thrust over sand, followed by splashing of water.

"Quiet, ye dogs!" The voice growled in Greek, and though it was hushed, Ulf recognized it.

"Georgios!" he chuckled softly to the wind, and tugged at the bundle under his arm.

One after another, the ten beached ships were run out, now and then fouling in the dark with a thump of wood on wood that drew stifled curses from Georgios. There came splash on splash as men waded into water they could not see, the rattle of chattering teeth as the cold bit them, the jangle of armor as they swarmed over the sides, climbing by the oarports. The chock of oar against oar, and the drip of raised blades gave warning that the Greeks had taken the bait.

Ulf rose stiffly, his eyes trying to pierce the murk in search of the disappearing ships.

"They must keep close to the seawall to avoid running into the fleet," he muttered. "Trust Georgios to think of that!"

Impatiently he waited, brittle with cold, his ear cocked to catch the dimming noise of the oars, till the rain drowned out all sound but its own pounding.

"Now!" Ulf breathed. Opening his packet, he struck flint on steel. His fingers were so numb that he tried thrice before his first flare caught. It sputtered in the rain, spat, and burst into a stream of light. A second, and a third, flung their streamers across the dark.

Then, as if in answer, the carousing aboard the thirty pamphylians ended in one wild yell; while from the city wall great fires, fed with naphtha till they became pillars of flame, threw the whole north end of the harbor into bright relief. Three thousand oars bit the water as one; the steady beat of drums and the grunt of the laboring oarsmen thrummed in diapason to the yells of excited men.

His eyes straining out over the illuminated water, Ulf saw ten lean shapes silhouetted by the flare from the walls. With shouts of alarm, their crews sheered out to find cover in the darkness beyond; and as they did so, other shapes, dimmer, shot from the dark and took form to south and east of them.

"Caught!" Ulf danced to keep warm, laughing and hugging himself.

GEORGIOS WAS INDEED caught, and knew it as soon as the fires soared from the city wall. He had need to hug that wall as close as he dared, till he passed Ortygia; for he was in no mind to bump his ten stolen ships into the main fleet. The thirty carousing Norse crews lay well to the south of him; but he had less fear of them than of the more silent companies that slept, sober, aboard the other ships.

But as soon as the roaring fires brought his ships into sharp relief against the restless waves, he turned perforce, fearing showers of stones from the battlements, and seeking the cover of the darkness.

His only hope of escape lay in putting behind him that broad band of water irradiated by the leaping flames, and nosing, under cover of the dark, between its edge and the northward end of the anchored fleet. He dared not raise a single sail, lest the violent rain squalls drive him against the cliffs under the walls; he could trust only his oars; and he dared neither light his lamps that his rowers might see, nor have the drums beat to give them time, for fear he betray his position. Accordingly the oars lashed the water in a frenzy of mistimed strokes, blade clashing with blade, losing speed and giving the helmsmen a bitter struggle.

But other drums could beat: drums aboard those lighted ships, from which no longer came drunken shouts, but the steady, even chock of oars dipping in perfect rhythm. A long, lean prow shot athwart him; another, and another. Here and there the flames on the wall mounted, revealing a white rag of sail to the east. Some of the thirty had set their lateens, to run before the wind, get well ahead of him, put about, and turn him back!

It was all over; but Georgios, having put all to the hazard, was not minded to give in. Lights gleamed to starboard, lights ahead; to port and astern were the cliff-lined walls, and the flares that reached out to expose him. If he could make speed, ram or drive between those who blocked his way, he might yet win free.

The fires rose higher, their tongues of light pursuing him. A shout across the water, savage yells, and the clang of arms!

"Heave to!" cried a voice; and Georgios cursed in frenzy. "Row!" he bellowed.

But his oarsmen, walled-in, defenseless below decks, dropped their oars and ducked beneath the benches. One after another his ships lost way, drifting, tossing in the choppy waves. His fighting men gathered on the fore-and-aft bridges, ready to sell their lives dearly for him; but the rowers, whom battle always caught in a red shambles, would not stick it out.

A sudden shock almost threw Georgios from his feet. The crash of wooden beaks on plank told him that the pursuers were driving into his ships one after another. The loom of prows overhung him. The whistle of arrows beat through his rigging.

"You are surrounded!" boomed a voice from the dark. "Throw down your arms, or die!"

HE GAVE NO answer, but clutched his sword hilt. He could die. But the thrumming drums, slower now, yet steady, and the reel of his decks, gave proof that the nosing prows were pushing his little fleet on, toward the flame-lit city wall. He would be held there, imprisoned by thrice his weight of hulls, till he was crushed against the rocks.

His men understood, too, and their courage melted. They knew they could not board their more numerous foes, knew they must die either against a wall of spears or a cruder wall of storm-lashed rocks. They pressed about him, begging him to yield, to save them.

He had drifted in now, under the glare of the fires, which shone full on the gleaming helms and spear-points of his foes. Every ship of his was menaced by them, across his bows, to starboard, and astern. Rail grated against rail; and the Varangian bulwarks were packed with grinning faces and thirsty ax blades.

Georgios hurled his sword to the deck, and his men, only too willing, followed his example.

Then the Varangian decks vomited men. Over every beaten ship they poured, surrounding, overpowering the dejected Immortals. Caught in the press, Georgios was flung from his feet, overborne by a living torrent, bound hand and foot.

He wondered dully why the ships did not crash against the cliffs; and only when lifted to his feet did he see that the conquering Northmen had thrust out the captured galleys as well as their own, and were forcing their crews to pull back inshore. He was beaten, as he had been beaten at every turn, by the cursed barbarians.

Ungentle hands thrust him under a newly kindled deck lantern. He looked up, to find himself eye to eye with Harald.

"You will not be Emperor this year, Greek," Harald said.

Georgios gritted his teeth. "What will you do with me?" he demanded.

Harald stood with feet apart, braced against the roll of the ship.

"Take you in chains to the city," he answered, "as I promised John."

Georgios cursed and tore at his bonds till the breath went from him.

"And my men?" he finally found grace to ask.

"I shall do with all of them what you meant to do with all save the thousand you put aboard stolen ships: leave them in Sicily, to fight the Moslem."

Georgios felt the shame of it. He had fallen full into a trap, cunningly laid for him; and it was bitter to know it.

"You dared not take all your host," Harald went on mercilessly, "and you did not hesitate to leave the rest to face my anger when I should wake to find you gone. Fear not for them: I shall leave all my Varangians save my own house-carles, to protect your Immortals from the Saracens! Likewise I shall leave all but a few ships of the fleet, lest good soldiers be caught in a hostile land without means of retreat. My men will see to it that yours depart not till they have made a good fight for the faith."

Georgios gnawed his lips, thinking of what might be in store for him at Constantinople. Stephanos, in the hands of two Varangians, came into his sight. A faint hope lighted Georgios's dark face.

"But John, who ordered me seized, is dead!" he exclaimed.

"So Stephanos told you, knowing no better," Harald answered. "John lives!"

21

RETURN

IN THE TEETH of the rising gale Georgios was transferred to one of the treasure ships, and his men held on board the captured galleys till the wind should allow them to be landed in safety. Then, leaving the crews that had taken part in the surprise with instructions for the fleet, Harald warped out his five treasure-laden ships and Stephanos's galley to the open bay, and with reefed sails ran before the wind.

Day followed day, the breeze always brisk, but not always following; so that the crews must fall to the oars and pull their gold-laden keels eastward. Scarce a sail they saw, for both Greeks and Moslems find even Mediterranean winters too chill for hot blood. On the sixth day they left Crete behind and entered the waters made safe by the power of Constantinople. Three days more of tracking through the dotted Grecian isles brought them to the Sea of Marmora.

At San Stephano they beached keels, and held a ship council.

"We bide here till night," Harald declared. "I have no mind to show myself to Constantine's patrols. Under cover of the dark we shall slip by them."

"And be caught, as we caught Georgios," Halldor objected.

"If so, we shall put up a better fight," Ulf retorted grimly. "We have fire-tubes of our own. But," he conceded, "when we put in at the imperial port, we shall be taken like rats in a burning shed."

"That we shall not," Harald answered with conviction. "We shall creep through the Bosporus, and so into the Golden Horn, making port in the Zeugma Harbor, where those on guard are Varangians. Moreover, we shall put a score of house-carles aboard Stephanos's cutter, and send her on ahead. If we are challenged, Stephanos shall answer for us. They will not question him."

"Harald is no fool, you Iceland lads," Eilif reproved them. "If aught goes amiss, he will give you good fighting; but there will be no blood spilled for lack of a well-laid plan. Give the oarsmen wine, Harald, that they may row well for you to-night."

ALDHELM STARTED FROM sleep, to find the tousled head of Ulfgar bending over him.

"What now?" he growled drowsily.

"Enough, Prefect. Harald Sigurdsson has landed."

Aldhelm leaped up. "Where? When?" he demanded, wide awake. "In the city?"

"Almost," Ulfgar replied. "One of the port watch rode in from Zeugma Harbor with word of his coming. He stole through the patrols like an owl in the dark—a swift shadow, and gone—and had his six ships under the wall almost before our lads there could challenge."

Aldhelm was dressing as fast as he could make his fingers move.

"What force has he?"

"His house-carles, what the wars have left of them. Something under four hundred."

"They have had good fighting then. But how did they get free of Georgios?"

Ulfgar laughed silently, showing all his teeth. "They brought him along, trussed like a beef for slaughter."

Aldhelm invoked the saints. "A hard man, Harald, by my salvation! But I knew not he was bold enough for that. This is a bad time for him to come, and with so few men. Constantine will have his head before noon to-morrow. I would he had brought greater forces. What does he mean to do?"

Ulfgar grunted. "That is what he means to tell you, doubtless. He has sent for you."

Snatching up his sword, Aldhelm ran for the door. "Fool!" he called, running. "Why could you not say so?"

"Your horse is saddled at the gate," the officer shouted after him. While the rapid pound of his chief's feet still rang on the stairs, Ulfgar was on his way to the guardroom to share his news.

Aldhelm rode pell-mell through the echoing streets, caring not how many waked at the sound of his horse's hoofs. He neither slackened pace nor halted till he clattered under the wide arch that gave on the battlemented Zeugma Port. Here he reined in with a pull that brought his horse back on its haunches, sprang from the saddle, and tossed the reins to a waiting Varangian of the port watch.

A group of men waited him in the shadow of the merlons. Torches shone on their mail and outlined their faces.

The captain of the port hurried forward, but Aldhelm leaped past him and grasped Harald's hand.

"Hail, and welcome, Harald!" he cried. "You, too, Thiodolf—and Eilif, Halldor, and Ulf!"

Each in turn wrung his hand; and not till then did he turn to Helgi, the port captain.

"You have done well, Helgi, to send to me so promptly," he commended.

The officer showed white teeth. "It was Harald's will. He is safe here with us—till morning. After that there will be no hiding so many men."

"Too many to hide, too few to fight," Aldhelm said with distress in his manner. "Where are the two good themes you took to Sicily, Harald?"

"Carrying on the war, I hope," Harald answered. "But we are none too few either, if you are still my friend, Englishman."

Aldhelm's eyes reassured him. "As to that, I have five thousand men who will go to purgatory for you. But there are thrice as many Paphlagonians encamped between the walls."

"Let them stay there. Who guards the palace? Paphlagonians also?"

"Six hundred of them," Aldhelm replied, "and six hundred Varangians. We of the guard put Constantine in power, and he thinks it prudent to keep our friendship; but like all Greeks, he trusts no man fully. Varangians hold the Chalke; Paphlagonians hold the Daphne and the rest of the palace as a guard of honor for him."

"Will the Varangians obey you if you bid them quit the Chalke?"

Aldhelm shook his head. "A Varangian on post obeys only the Emperor and his own grand commander. When men of my police were detached to guard the palace, they passed from my authority."

"**WHAT OF THE** Empress?" Harald asked.

"Shut fast in the convent on Prinkipo by Constantine's orders."

"What?" cried Harald. "The people endure this? The Varangians permit it?"

"The people know it not: Constantine has given out word that she lies sick of a slow fever in the palace, and has made him her heir."

"But you! The Varangians have ever been true to the Crown."

Aldhelm shrugged. "I waited to hear from you. If Georgios had slain you I should have struck; if not, I held it best to wait for your orders. Then there were the Paphlagonians to reckon with."

"Why did Constantine not bring them within the walls?"

"Because he feared to quarter them on the folk, lest they breed trouble; and because I warned him that I, as prefect of police, would not allow the law to be broken without a fight."

"Well done!" Harald approved. "You have saved the lives of good men."

"But I see not what you can do," Aldhelm lamented.

Harald turned to the port captain.

"Fetch the Greek Stephanos," he said.

Stephanos came, under guard. He seemed shrunken, stripped of all dignity, among the tall Norsemen. He turned instinctively to Harald, who opened on him brusquely:

"Constantine has ordered my death. How will it fare with you when he learns you came hither with me?"

The Greek shivered so his lips could not frame speech.

"You hold your commission from John," Harald resumed, "and John is a prisoner in the Prefecture, unknown to Constantine. I can bring him back to power. If I do, it were well for you to be on his side and mine."

Stephanos gazed from one Northman to another with shifty, troubled eyes.

"My life is in your hands," he answered huskily.

"You may save it if you obey me; otherwise you die before morning. You are to hasten to the palace, demand audience with Constantine, and tell him that Georgios, with all his ships, has been sighted off Chios. Aldhelm will go with you, and return here with you, to make sure that you say neither more nor less than I bid you. Aldhelm, is the Bucoleon Port guarded by Varangians?"

"Nay; by fifty Paphlagonians detached from the palace guard. We hold all other ports as well as the walls; but the Bucoleon, where an alarm from the outer coast patrol would be bound to come, is the key to the palace; and the usurper has it garrisoned with men of his own race. Few though they be, they can hold it: their fire-tubes command the channel, and only an insurrection within the city would menace them."

"Then," Harald decided, "Stephanos cannot say he hastened hither from Chios by sea to bring the news. He must say that he lost his ship, was cast ashore, and took horse from Assus, using the imperial post stations to make the more speed.

"You, Aldhelm, will tell Constantine that your men admitted him at the Kaligaria gate, and that you made all speed with him to the palace. We must convince Constantine that Georgios, having heard of Michael's death, means to seize the throne at once. If you convince him not, Stephanos, and if you are not back before dawn, I will have your head!"

Aldhelm vanished, half carrying the Greek with him.

When they were gone Eilif asked: "What means this?"

"What would you do," Harald countered, "if you were Constantine, and heard that one like Georgios was on his way to overthrow you?"

The Swede considered. "If I heard he was off Chios when the messenger who saw him took horse, and if I had three themes outside the city, I would send them at once to the forts commanding the Hellespont, to stop him."

"YOU SEE MY purpose," Harald nodded. "It is to get those troops out of my way."

Eilif chuckled. "When did Harald learn to think like a Greek?" he mocked.

"When a Northman wants a thing, he goes straight to it," Harald answered. "A Greek goes roundabout, thinking it safer. These Greeks have so enmeshed me with intrigue that I have learned to play their game, lest I perish. I but ask myself what I would do if I were a Greek, and then trick them into doing it."

"All very well," Ulf growled, "but what is there for us to do?"

"Much. Two of the swift pamphylians we brought from Sicily Eilif shall keep here, ready for departure. The rest of the loot Helgi shall hold in trust for the Varangians I left in Sicily. You, Thiodolf, take Stephanos's cutter, sail for Prinkipo, and bring back the Empress. There will be none to resist you but nuns, and you should be back within two

hours. Then put the house-carles aboard the two pamphylians and see if you and Eilif can get them off the lighthouse south of the palace as secretly as we came hither."

"If we fall foul of the patrol?" Eilif questioned.

"Then sink it, or go down! But avoid the patrol if you
can. I think the word I have sent Constantine will get rid
of them. And if you keep all armed men below decks, you
will doubtless be taken for part of the patrol yourselves. All
pamphylians look alike."

"Fair orders," returned Eilif, and swung down the wharf.

"You, Halldor and Ulf, bide here with me. Have you
wine, Helgi?"

Within the port blockhouse they sat and drank till a
soldier announced Aldhelm's return. Harald rose at once.

"Well?"

Aldhelm looked happy. "The message was delivered,
and Stephanos is here. Constantine is badly frightened.
Orders have gone to the Paphlagonian themes to march at
once to hold the Hellespont. I have orders to put half my
companies on the walls and keep the rest on police duty."

Mellowed by the wine, the Northmen burst into shouts
of gratified laughter.

"Sit down and drink, Englishman," said Harald hospi-
tably. "Then you shall take Georgios to the Prefecture
and hold him safe there. Place your men as Constantine
commanded: they need not stay there long. In the morning there will be uproar in the city: when you hear it, send
every Varangian under your command to the palace. They
must be there before the mob."

"Mob!" exclaimed Aldhelm.

"Aye. I will see to that. But you are to lead the mob, not

fight it. Helgi here will send out his lads as soon as folk gather in the market places for their morning trade, to spread the report that Constantine has imprisoned the Empress in a nunnery. The folk love her, and will fight for her. They must be told that the Varangians will arm them from the arsenal at the Strategium, and join with them. Halldor, Ulf, and I go now to the palace."

Ulf gasped. "To the palace! You will thrust your head in a noose!"

"Not I," laughed Harald. "Are we not plainly Varangians? Who will think to challenge three of the guard in a city policed by Varangians?"

Ulf pointed to the medallion on Harald's breast. "Hide that then, and your face," he advised.

"So I shall, thou old gray wolf. Come!"

To the palace they sped, Harald setting a sharp pace. The streets were empty, save for an occasional night prowler, till they reached the Forum of Constantine. There they ran full into a marching column of Varangians.

"You take the wrong way!" the officer spoke sternly. "To the walls!"

Harald muffled his face closer in his cloak. "We are held for police duty," he answered, and passed on.

"**CONSTANTINE MOVES SWIFTLY**," he observed to Halldor.

"Aye, when he is frightened. Mayhap too swiftly for us."

"I will have his life," Harald spoke through set teeth, "if I meet him in hell the next instant!"

They had fresh proof of the Greek's energy when they neared the palace, where, from the subprefecture close by, a second troop of police passed, marching at the double. At last the three came to the gate of the Imperial inclosure.

Before the Chalke gates a dozen pikes halted them.

"Stand, Varangians!" a voice challenged. "Your errand?"

"A good one, brothers," Harald answered. "Where is your officer?"

The captain of the guard came forward, still wearing the insignia of the police, but bearing on his breast the double eagle of the Imperial bodyguard.

"Constantine keeps good watch, to hold Varangians here," said Harald.

"He admits none who have not business here. What is yours?"

Harald let the cloak fall from his face, and the officer seized his hand.

"Aldhelm said you were here or I should have thought you a ghost!" he cried.

"I am more alive than Constantine will be by this time to-morrow. By noon the Empress will be free and on her throne again."

"But—"

"She is sick, you would say? Nay; just now one of my ships has gone to bring her hither from the nunnery into which Constantine thrust her. You of the guard have always been faithful to her. Will you be faithful now, or take orders from her oppressor?"

The captain flushed. "He has lied to us, then? He told us she was here, and that we must guard her with our lives against all who sought to harm her. Our duty is to her; only from her and from you, our Grand Heteriarch, can orders come which will bind Varangians."

"Good. Hide us here to-night. When morning comes, I will give you further orders."

"There will be fighting?"

"There will, but not for long. How well is Constantine guarded?"

"Too well for you to come at. He sleeps in the far wing of the palace, the Daphne, with his Paphlagonians about him. Will you order us to take him from among them?" The officer's tone was hopeful.

"Nay, there are ways that will cost less Norse blood. Have you any news of the harbor patrol?"

"The ships? Constantine has sent them to the Hellespont, with orders that every sail in the ports shall follow. What news of Georgios?"

"I am weary," Harald answered, "and there is toil ahead. Georgios is in my hands. Where do we sleep?"

The captain of the guard led them to his own quarters, a well furnished apartment off the guardroom. As the door closed on them, they heard the clank of armor, and knew that the guard was changing.

"Your plans," Ulf growled, "are like a sword of fine steel, ground to sharpest edge, and with a gross flaw below the hilt."

Harald composed himself on his couch. "The flaw?" he inquired.

"When Constantine learns you have roused Varangians and the folk against him, he will slip away by the water gate, the Bucoleon Port. The Paphlagonians in the Daphne will cover his flight, and the Bucoleon is fortified."

"I have prepared against that," Harald answered drowsily.

22

ON TO THE PALACE!

THE DAY DAWNED in a splendor of crimson fire against ragged clouds, and a keen wind from the sea. Cocks crowed from farmyards far outside the walls; the famished dogs of the city streets howled back at the cries of early venders.

"Harald will want us soon now," Ulfgar observed, stamping restlessly along the battlements, to warm his feet.

"At the first sign of turmoil down yonder," Aldhelm replied, staring out over the city. "Constantine suspects nothing; the Paphlagonians he sent from the palace found us on the wall as he had ordered. Curse these Greek dogs for lazy lie-abeds! The sooner they arouse and get the business over, the sooner our men may eat."

Yet the folk were in truth up early, merchants opening their booths with the sun; beggars stretching on church porches and automatically holding out their hands as their eyes opened; citizens walking abroad to make purchases for breakfast; roisterers reeling home from the night's debauch.

The hum of many folk suddenly swelled on the keen air, burst into a clamor, then into a howling. From square to square, wherever the throng was thickest, came shouts and uproar. From his height Aldhelm could see the gatherings thicken. From colonnade and arch they streamed, gaining speed and density; alleys disgorged their rivulets of running forms into the greater channels of the main streets. Down the Mese, from the Forum of Theodosius, rushed a screaming multitude. On the housetops clustered women and children, leaning over to see and hear.

"Look yonder!" Ulfgar's eyes lighted. "The whole city is out!"

A bell began to peal; men yelled at every corner; here and there knives flashed. In the forums, where the press was greatest, a ripple of light above the heads of the throngs marked armor.

"Soldiers speak to them!" Aldhelm observed.

"Varangians!" Ulfgar added. "Helgi's men from the Zeugma Port! They are Harald's wasps. May they sting deep this day!"

"Come!" Aldhelm called, running for the nearest stair, "ere they fill the streets so thick we cannot pass!"

Once down the stair, Aldhelm ordered the advance sounded, and strode off at the head of his men. The Varangians advanced at the double, their column at first filling the street from side to side, brushing from its path the stragglers of the growing mob; but as the press thickened, they were forced to break up and work their way down whatever byways were open.

As each battalion converged on the Mese, it dragged along a disreputable train of excited Greek rabble. A second and vaster mob stretched out before them, radiating from the Forum of Constantine; and as the Varangians shouldered through—none too careful of ribs and toes, yet cheered to the echo—they caught the gleam of arms and the ripple of mail.

"Helgi has thrown open the Strategium, and armed them!" Ulfgar rejoiced. "See, how the fat burghers strut in soldier's finery! Pah! They hold their weapons like women!"

"They will use them like fiends!" Aldhelm answered.

For all their efforts the troops could not penetrate the Forum, and were forced to turn back and make a circuit. When they emerged from the side streets, they were at the very head of the multitude, and halted to learn how far matters had gone.

The sight of their marshaled spears drew howls of delight from the populace.

"They were ready enough to set their mangy curs on us once, or to hurl pots down on us from the housetops!" Ulfgar grumbled. "But to-day, when they need our help, we are heroes!"

Standing on carts above the folk, men from the Zeugma Port had been haranguing the throng; and as soon as the cheers for the Varangians died down, these took up their speech again:

"Behold! These are the men who will help you rescue your empress! Follow them to the palace! Tear the usurper's head from his shoulders!"

Once more rose that monstrous howl of mingled excitement and blood-lust. Men in rags, men in silks and velvets, men scarce clad at all—and every fourth man wearing mail looted from the arsenal that Helgi's lads had flung open— shrieked and clamored for Constantine's life. Their armor, made for Northern limbs, flapped and rattled on those lesser Eastern folk like the trappings of a scarecrow; but all brandished arms, and all were in a killing frenzy.

AS THE VARANGIANS debouched into the vast vacancy

of the palace square, the rabble at their heels, a single man stepped to meet them from the porch of Santa Sophia. At sight of him, cheer on cheer burst forth, like the roll of waves on the strand: first the crashing salute of the soldiers, then the prolonged roar of the mob. All near enough to see him knew his proud height, his scarlet cloak, the gold medallion of his rank: the Grand Heteriarch, Harald, champion of the true crown.

The enormous square was filling, as the folk streamed out from behind the Varangians and poured forward. As well as he could, Aldhelm set his men to herd them back, lest they rush the palace before Harald was ready.

Harald looked at the mob, one sea of heads and tossing weapons, those behind struggling forward, those in front thrust back by the soldiers. Behind them trailed a flood of late comers, themselves innumerable; and in their wake the shrubs and lawns of the gardens were trampled into desolation.

When the stream had trickled out, and square and garden were packed with frenzied men, Harald gestured for silence. Then he shouted to them:

"Look at the gate!"

Every eye obeyed. The bronze leaves of the archway guarding the imperial inclosure were shut tight; spears bristled from its sentinel towers. Beyond, on the battlements to either side, the sun smote flame from helmets and weapons. Cordage creaked as catapult-arms were drawn back on the palace ramparts beyond.

"Those are Varangians!" Harald called aloud to the mob. "They take orders from me. When the time comes, they will open that gate to you. Wait till their trumpets sound—then advance, and take the palace. I go to prepare your way."

He came on past the troops, stopping for a word with Aldhelm.

"Give me half your men," he commanded. "And bide here to see that these fools do not go mad and rush the wall. There are enough engines on the Daphne to kill thousands—and the Daphne is held by Paphlagonians."

"What will you do?" asked Aldhelm.

"Make a feint at the Bucoleon Port. Ulf and Halldor went off before dawn to bring up Eilif and the ships. They will deliver the real attack under cover of our threat. When my trumpets sound from the port, the Varangians in the Chalke will open these gates, and we shall attack the Daphne from two sides at once. If all goes well, Constantine cannot escape."

Harald spoke with deliberate calmness, but the hard flash of his eyes betrayed his repressed impatience.

Aldhelm detached Ulfgar with three thousand men to follow Harald; and they marched south along the great wall, just out of missile range from the Daphne, amid tumultuous cheers. As they advanced, a few scattered engines hummed, and great masses of jagged stone hurtled at them, to fall short and smash on the pavement in a cloud of dust.

The crowd stood its ground, watching them depart. An hour passed; two hours, the breeze tempering the heat of the mounting sun. The mob's spirits rose still higher as their bodies warmed. They shook their weapons at the palace, yelled curses, pressed forward as far as Aldhelm's men would let them. They would have swept him aside, to batter at the gate and the resisting walls, but that a few stones lobbed over the Chalke from the Daphne wall taught them caution.

HARALD'S MEN HASTENED on to the shore, where the rampart thrust its foot into the very brine; nor did they heed the threats hurled at them from the helmet-lined parapets of the Daphne. Down beyond them lay the Bucoleon, "Port of the Lion," the emperor's private harbor. They could see its walls, shutting off assault by sea; and above the ramparts rose the masts of two ships. From their tops floated the double eagle banner of the empire, to deceive the Paphlagonian garrison; but in signal to Harald, a small red streamer rippled above the eagle.

Harald saw. "Blow trumpet! Rush the wall!" he commanded.

The Bucoleon was a walled triangle, her longest side the main rampart of the imperial inclosure; her base the sea wall, the third side giving by a gate on the palace gardens. On the sea side she was further protected, by the square tower that also served as a lighthouse.

Straight for her long wall the Varangians rushed, shields raised to protect their heads from dropping arrows. Their trumpet call, their battle cry, drew to the rampart a line of mailed Heads; then a drum beat the alarm, and shafts began to fly.

The Northmen, skilled in the siege-warfare of the East, drove through the hail of arrows and darts to the very foot of the wall; there they clambered on each other's shoulders, forming a living pyramid to scale the battlements. This wall had no gate; the only entrances were the sea-gate, and the archway giving on the gardens. Sure there could be no attack on those sides, the garrison all gathered on the long wall of the inclosure, to repel the fierce assault of the Varangians.

Simultaneously Harald's trumpet blew the recall: it was not his purpose to storm, but to hold the enemy's attention till Eilif and his crews could come into action. But his men for once paid him no heed: they were not his house-carles, but Aldhelm's police, who for months had been cooped in the city, spoiling for action—and they had seen their comrades stricken down by Paphlagonian arrows. They pressed the assault.

The defenders were few, being drawn from Constantine's scant six hundred of the Daphne guard; but they fought desperately, and from the advantage of towering walls. Some plied their bows as fast as they could strip their quivers; others rolled great stones to the merlons and thrust them into the thick of Harald's men. Thrice they shattered the Norse pyramid, and the Varangians withdrew to reform, leaving crushed and writhing bodies behind.

Harald ran to the rear to get another sight of his two ships, and came back exultant.

"Storm on!" he shouted. "Help comes!"

Once more they gathered, this time in two smaller bodies, to divide the resources of the defense. One pyramid rose at the apex of the walled triangle; the other midway to the shore. Desperately the Paphlagonians strove to meet this double threat, raining down huge missiles and thrusting with long spears.

The first pyramid wavered, crumbled, and came down in a welter of tumbling bodies; the other was held upright in spite of all by the sheer mass of men behind it. Ulfgar and three more reached the top, scrambled over the parapet, and lashed in with red blades to hold their own till help should come. About them the Paphlagonians swarmed and hacked. One Varangian went down, another, till Ulfgar was left alone. Then Harald sprang to his side, and four more; and the whole pyramid collapsed under a rain of stones.

The six Northmen set their backs to the merlons and fought for life. Ulfgar was bleeding from a gash in the thigh; another Varangian, half disemboweled, struck on with diminishing strength. The ax Hell rose and fell furiously; then, pressed too close to use its edge, Harald thrust savagely with its edge horn. Half the garrison were plucking at them, while the other half struggled to prevent the pyramid below from reforming.

SUDDENLY THE WOLF-PACK that leaped and slashed at the few Northmen on the wall hesitated, gave back, half turned. From below them, at the sea-gate, came the thunderous beat of axes on the doors. As the Paphlagonians turned to meet this new attack, Harald was among them, Ulfgar and one other at his side. The three fought like demons, hacking, stabbing, leaping back to dash in again.

Then over the wall poured a wave of men, the crest of the reformed pyramid; and while the Paphlagonians wavered between them and the force below storming the sea-gate, there rose over the seaward rampart a stupendous sight. A mast, dangling a crimson war-shield, thrust over the wall a ship's boat lashed to an improvised boom, and filled with Northmen. Then another mast thrust out a second boatload. From both boats the house-carles tumbled over the battlements, and fell on the foe.

The Paphlagonians were rolled up, overpowered, and

disarmed. The house-carles set to work binding the beaten men, tossing their surrendered weapons into the water, opening the sea-gate. Through this, too late for the action, poured a third mass of house-carles from Harald's ships.

Harald ran to the stair giving on the archway and the palace gardens. He tugged at the bars, threw them aside, and sounded his trumpet.

"On!" he commanded. "On, or we are too late!"

He drew back to let the host surge past him into the gardens, and caught Eilif as the Gautlander would have followed.

"The Empress?" Harald panted.

"Thiodolf found her not on Prinkipo," Eilif answered. "We think Constantine must have her."

Harald released him and ran down after his men, using all his fleetness to catch up with the foremost, wondering the while if the Empress had already been murdered.

Through the gardens the Varangians rushed, breaking through a maze of hedges and trampling the flower-beds, their hungry eyes fixed on the gleam of the white building ahead, with their untold treasures.

"Ye had no palace-spoil when Michael died!" Harald roared. "Take it now!"

With a yell of joy the men scaled the terraces of the palace's middle wing and poured through its sacred doors. All save the house-carles swarmed through its halls and corridors, smashing and looting. The carles followed Harald along its wall to the water gate of the Daphne. As they made for it, they saw a pamphylian resting on her oars at the end of the long garden walk that ended at the beach, while her boat waited at the strand.

"He has not fled yet!" Harald exulted, and led the way up the stair to the garden entrance of the Daphne.

Once within, the house-carles, dazzled by untold wealth, would also have scattered to loot; but Harald summoned them together with a blast of his horn.

"Our work brooks no delay!" he thundered. "We have Constantine to capture. Take fifty men, Ulf, and hold the door. Come, lads!"

Through chamber and passage they poured, till they came to a halt, astounded, in the gold-lined throne room. Raging, Harald ordered them on:

"Hunt, ye dogs! There is time for gold afterward!"

A tremendous roar drowned his words, mixed with the clash of arms. It so echoed through the enormous building that none could tell whence it came; but it was instinct with awful menace. After a bewildered moment Harald understood; the larger part of Constantine's Paphlagonians was at bay between Chalke and Daphne, fighting loyally to prevent the entrance of Aldhelm's police and the mob. Constantine would not be where there was bloodshed; and he and Zoe must be found.

Thudding on as fast as they could, the house-carles burst into a splendid peristyle, from which a dozen rooms opened off. Harald brought them up to a sudden halt. He was at a loss. One way led to Constantine, and only one. But which?

"Shout and clash your shields!" Harald commanded, and the men obeyed lustily. The din brought armed heads through one of the doors.

"That way!" shouted Harald, pointing with his red ax, "He will be among his guards!"

The heads disappeared more suddenly than they had come, their owners running headlong to warn their master. Close on their heels the pursuers rushed, up a wide marble staircase, into a corridor, up a second, narrower stair. Breathless, they emerged on the battlements.

ON THE EDGE of the parapet stood Constantine; and beside him a woman, clad in imperial robes, her head veiled in cloth of gold. About the two were perhaps two-score wild-looking soldiers; and along the merlons were posted three-score more, waiting with bent bows, or standing ready at the catapults. Now and again they loosed, picking their targets carefully.

As the Varangians massed, Constantine turned, saw, and went suddenly pale. He was mailed and helmeted, and wore a sword; but he looked as unlike a soldier as a man may.

"Hold them off!" he squealed, just able to raise his voice high enough to be heard. His Paphlagonians rushed from their stations to form a pitifully thin screen between him and his foes.

The Varangians would have charged, but Harald waved them back. His eyes blazed, but there was a thin smile on his lips. He stood a moment, listening to the din of the mob below, and the hammer of steel on shields in the Chalke, where, with all the advantage of position, but desperately outnumbered, three hundred Paphlagonians were fighting their last fight to save their coward master. The Chalke would certainly be filled with battling Varangians, whose numbers alone still held the furious mob in the square from following at their heels.

"Our settlement is at hand, Greek," Harald spoke. "Within the hour you shall be dead flesh!"

While his men and Harald's waited, weapons quivering to strike at the first word of command, Constantine forced a wry grin.

"What have you against me, Heteriarch?" he asked unsteadily. "What, madness has turned all Varangians into traitors? And what do you here," he stiffened with a great effort, "away from your command in Sicily?"

Harald rested, the horn of his ax on the flagstones.

"I have come," he said deliberately, "to render payment for the hands of Cyra: Your brother will rejoice to learn how well I have paid."

Constantine shook visibly, and a look of desperation came to his face. He leaned over the parapet and called down to the mob:

"Ye folk of Constantinople! They have lied who told you I imprisoned your Empress. Behold her here beside me, who am her most obedient slave!" He grasped one of Zoe's hands and raised it high in his own; and so stood a moment, trying to force her forward.

"It is the false Varangians who strike against her, seeking to make Harald Emperor. Smite them, and save her!"

A wild shout burst from the myriad throats in the square below; a shout of mingled rage, hate, and bewilderment.

Zoe pulled back on Constantine's hand, striving to keep herself out of sight of the folk. Constantine dragged her forward.

"Show yourself!" he hissed at her.

She drew herself up proudly and stood forth between two merlons, where all could see her; quietly, like a statue.

The yells of the mob redoubled; yells of joy now, and wild acclamation. Then, so quickly that the act was done before it could be guessed, she snatched off the veil of gold that shrouded her face, Constantine caught at her arm in vain. The veil fell; her head shone golden in the sun; but her glorious hair was shorn.

As they saw the clipped locks of their beloved Empress, the people raised a howl of fury. They knew what it meant. It was true, then: Constantine had forced her into a convent, and brought her forth again to save himself from their wrath.

He had meant her presence to convince them of his loyalty to her, but her rage against him had shown her a way to turn his cunning into his ruin. Zoe ran her fingers pathetically through her shorn hair, and stretched her arms out toward her people with all the appeal she knew how to put into such a gesture. The multitude fought to crowd past the backs of Aldhelm's battling Varangians, brandishing their weapons, shrieking like demented beasts.

MADDENED BY HIS failure, Constantine wheeled on his Paphlagonians.

"Drive yonder dogs from the ramparts!" he screamed. "To the ship!"

"Sweep them over the edge, Northmen!" Harald shouted.

Then two forces met with a crash. The clang of blade on shield deafened the ears; the stones underfoot grew slippery with blood.

At first, desperation lent the Paphlagonians strength; but as soon as the long Northern axes and mighty Northern limbs gave the house-carles clearance for their strokes, the Greeks were pushed back closer and closer to the battlements. The fight swirled in a score of eddies here and there about the parapet. Now and again some soldier, torn with wounds, was hurled from the merlons; and at sight of his armored body flashing and whirling in the sun, the mob raised a cry of wild blood-lust.

His ax circling, Harald strove to cut a way to Constantine; but the cunning Greek evaded him, dodging behind the backs of his men. At last, with a sudden rush, the house-carles broke their foes; but, carried too far by their charge, they left a wide gap open before the stair. Constantine saw his chance, and fled through it under the very fall of Harald's ax. Nimbly the Greek ducked, doubled, and sprang down the stair. Recovering, Harald sped after him.

As fast as he ran, Constantine was faster, his feet winged by despair. From room to room, through hall and chamber, the pursuit went on; till a sudden rush of many feet and the sound of bloodthirsty yells from the court between Daphne and Chalke warned the fugitive that the mob was in the palace, and his last guards overpowered or slain.

The Greek turned like a hare, and made for the gardens. As Harald pressed after him, the Varangians of the palace and Aldhelm's police burst into the Daphne. Behind them roared the mob, waving their weapons, just in time to see Constantine flash across the gardens. Forgetting all else, they flooded in pursuit, howling for his blood.

With a frenzied burst of speed Constantine made for the water gate beyond the farthest hedges. From the ship's boat at the shore a knot of sailors came to meet him; but Ulf and his fifty, darting from the door where they had been posted to meet such an emergency, cut the seamen off.

With his last strength Constantine sped between the

two groups and made for the boat; but just as safety was in sight he stumbled and fell. Harald was on him ere he could rise. Dragging him to his feet, the Northman set him with his back against a tree.

"Draw sword, dog!" he panted.

Constantine cowered against the trunk, wholly unmanned. His hands shook, unable to grasp the hilt.

"Draw, or I give you to the rabble!" Harald threatened.

Fumblingly Constantine's fingers touched his hilt; then, with a snarl like that of a cornered beast, he snatched out his sword and leaped forward. His treacherous, furious thrust turned Harald's guard, ripped through the good mail, and brought up against a rib. Harald swung once, and beat the sword from the Greek's hand.

Constantine stood still, disarmed, licking his dry lips. Harald picked up the fallen blade and thrust it upon him.

"Will you die in cold blood?" he asked.

Constantine looked at the sword in his nerveless fingers, as if uncertain what to do with it. Then, as suddenly as before, he thrust again; but this time Harald was ready. The ax whirled, fell, and severed Constantine's right hand at the wrist.

"One for Cyra!" Harald cried, and whirled up his ax again.

In his triumph he had forgotten the populace. They streamed up to him now, shouldered him aside by their very numbers, and flung themselves on their Empress's oppressor. In one wild rush they bore Constantine down. The next instant they pulled him to his feet again; but in that instant he screamed horribly. When they raised him to their shoulders, his eyes were two bloody holes.

Shouting and singing, they formed a ragged procession, and bore the mutilated Constantine in ghastly exultation back to the Daphne.

"Show him to the Empress!" the mob roared. "Show her how her subjects punish her foes!"

Back in the garden Harald reeled against the tree where he had stood Constantine. His side was bleeding, and his stomach felt faint.

"By all the saints!" Harald gasped. "This city is hell, and its people devils!"

IN THE WIDE court between the towering walls of the three palace wings, the victorious Varangians herded their prisoners. Above them, on the portico of the Daphne, Zoe sat in judgment. Beside her stood Harald, his flesh wound bandaged. From the palace square came the shouts and cheers of the folk, now acclaiming the Empress they had helped to restore, now scrambling for gold thrown down from the ramparts by palace eunuchs who had skulked like rats during the fighting.

Zoe, her shorn hair hidden by a skillfully arranged coif, bent angry eyes on the captive Paphlagonians—a scant two hundred who had escaped Varangian steel and the fury of the mob.

"Crucify every tenth man!" she ordered.

Harald interposed. "By your leave, Augusta, it is an ill thing to slay surrendered prisoners, and the Prefect Aldhelm promised them life."

Zoe frowned; and her cheeks, which she had not had time to smooth with her marvelous cosmetics, showed fine wrinkles.

"They have borne arms against their Empress!" she

exclaimed; but as her eyes met Harald's, her anger faded in a smile.

"Since you ask it, they shall be pardoned. Where is Constantine? That traitor shall not be forgiven, even for you!"

"I should not ask it," Harald replied; "but he is dead of his hurts."

"Then justice is done!" and Zoe leaned back in her chair with a sigh. "There is one more offender," Harald interposed. "Ho, you who command the Palace Guard!"

The captain of the Chalke guard came forward, his eyes downcast.

"I ordered you," Harald reproached him coldly, "to admit the police and folk as soon as my trumpet sounded from the Bucoleon. You delayed in obeying; otherwise Constantine's men would never have gained time to hold the passage to the Daphne."

The officer raised his head and met Harald's gaze.

"I was wrong," he said. "Constantine sent me an order to hold the gate. I answered that I had your command to open it. He prayed me then to wait, declaring that the Empress was safe in the Daphne, and by making terms with the mob he could save good Varangian lives. I hold it an officer's duty to spare his men; and I knew you had with you force enough to take the palace."

"You spared your men, and in consequence men of mine perished," Harald said sternly. "Had you opened when I bade you, the foe would have surrendered at once rather than face the folk."

The officer fell to his knees. "I have said I was wrong," he repeated, "and am ready to pay. Strike."

He thrust out his neck and waited for the blow.

Harald threw down his ax. "Blood enough has been shed this day. Go free. But if ever I give you an order again, obey!"

Zoe rose and laid her hand softly on Harald's arm.

"Take me to my chamber," she commanded, yet with a gentle grace.

Harald removed her hand, and shook his head.

"Your pardon, Augusta; I have business. I will come later."

The Empress's cheek flushed. "You are too much the barbarian," she said coldly, "to know that the invitation of the Augusta is a command. Remember the duty of a soldier, as you but now taught it to yonder captain; and if ever I give you an order again, obey!"

She paused, and a weary look came over her features. "Where is my woman Maria? I have not seen her since they seized me. Is she alive?"

Aldhelm spoke up: "I will send her to you at once, Augusta."

With a curt bow Harald turned his back on Zoe, and made his way with Aldhelm toward the Prefecture. As they passed through the imperial gate, the folk, just dispersing, greeted them with rapturous cheers.

Zoe stood gazing after them, biting her lip.

23

HARALD'S WAY

"**HAS GEORGIOS BEEN** sent to the palace?"

Aldhelm nodded. "As you ordered, Harald. He will do no more harm now, for Zoe has had him cast into prison. A hard fate for a man who, for all his faults, was a brave soldier."

"Fetch John to me."

The Eunuch came, guarded by two Varangians. Harald met him with a hard stare. John was well clad, well fed, but his face had lost its inscrutable calm, and was openly troubled. At sight of Harald, however, something of his old self, a smooth graciousness, came back to him. He held out a hand in greeting. Harald ignored it.

"Aldhelm believes you have kept faith with me," he began, "and that it was Constantine alone who plotted my death, and murdered the girl Cyra. He sent her hands to me in a coffer, just as I sailed, with a letter offering them as a gift from you."

John's face showed utter dismay.

"A foul trick!" he cried. "A dog's deed! By my faith, I had nothing to do with it! I set a price on his head for murdering her. He even planned to poison me. But, by my soul, I knew not he had sent her hands to you!"

Harald regarded him narrowly. "But it was you who first imprisoned her?" he demanded.

"I meant but to frighten her, lest she run Zoe's errands too often," John insisted. "Am I a fool, to anger you, on whom alone my plans against Georgios depended?"

Harald's face cleared, and he took John's hand. John smiled, a smile of keen relief mixed with genuine friendship.

"You are a dangerous man to cross, Harald," he said. "That you are here, and Zoe on the throne, means that my brother is dead. I loved him once; but he broke my heart, and I do not grieve for him now." He raised his eyes calmly to Harald's. "Once I held your life in my hands," he continued; "now you hold my life in yours. What will you do with me?"

"What you will, except place you in power again. God send Zoe wise and good ministers who will not betray her!"

John sighed. "I had hoped," he said, "that you had learned I was the best ruler this realm could have. There was a bargain between us; I kept my half."

Harald's eyes flashed. "And I kept mine! I swore to support you as long as you kept faith with me. You have not harmed me, it is true; but you lied to me. It was you and your dead brother who slew the old emperor—not Zoe, as you said. A murderer and a liar is not fit to rule. You had best leave the realm. I will give you an escort of Varangians outside the city; and it will be well for you if Zoe learns not that you still live!"

"You are young and a king's son," said John, looking thoughtfully at the tall Northman. "Some day you will reign. You, too, are a hard man. It may be you will yet learn that such men as you and I must lie and murder to keep either power or life. Farewell!" With a step that dragged a little, he left the court.

"What will you do now?" Aldhelm asked. "Go back to Sicily? Or rule Constantinople in Zoe's name?"

"I have had enough of this land." Harald shuddered. "It is an evil place, where a man must choose between dishonorable prosperity and death. I have done with it! I have ordered my carles to have all ready to sail to-night on the tide, when I have said farewell to the empress."

"It is an ill thing to lose you, Harald," Aldhelm rose and took his hand. "We have been friends so long, and have done such deeds together."

"Why should we part, comrade?" Harald asked, his stern face softening. "Come to Norway with me. Ulf and Halldor sail with me, and Thiodolf. In my ships I have much gold, and some steel: both ready to win back my kingdom. There will be a place for you at my side."

Aldhelm's eyes dimmed, and he slowly shook his head.

"When I leave this place, I, too, go home. There is a little stead in Sussex, where the fields are very green. But there is another thing, Harald. You are such a man as I could follow to the death—now. But John said a true word. The time may come when you will be too hard for men like me to love. It were better to part now in friendship, than later as foes, Harald Hard-Measure!"

Harald stared at him, and his eyes were troubled.

"Mayhap you are right, Englishman. I do not brook opposition. Well, I have known you, and that has been a gift from the saints. Where is the girl Maria, whom you said you had here?"

"I sent her to the palace to be with the empress. Men say you love her, Harald. It is also whispered that Zoe loves you. Beware both mistress and maid! A Greek is no fit mate for a Northman."

"Good advice, whoso will take it," laughed Harald. "Now let me have food and a bed. It is long since I have slept. And be here before sunset to wake me, and bid me farewell."

Aldhelm put both hands on his friend's shoulders. "My men will wake you. I will say farewell now, comrade. It is not good to draw out partings. If ever you come to England, may I be there to welcome you!"

SHORTLY BEFORE SUNSET Harald left the Prefecture and trod the Mese for the last time. His men were all on board the two treasure ships. A boat was to pick him up at the water-gate after his audience with Zoe.

"Norway!" he whispered, and smiled. His longing for home brought the mighty peaks and winding fjords so close that he could almost see them. He was roused from his dreams by the challenge of the guard at the Chalke; and the same officer whom he had pardoned that morning, opened the gates to him.

"The Augusta expects you," the man said. "Good fortune—Augustus!"

Harald started: the Varangian had greeted him with the title of emperor!

"Thanks, Sultan of Egypt!" he retorted mockingly, and passed on.

Others than Aldhelm knew, then, the offer Zoe had made him so long ago. The palace was full of eunuchs with double-hung tongues to spread the rumor.

Instead of going through the Daphne, he crossed the

open court between the Chalke and the throne-room, irritated that the jaded favor of the empress had fallen on him, and that she thought to make him emperor in spite of himself.

There were no guards at the entrance to the empress's apartments—no one, save a white-robed eunuch with drawn sword. At Harald's approach the eunuch prostrated himself; and the door opened quietly. Maria stood there, beckoning him in.

He had not seen her since his departure for Sicily. The clean air and hard-fought fields of the great island had almost driven her from his mind. A man of action, he had thought first of the things in hand. But now he forgot all else—his interview with the Empress, even his longing for home—in the beauty of her eyes. He stood and stared at her.

"Will you keep Augusta waiting?" she whispered.

He moved within, like one in a dream, feeling her follow close behind him. Her nearness, the remembrance of her promise to him, made his anger at Zoe keener.

With her wonted grace, that alone made her seem lovelier than other women, Zoe lay on her low divan; her delicate complexion freshened, her shorn hair trimmed and curled till it was almost as fair as in its unrestrained glory. She smiled enchantingly, and held out her hand in a languid gesture. Behind her stood the Patriarch.

"You have saved me my throne, as you promised," the Empress spoke. Her voice; low and rich at all times, was happy now. "You have been ever faithful, daring all things, overcoming all things. Your reward shall be as great as your desserts."

"I ask no reward," Harald answered.

The Patriarch struck in with a flash of his former fire.

"Whether you ask or no, you shall receive! You have overthrown the usurper, saved this city and land from the enemies of God! Aye; and those sacrilegious hands that oppressed the head of Holy-Church have been palsied by your might!"

The Empress nodded in agreement.

"What mean you, Holy Father?" Harald asked wonderingly.

"You did not know?" Zoe smiled. "This very day my servants, spying out those who had befriended Constantine, found our holy Patriarch imprisoned in the house of the Syrian Demetrios, foully treated, and weak with abuse. Had you not saved me, how could I have saved him? The Syrian dog and his brother are even now atoning their crimes on the cross. And you ask no reward! Tell him, Most Holy, the honor in store for him."

THE PATRIARCH'S WAN face grew warm with zeal.

"My son, at the command of the Divine Augusta I have proclaimed throughout the palace that this night shall see you espoused to the Empress and crowned Emperor! Nay, protest not! It is announced, and so cannot be undone."

Harald met their eyes. Zoe was smiling happily, triumphantly. The Patriarch's face showed open exultation. On Zoe's other side stood Maria, demure, her eyes cast down, but her hands were tightly clenched.

These Greeks, who thought that to proclaim a thing made it real! Harald raised his head high.

"I sail to-night," he said, "for Norway—free of all Greek fetters!"

Zoe's eyes lowered; but almost instantly she looked up, the smile again curving her lips.

"You will never see Norway again," she murmured. In her confidence she was subdued, and her stilled excitement made her very lovely. But Harald's eyes sought Maria, silent and shy.

"You have ordered your ships made ready," Zoe's musical voice went on, "but you will never reach them. The vestibule is full of soldiers—Paphlagonians. One step across this threshold, and you run into their points. You have no choice but between me and death!" She laughed softly, beguilingly, as if she invited him to join in her amusement at his helplessness.

Harald's senses leaped to wakefulness. A twist of his shoulders brought the ax Hell under his hand. His fingers, hidden by the folds of his cloak, grasped it. With his left hand he tore away the medallion of his office, and cast it at Zoe's feet.

"Give me death, then, and freedom!" he answered.

The Empress sat up, tense with anger. "It may not be death!" she stormed. "Fool! Perhaps a prison, dark and foul, where you shall rot till you change your mind! Think not you can escape from me, either in life or in death!"

She clapped her hands and the door flew open. Through it spears twinkled, and the lamplight fell on mailed bodies. They were sturdy men, thick-set, with black hair and gleaming eyes.

"Take him!" Zoe commanded.

They came on, but the door was too narrow to admit more than two together. Harald swept the ax from his baldric and sprang—straight at the Empress. His left hand tore her from her couch; his right poised Hell's blade above her head.

"Back, dogs, or I strike!" he cried sternly.

The Paphlagonians stopped so suddenly they stumbled. Their eyes filled with horrified amazement, and they glanced uncertainly at the Augusta.

The Patriarch flung himself on Harald's back, clawing and tearing with all his feeble might. Harald hurled him off with a shrug, never taking his eyes from the soldiers; and so he did not see Maria creep up behind him.

Zoe's face paled beneath its artificial color. Her love, or the desire she took for love, was no match for her love of life, her abject terror of death.

"Back!" she screamed at the soldiers. "Withdraw!"

The Paphlagonians drew away from the door, but they hung about the vestibule like hungry wolves. Harald, still clutching the Empress to him, sprang to the doorway. There were a dozen of the soldiers, armed with swords and pikes. As he watched them, his ax lifted, something smote him hard between his mailed shoulder blades. He half turned, his blade still threatening Zoe, and saw Maria and the Patriarch behind him. On the floor lay a broken dagger.

"A shrewd blow for old hands, father!" Harald laughed. "Take the lamp, girl! Go before me into the gardens, straight to the water gate. Now, ye jackals! Stand back, if ye would save your Augusta's life!"

Maria sped out into the night, flashing by the astounded group of Paphlagonians, who snarled at Harald, not daring to touch him. For herself, Maria could find the gate in the dark, blindfolded; the light she carried was a beacon for Harald.

She held it as high as she could, thankful there were no shrubs taller than her reach between Harald and the gate. Sobbing she ran, but none the less fleetly, her heart aching to know how Harald fared, yet afraid to pause an instant to look back, lest some one be in pursuit.

SHOULDERING THE WRETCHED Zoe like a sack, Harald strode out of the chamber, glaring fiercely about him. The soldiers closed in behind, points lifted, creeping as close as they dared; but the cruel ax edge threatening their mistress's throat, they shrank from attack. So Harald passed into the darkness of the gardens.

Now was the moment of real peril. In the dark and in the open, he could scarce hope to keep the Paphlagonians off for long. They could steal about him, ahead, behind, on both sides, and thrust before he could see them. His eyes straining for the black loom of trees, he took advantage of what shelter he could, leaping from one dark patch to another. And always he must look ahead for the flickering glow of Maria's lamp.

He stumbled on the root of a tree, and a spear hummed past his head.

"Hold your weapons, or she dies!" he shouted. And there was silence—silence broken only by little tinklings of mail, as the men who dared not strike crept closer in upon him.

Then the light that danced ahead stopped, and there were distant voices. A shout:

"Harald! We come!"

Footsteps, heavy and swift, mingled their crashing fall with the snapping of twigs. An impact, followed by the sound of mailed man striking mailed man, and the clang of weapons. Then, as the Paphlagonians gauged the number of their foes, magnified by darkness and the noise of their approach, there came the stealthy sounds of men slinking away.

"Harald!" came the shout again, close at hand.

"Here! Who comes?"

"Ulf. The Englishman sent us word you might be in danger at the palace. We were waiting at the landing, and sent back for another boat's crew. There are a score of us."

"The girl with the lamp?"

"Thiodolf has her."

Harald set Zoe down. Feeling her life no longer in danger, she began to hiss with hate and ruffled dignity, like a disturbed cat. They stood so close together that, even in the dark, he could see the flame in her eyes.

"So I am free in spite of you!" he exulted. "Harald Sigurdsson chooses his own land and his own wife, and prefers the maid to the mistress. Farewell, Augusta!"

He ran toward the light, his men following as close as they could. When they came up with Thiodolf and Maria, Harald snatched up the girl and ran on, calling:

"To the boats!"

Maria was struggling in his arms, the pounding of her fists like the thud of velvet paws against his steel shoulder.

"Zoe!" she wept. "What have you done with Zoe?"

If Zoe were hurt, all Maria's longing was to minister to her. She had helped to save Harald's life, loving him too well to see him perish; but to be carried off by him far from her mistress and Constantinople was no part of her plan. But Harald held her fast, the only loyal Greek he had found in all the land.

A FEW YARDS beyond lay the shore. A voice challenged

from the dark, in good, mouth-filling Norse. Answering, Harald found the loom of the boats, lowered Maria gently to the stern thwart, and thrust off. She was crying softly, but with abandon, as if she would never stop.

"Give way!" Harald shouted. The boats slid from the sand; the oars dipped.

A few swift strokes brought them to deep water; and a single light displayed twice, then hidden, brought an answering gleam from the two treasure ships. Stroking up quietly, the oarsmen brought the boats under the looming hulls, and all climbed aboard, Harald tenderly lifting Maria to the deck.

"Cut the cables!" he commanded. "To your benches, carles!"

The great ash oars were thrust out as soon as the ships' boats were hauled aboard, and the two pamphylians headed into the wind. Thiodolf and Eilif at the steering oars, they fended off the shore and bore north, the palace lights giving them their direction. The breeze blew steadily, holding them back, making sails useless; but the huge-limbed house-carles tugged at the oars like men. Slowly at first, then faster, the lights of Mikligard the Great dropped behind.

On the high poop deck Harald stood above the crouched figure of Maria. She turned from him, and stretched her arms out over the water.

"Oh, my mistress!" she sobbed. "Shall I ever see you again?"

"If she sees you again, she will slay you, from jealousy and disappointment." Harald spoke softly.

Like cold steel the words fell on Maria's heart. As

Harald uttered them, she saw their truth clearly, and shivered. Maria was young, and as Harald gently placed his cloak about her she was beginning to realize how sweet life might be. Her face brightened and the heaviness went from her posture, but she still seemed deep in thought.

"She was my lady, my Empress, and she trusted me." The girl again bowed her head. "But—I loved you, and when the Patriarch plucked my own knife from my girdle, and struck you with it from behind—I forgot Zoe. I obeyed when you told me to take the lamp and guide you." She raised searching eyes to his face.

Harald laughed softly, slowly, holding her glance: "Believe not that I would have killed your Empress, lass. I am called a hard man, but I am not that hard. I but knew the Paphlagonians believed I would slay her, for so would they have done if they were in my place."

At once the girl rose and stood by his side. Her hand sought his. Together they looked back over the water murmuring in their wake.

"Why do her ships not pursue us?" Maria asked presently, her wondering gaze scanning the dark waters of the empty straits.

"Her ships, sent out by Constantine, still watch for Georgios, off the Hellespont, not knowing Zoe has him in prison," Harald smiled. "We are safe."

As long as the faintest gleam of the city, fast dropping astern, reached toward them over the water, Maria watched it. When night had swallowed it wholly, and nothing seemed astir in the world but the ships and the water that lapped their sides, she turned and looked at Harald with quiet eyes.

"Zoe loved you," she said.

Harald's eyes sought the far northwest, where, beyond two seas, lay Norway. He shook his shoulders, and the ax Hell stirred between them.

"I shall have a better kingdom, and a better queen," he said.